Praise for

THE EDEN THRILLERS

Chaplain (Maj.) Jaime Richards makes a promising debut as a savvy-but-nurturing minister to American troops during the early days of Operation Iraqi Freedom. Though she's an unconventional thriller protagonist, Richards leaves no doubt she's up to the task.

—*Publisher's Weekly*

"A hallmark of Eden Thrillers is their highly compacted timeline, which propels the story forward at a breakneck pace. This is a thriller for the thinking mind; it raises fascinating questions regarding faith, politics, and the monetary system. The heroine's amazing voyage of discovery has taken her to a fantastic world, but it also reinforces the need to fight for the survival of our species and planet. Awesome!"

—Jill M. Smith, *Romantic Times Book Reviews*

The latest action packed Eden thriller is a terrific tale that combines biblical references with modern day intrigue. The story line grips the audience from the onset . . . . Jaime is a fabulous protagonist. A superb entry in a fascinating saga."

—Harriet Klausner, *Mystery Gazette*

"An absolute page-turner. This book has 'you are there' insider details that make you question everything you read in today's headlines. A thrill-a-minute read!"

—Christina Dodd, *New York Times* bestselling author

ALSO BY
SHARON LINNÉA
AND
B.K. SHERER:

Chasing Eden
Beyond Eden
Treasure of Eden

BY SHARON LINNÉA

These Violent Delights

PLAGUES OF EDEN

SHARON LINNÉA
B.K. SHERER

This is a work of fiction. All the characters, organizations, and events portrayed in this novel are either products of the authors' imagination or are used fictitiously.

PLAGUES OF EDEN

First printing September 2014

Cover design by Christian Fuenfhausen. Interior design by Mie Kurahara.

For information:

Info@ArundelPublishing.com

ISBN 978-1-933608-12-9

For William Diderichsen Webber

Gardener Extraordinaire

whose example has shaped the authors

in ways too numerous to count

CONTENTS

PLAGUES OF EDEN

“And now faith, hope, and love abide, these three;
and the greatest of these is love.”
1 Corinthians 13:13

“Everyone brings out the choice wine first and then the cheaper wine after the guests have had too much to drink; but you have saved the best till now.”—John 2:10

PROLOGUE

SATURDAY, NOVEMBER 10, 2007, 6:38 P.M.
TEL EL-BALAMUN, EGYPT

DR. SAMUEL GOLDING SQUINTED, trying in vain to focus on the mud-yellow brick from the porch of the ancient temple he was unearthing. The young archeologist had spent the last three hours on his knees, painstakingly brushing silt and dirt from the object. With a sigh, he leaned back to squat on his heels and survey the dig site. The temple was much older even than the third century library sitting above it, and he no longer had enough light to continue working.

Another day was now over on this, the strangest dig he'd ever worked.

Sam was the Assistant Project Leader for the British Museum excavation at Tel el-Balamun and the de facto project head, since the team leader was not available due to the unusual timing of this off-cycle dig. This project in the Central Nile Delta of Egypt would not unearth the type of tourist-frenzied structure like Luxor or Giza—which suited him just fine. The team's work on these ancient Egyptian temples could progress with little outside interference.

He started packing up his tools for the day. The porch would wait until tomorrow. It wasn't going anywhere.

"'Night, Boss," said his assistant, Ibrahim. "Going into town tonight?"

"Don't think so," Sam replied. He brushed the dust off his signature Sandhurst t-shirt and shook out his cargo pants.

It wasn't simply that he was tired. He wanted time to mull. Odd things had been happening on this dig, and he wanted some peace and quiet to think.

He sat down on a canvas camp chair and poured himself a glass of Chardonnay from a bottle he kept in his cooler. Sometimes, these bricks seemed to him to be miniature time machines. When he touched one, it was as if he were propelled back, hearing the voices and conversations of those who had stood in this place many centuries ago. He envisioned what they were wearing, heard the sounds of the city around them, smelled the odors of animals and incense.

But now there was a discordant note. He had found several objects in this dig that, while ancient, were not from this place or time period. In fact, not even close. How to report these?

He didn't want to do anything that would call the validity of the whole dig into question. And yet...the pieces didn't fit.

It was the time of evening the military called EENT, or early evening nautical twilight. The horizon was becoming indistinct and stars were just beginning to twinkle. It looked like there would be little haze this evening, and the clear Egyptian night would provide a nice backdrop for the heavens in all their glory. Maybe he should have been an astronomer instead of an archeologist. No, scratch that. He could enjoy the night sky without knowing how far away the stars were or what made them shine. But he could not pass by a mound of earth without wondering what ancient treasure might be hidden beneath.

Sam sipped his wine and looked to the northwest just in time to spot a falling star.

Wow, what a nice tail on that one...

But it didn't fade.

Instead, it seemed to grow brighter, larger.

What?

He stood and stared, unmoving, as the fireball plummeted, hitting the ground with a loud explosion a half mile to his east. In one fluid move he dropped his glass and dove behind the nearest dirt pile, his mind flashing back to bombs exploding when he was a young officer in Northern Ireland.

Heads began popping out of tents, just in time to see another "falling star" close in and burn up just before hitting the ground a quarter of a mile to the west.

Within moments, the camp was in pandemonium, everyone running back and forth, searching for cover. Ibrahim and one of the local diggers, who were heading into town, were caught between the tents and the dig's rattletrap car. They both made a run for the extra protection of the vehicle. It was a rusty old station wagon that had survived twenty years as transport for the team. Sam watched as they each dove in a door and rolled up the windows. He wondered if he would be safer joining them than lying sprawled behind a dirt pile.

What was going on?

And then there were more. It was like a hailstorm—if the hail was made of fire.

A much larger piece headed straight for Sam's hiding place, then split in two at the last minute. One part burned up before reaching the ground, the other impacted the car where his fellow workers had taken cover.

The largest part had crashed through the roof of the car; other parts had shorn off and hit the doors of the vehicle. One had apparently ruptured the gas line. From where he was, Sam now smelled gasoline mingling with the burning sulfur from space.

"Get out!" he screamed, standing and rushing for the station wagon.

But it was too late.

Fire continued to rain down, and some landed, still burning, close enough to the vehicle that the fumes, then the spilled gasoline on the ground, and finally the remainder of the tank, ignited.

Sam threw himself down and covered his head but he felt the ground shake as the car exploded. He stayed flattened against the sand, fully expecting to be hit by debris from the explosion or the sky, fully expecting the next second to be his last on Earth.

It took a moment after the explosion for the ringing in his ears to stop, and for him to regain enough equilibrium to discern which way was up. Then he raised his head, saw the burning vehicle, and launched himself toward it.

He disregarded the continuing rain of fiery meteors as he tried desperately to get to his friends. He circled the car, looking for an opening, but the fire was so hot he couldn't get close enough to open a door. He looked through the flames for some hint of movement within, but saw and heard nothing. Several others had seen what had happened and also ignored personal safety to try to help.

There was nothing to be done. The car was obliterated.

Another five minutes of chaos, and then darkness, and silence. As suddenly as the firestorm had begun, it was over.

Team members began emerging from tents, moving slowly and carefully in case the danger wasn't over. Grabbing flashlights, they looked for anyone who might require assistance.

What they found was Dr. Sam Golding standing motionless in front of a burning station wagon, wondering how the ancients would have responded to the gods showing their anger by sending a mighty firestorm to annihilate whatever and whoever was below.

For this was an act of destruction, one whose consequences would reverberate for years to come.

Why had it come into their dig? Their lives? Why had it taken two of their own?

Strands of horror, hurt, anger, and loss wove together inside of Sam, a feeling as primal as had been felt in this very spot, millennia before. He dropped to his knees, screaming from his gut, until he could scream no more.

SATURDAY, NOVEMBER 10, 2007, 6:48 P.M.
ANDRIA, ITALY

TEN YEARS.

That's how long Savino Latorre, together with the mysterious business mogul Shanlei—Mountain Thunder—had been working to prepare this world-shaking modern display of the plagues visited on ancient Egypt by the God of the Israelites.

And, as last time, the plagues were meant to send a message. To bring certain world governments and policy makers to their knees. Well, that was Shanlei's motive.

Savino was in business with Shanlei, of course. But there was another group whose attention he sought to arrest, and a specific person whose affections he meant to secure. This part of his plan had been in the works not for ten years, but for fifty.

Since the dawn of time, men have made grand gestures to impress the women they love. Nebuchadnezzar the Second is said to have built the Hanging Gardens of Babylon for Queen Amyitis. Shah Jahan built the Taj Mahal for Mumtaz Majal (granted, after his favorite wife was dead), and Richard Burton bought a 69.2-carat diamond for his Elizabeth.

To his mind, Savino Latorre had created something that outshone them all.

It was, coincidentally, about the size of a seventy-carat gem; in hue, something between midnight blue and deep purple.

It was a grape, yielding wine whose exquisite flavor was as yet unknown in the Terris world. This grape was named the Analucia, after Savino's love, and when it blended in correct proportions with the Negroamaro grape, grown only in the region of Puglia, Italy, it produced a full-bodied, smooth wine that was an unparalleled taste of paradise.

Savino removed his coal grey Armani jacket and carefully folded it over his arm. He stood at his full six feet four and took a final look at his vineyards for the day. Beyond the intertwined, centuries-old olive trees, they stretched, nearly as far as the eye could see, wave after wave of curving grape vines, fanning out from the river.

He had not yet released the Analucia wines for public consumption. He would do that with Ana beside him, once she walked freely on the Earth.

Which led him to the work still at hand. Shanlei should be happy. If all had gone well, it should have happened by now: plague three, Burning Hail from the Sky.

And very soon, the murder of the man responsible for the greatest of his woes.

A man known simply as Sword 23.

SATURDAY, NOVEMBER 10, 2007, 6:14 P.M.
TIME ZONE 1

IT HAD ALL COME DOWN TO THESE THREE DAYS.

Within the space of seventy-two hours, the world would change. Twelve key government and industry players would be brought to their knees, and would capitulate power. Every continent would be represented. These dozen could not imagine how their bright square of fabric would weave into the large quilt that would lead to a tipping point of resource redistribution.

Shanlei understood the importance of story, of weaving together the narrative that would cause these mini-pharaohs to yield. Shanlei didn't remember who had first come up with the idea of recreating the ten plagues that the Western God had visited upon the Pharaoh of ancient Egypt—whether it was Savino Latorre himself, or one of his psychotic geniuses. But the triggers for each plague were in place.

And for those who refused to yield?

The countdown to the final plague: Death of the Firstborn.

The countdown clock had started now on the homepage of WheelofPlagues.com.

The firstborn had seventy-two hours to live.

Perhaps the parents would each acquiesce in time. Shanlei secretly hoped not.

Tuesday would be a celebration, in any case.

Had the Western God felt this smug satisfaction, knowing

that Pharaoh was going to refuse Moses' demands, making it open season?

It didn't matter. In less than three days, those players—in fact, the world—would be convinced.

SATURDAY

SATURDAY, NOVEMBER 10, 2007, 12:22 P.M.
CADET CHAPEL, UNITED STATES MILITARY ACADEMY
WEST POINT, NEW YORK

IS THIS KID ASLEEP OR DRUNK?

Chaplain (Lieutenant Colonel) Jaime Richards almost tripped over a body at the bottom of the spiral cement staircase. Her heels were no help as she leaned down to get a better look at a handsome young man sprawled on the bottom steps and had her answer. He smelled like a brewery.

Seriously?

Jaime shook his shoulder. As she did, she could see he had one golden bar on each shoulder of his army dress blues. A "Butter-Bar." It figured. Leave it to a brand new 2nd lieutenant to come drunk to the basement of Cadet Chapel, the most identifiable site on the U.S. Military Academy at West Point.

She shook him harder, and he started to rouse. "Lieutenant! What are you doing here?"

"Wha...Wassup? What time is it?" Frantically he looked at his watch and tried to stand, almost falling over. Jaime grabbed his arm. Fortunately, he was in the front end of the basement, which included a sitting area, and she half walked, half dragged him to a nearby couch. He was half a foot taller than she was, and it took all her strength to keep him from falling. They reached the couch and she let go. He swayed for a moment and fell back onto the cushions.

"Lieutenant..." she looked at the name tag on his uniform, "... Pellman, why are you here?"

She thought quickly as she waited for him to answer. There were no concerts that afternoon, only three weddings, one of which was in full swing above them. "Are you here for a wedding?"

The young man tried valiantly to focus his gaze on Jaime. He nodded his head with vigor.

"Attend a bit of a wild bachelor party last night?"

He had a very solemn look and shook his head no. At first Jaime was confused, then she began to put the pieces together.

"Wait. Are you here for *your* wedding?"

Very slowly, with a pained look, he nodded his head yes.

Oh boy, now what? "Is it at fourteen-hundred?"

Another nod. Now he just looked sad.

Jaime looked at her watch, did a quick calculation about how much time she had, and sat down on the couch next to the obviously miserable young officer. His eyes were focusing more as his head seemed to clear. "So, what's wrong?"

"I don't know if this is going to work." His words were slightly slurred, but understandable. "I really love Melissa, a lot, I mean, well, maybe too much."

He rubbed his hands hard across his face and shook his head. "We've been planning this wedding since we were Cows. It all seemed perfect! Graduate in June, attend our officer basic courses, then get married." He counted off each step on his fingers as he spoke. "But at basic she decided to specialize in EOD."

"So your fiancée is going into explosive ordnance disposal. That sounds pretty exciting. But I take it you don't think so."

"I know that any job in the Army can be dangerous, and I thought I could handle it if Melissa had to go to combat. But this really hit me. I think of her heading up an EOD team and I just can't take it! It just gives me the willies."

Jaime nodded, conjuring up images of the dangers of bomb defusal.

"And then," he started, rallying, "then I asked her, 'What kind of a job would that be when you get pregnant?' And she just looked at me and said, 'Pregnant? I'm not getting pregnant! At least not any time soon.'"

The young officer looked down to inspect his fingernails, trying to hide the tears welling up in his eyes. "I want to have children, and now I'm not sure when, or if, we will."

"Have you told her this? Talked about how you feel?"

"I hinted at it. I mean, when she told me she wasn't getting pregnant any time soon she had to know that I wasn't happy about it!"

"You hinted? So now she's expected to be a mind reader?"

He looked chagrined. "Well, I guess…"

Jaime shook her head. "Okay, here's the deal. Do you love her?"

"Yes!" He sounded almost offended.

"Has this issue made you love her any less?"

"No! I really, really, really love her, that's why this EOD thing scares me. I couldn't stand to lose her."

Jaime grabbed his head, one hand on each side of his face, so she could look straight into his eyes. "Then tell her how you feel. Don't hold this in. Especially don't go off drinking on your own. That won't solve anything."

"But should I still get married today?"

"Oh, don't suck me into that one! I'm not making that decision for you." Jaime quickly stood and almost tripped over the hem of her dress. She straightened up and smoothed a few wrinkles from her skirt. "The only advice I will give you is: don't think you have to get married today just because the wedding is planned, and don't think you shouldn't get married just because you have had one disagreement. You're looking at the rest of your lives together, and this is just the first of many challenges you'll have together as a married couple."

Jaime reached out her hand and squeezed his shoulder. Just as she was about to suggest he get a cup of coffee, another young man in dress uniform—this one a cadet from one of West Point's international partners—came racing down the circular stairs. He gave a loud sigh of relief when he saw Lieutenant Pellman.

"There you are!" he said. "I've been looking everywhere! When you asked me to be best man, I didn't realize it would be so much of a challenge."

"So you're his best man?" Jaime asked. "You do have a challenge here, Cadet Bak. He has an hour."

"An hour, fourteen minutes," said the newly-arrived cadet, with a nervous smile.

"He's all yours," Jaime said. "And he's gonna owe you."

The first notes of the organ recessional reverberated from the ceremony a floor above them.

"Oh, cripes!" Jaime looked distressed. Lieutenant Pellman and Cadet Bak stared at her. It finally registered to them both that she was wearing a floor-length ivory sheath.

Confused, Cadet Bak said, "Hey, are you getting…?"

"Yes," she cut him off quickly as she began to run down the hall. "He's the two o'clock wedding; I'm the one o'clock. I'll say a prayer you make the right decision!"

SATURDAY, NOVEMBER 10, 2007, 7:02 P.M.
CASTEL DEL MONTE
ANDRIA, ITALY

THEY HAD DONE IT. They had freaking done it.

Bradley Kluge sat on a stool in the middle of a sophisticated command center hidden in the rock beneath Castel del Monte, a thirteenth century fortress built on a hilltop in Andria, Italy, by Holy Roman Emperor Frederick II.

Gleefully, he watched the half-dozen live feeds on television screens affixed to the walls of the secret, modern fortress beneath the ancient castle. One by one, regular programs on the twenty-four hour news networks were interrupted with breaking news, reporting fiery hail from the sky.

Bradley pumped his fist in the air at each, punctuating the move with a loud "Yes!" Today he had put to use his undergraduate degree from MIT in computer science and graduate degree in aerospace engineering, both of which he'd achieved before the age of twenty-one.

Let's see who would be first to confirm what had actually taken place.

Someone had been able to grab video of some of the fires at the dig in Egypt. As he watched screen after screen light up with footage of orange-gold fire against the night sky, his employer, Savino Latorre, finally walked into the room. While Latorre stood tall and elegant, shirt crisply laundered and wool trousers pressed with a flawless crease, Bradley was a lanky, gangly, fashion photographer's nightmare in frayed blue jeans and layered t-shirts of bright, clashing colors. His bushy hair, unruly and in dire need of a trim, stuck out in clumps around his headset. Purple flip flops underscored how seriously he took his role as a creative genius.

As soon as his boss entered the room, Bradley stood and removed his headset.

"O, Supreme Overlord," he spread his arms wide in welcoming triumph, "you've got to see the news outlets. The press is going nuts! We did it. Mission three accomplished!"

"Bradley, don't call me that." There was no hint of anger in the older man's voice, merely tired tolerance for a joke that had played out long ago.

"But, Savi, this is too good. We've successfully crashed four satellites owned by multinational conglomerates, and landed them all within a five-mile radius of our target. What says 'Supreme Overlord' better than that?"

Savino loosened his tie and surveyed his personal operations center, a collection of communications and information-gathering equipment that would be the envy of any senior military leader. Bradley knew he was thinking: *Does the kid genius have to be such a* kid?

Well, yeah, Supreme Overlord, I do.

But Bradley didn't say anything. Toy boxes with this many cool toys, and overlords with pockets this deep and assignments this crazy, were hard to come by.

This was his favorite plague yet.

CNN was the first. "Fire From the Sky" came down, and a graphic with the words "Crashed Satellites" went up.

Bradley grinned, and turned up the volume for the benefit of those in the room.

"...four satellites were pulled from low Earth orbit and crashed to Earth simultaneously," reported Wolf Blitzer, the first big gun they'd been able to get into the studio. "Governments and scientists are scrambling to discover who could have done this, and why. Is it an act of war? We have Dr. Angel Lopez, an astrophysicist and specialist in satellite tracking on the phone. Dr. Lopez, how on earth could someone blow up four satellites simultaneously and decide where to bring them down?"

Bradley turned the volume down again. Dr. Lopez wouldn't have a clue.

"The landings?"

"Perfecto."

It had been a tricky calculation, timing the retro-burn for each satellite so that all four would crash within a five-mile radius, but Bradley had enjoyed the challenge. Savino's young assistant enjoyed the fast-paced, ever-changing nature of the tasks the billionaire gave him: never a dull moment. And he also had no qualms about grappling with tasks that were not precisely legal. A match made in heaven.

Bradley looked beyond Savino to where one of his old MIT buddies, an ace programmer named Ben Carleton, stood looking perturbed, awaiting the moment to get Bradley's attention.

"What? What is it?" he asked Ben.

"There were people in the car that got hit. The satellites killed two people."

Was he kidding? Multiple crash landings and only two dead?

"Um, yeah. Fiery hail? It very easily could have hit the town, but it didn't. Good work."

Ben just stood there. "I don't...I mean, I didn't realize..."

"We'll talk later," Bradley said. Ben had to bring this up in front of Savi? He thought he was getting paid so much to write code for world plagues that wouldn't plague people? Ben backed away, shooting Bradley a look that said, "This discussion isn't over."

"A great triumph," Bradley added again, to Savino.

"And we're prepping the next?" Savi seemed not to have noticed the exchange.

"Yes, indeed."

"No one has connected all this with the website?"

"Nothing yet. But it's only a matter of time. I think we've got their attention. And look—the timeclock has started for Death of the Firstborn. It's all going according to plan."

Bradley looked at Savino's face as his overlord withdrew a bottle of wine from his satchel. It was one of *the* bottles, of the precious label that was as yet unreleased. That, more than anything, let Bradley know his boss was happy. Very happy.

Savino put the already empty bottle on the desk. Then he ceremonially drew out a decanter into which the wine had recently been poured. Apparently, in anticipation of the occasion, it had already been allowed to breathe.

Savino poured a goblet for himself, and offered one to Bradley.

Bradley swirled it and inhaled the bouquet. He then closed his eyes and took a sip.

Whoa. He knew all the words used to describe aromas and tastes of wine: chocolate, molasses, rose, apricot, peach, anise, geranium, burnt toast. But this wasn't any of those things. He could taste the dark berry flavors and earthen undertones which the negroamaro brought, but, there was something incredible about this wine. A taste for which Bradley had no comparison, no words.

Bradley looked again at his boss. He was an odd man. But he made a hell of a wine.

SATURDAY, NOVEMBER 10, 2007, 7:03 P.M.
TIME ZONE 1

SHANLEI WAS SATISFIED.

The first three plagues had gone off as planned: flies, diseased livestock, and now, burning hail.

The morbid results of the first three had been enough to subdue the mini-pharaohs in the locales of those plagues—Hungary, Australia, and now, Egypt. The call had just come in. Desired outcome in Egypt had been achieved.

The demonstration of power, and of the ability to deliver on future threats, had been enough to secure the capitulation of the political and business figures for which they'd planned the plagues of frogs and lice. Africa and Asia were onboard.

That meant that five of the twelve had brought their resources into line with Shanlei's master plan. The plagues of frogs and lice had, therefore, been canceled.

Shanlei didn't mind that the others needed more convincing. After all this work, it would be a pity not to get to execute at least some of the showier plagues that remained.

Five plagues left.

Seven targets that needed to submit. The final plague—Death of the Firstborn—was truly the finale. It targeted three of them, plus another high profile target chosen merely as an attention-getter. The hit men were already in place, had been for weeks. If one paid enough, it was possibly to employ la crème de la crème. Most surprising was how simple it had been to get the hit man into the US Military Academy at West Point. Truth be told, of all the things that could go wrong on an Army base, the targeting and shooting of a single cadet was probably not even on the radar.

But within seventy-two hours, it would all be accomplished in dramatic fashion.

On to the next.

SATURDAY, NOVEMBER 10, 2007, 1:05 P.M.
CADET CHAPEL, UNITED STATES MILITARY ACADEMY
WEST POINT, NEW YORK

JAIME STOOD IN THE BACK OF THE CADET CHAPEL at West Point, hidden from view by a series of screens and surrounded by her bridesmaids: best friend Lexi Kent Monroe, sister Susan and sister-in-law Dani.

Jaime didn't mind officiating at weddings, though given her druthers, she'd choose a funeral any day. At funerals, people were always grateful. Weddings—well, weddings were never quite the dream-come-true, and you were likely to run smack into a dozen sets of expectations.

For many years of her life, Jaime had assumed she would never get married. Not that she had anything against marriage, but she tended to fall for knight-errant types who were too busy slaying dragons to consider applying for a mortgage.

And yet, ten years ago she had become engaged to, and had married, her first knight-errant, her long-time boyfriend Paul, in the space of a week so their dying friend could help plan and host the wedding. Paul had been killed three months later. Case in point.

Even knowing the very real dangers of marrying a knight-errant, Jaime had managed to find herself another one. And this would be the fourth frigging time she was marrying him.

She had first married Yani in January, when they were dying in a cave in the Judean wilderness. Next, having survived, they'd been married in his home country of Eden, while she was still on mid-tour leave from Iraq. On return to the Terris world, they had been married by a justice of the peace in Hochspeyer, Germany, so that Yani would be recognized by the Army as her spouse; also, it didn't look so good for a single chaplain to have a strange man coming and going from her house at all hours.

Unfortunately, being married by a justice of the peace in a quick ceremony in Germany didn't fly with Jaime's brother, Joey. Joey had never quite gotten over the three years when Jaime had been missing, presumed dead, in Iraq. Now that she was back, he was insistent on being involved in the milestones of her life, and apparently felt her getting remarried was one such milestone. There was so much that Jaime couldn't tell Joey about the time she was officially missing that she had allowed herself to be guilted into promising to have a larger, "official" wedding wherever she was posted next.

It had seemed a simple promise. She had no way of knowing that, as Lieutenant Colonel, she would be assigned to the Military Academy at West Point and consequently expected by her family to be married at the huge, historic Cadet Chapel. She had mentioned the smaller Old Cadet Chapel to them, but, nope.

Yani thought this was hysterical, darn him anyway. Jaime wasn't sure if it was because he was so used to hanging off bridges and piloting dirigibles that getting married here was the only dramatic equivalent, or because he knew it was making her crazy to be the center of all this womanly attention. Picking colors, choosing dresses, selecting music—not exactly her thing. Yet she did feel she honestly owed her remaining Terris family and friends, so a spectacle wedding there would be.

Jaime's dress was a simple floor-length ivory sheath with a short cape. She'd gotten dressed by herself in the quarters attached to Cadet Chapel where she and Yani were staying. Not that she was shy, or hesitant about her body—which had some nice flat places balanced by some nice curves. But she also had some scars that were a little too interesting, and this wasn't the time or place to have that conversation.

Jaime also wasn't used to having her long, strawberry-blonde hair loose in public. But this was for her family.

"Oh!" Susan said softly, taking a step back, and looking at her from head to toe, "Oh, Jaime, if only Mom could see you. If only!"

Jaime met Susan's eyes and the sisters embraced. *She did*, Jaime would have given anything to tell her. *Mom did see me get married. In January. In Eden.* The hard thing was, it didn't matter. Whether their mother was dead or alive and well in Eden, it meant the same thing to Susan and Joey—life without her.

Jaime smiled. "I have you here, instead. Thanks."

"Okay, okay, I have to say it," injected Lexi in a stage whisper. "I can't believe Shepard's here! A freaking rock star! And you're not having him sing!"

The mention of Mark Shepard's name brought Jaime up short. The others were beyond excited about having an A-list celebrity among them.

"He sang at Jaime's first wedding," said Susan, then she stopped herself. "Sorry, I didn't mean to bring up Paul. Oh, I mean—"

"It's all right," Jaime smiled. "Shepard and Paul were close."

"Having him here is like having Paul's blessing," said Lexi.

Truth was, Jaime did feel like she had Paul's blessing. Paul would have enjoyed Yani.

However, unbeknownst to the others, Jaime no longer thought of Mark solely in the context of Paul. It was hard to hear Mark's songs or see photos of him without remembering a particularly wonderful afternoon in France in a hot tub—and remembering Mark's sculpted torso and the happiness she and the musician had shared in each other's company.

That particular night had not ended well, through no fault of Mark's or her own.

"Get a grip, Jaime," she breathed.

But why was he here?

"Is there another wedding after yours?" Susan asked, glancing at her watch.

"I hope so," Jaime answered.

The first notes of Handel's *Water Music* reverberated through the huge Gothic chapel, and everyone's adrenaline level skyrocketed. As Dani walked out from behind the screen and started up the aisle, Jaime closed her eyes. *You've been in war zones. You've been kidnapped. You've locked yourself in the trunk of a maniac's BMW. If you survived that, you can surely survive this.*

Susan was off, and Lexi was ready to move into place.

"Hello, Jaime," came the familiar voice that saved her, that pulled her back to herself. It was Abe Derry, under whom she had served during Operation Iraqi Freedom, and whom she had later discovered to be a fellow Gardener, as people from Eden called themselves. There was no one, save her own father, whom she would rather have walk her down the aisle. Not to mention, as a two-star general, Abe looked extremely impressive in his uniform.

And as a Gardener, Abe knew Yani in a way that very few others here did.

"You doing okay?" Abe whispered, in the deep rumble that she knew and loved.

"Yes," she said, "but am I crazy? If nothing else, to try to mingle my three families—my blood family, my Army family, and my Gardener family—for a whole day! What will they talk about? What if someone lets something slip? They each know very different parts of me!"

"Just be grateful," he said, giving her hand a squeeze, "that each of us know some of the best parts of who you really are. And everyone here loves you."

"Pshaw," she said, looking up at him.

He donned his serious face, but then glanced down at her one more time.

"You're marrying Sword 23, Jaime, really?" he said with a grin.

Yes, Sword 23—as Yani was still known—was a legend among Gardeners. And yes, she was marrying him.

At that moment, the first notes of the *Trumpet Voluntary* began, and she and Abe took their place at the center of the very long aisle.

Jaime looked forward, under the Gothic arched ceiling, past the flags hanging from the walls on either side, past the rows of brown wooden pews crowned with red hymnals. The bridesmaids had taken their places to the left. Her brother Joey and the other two groomsmen stood to the right, and Lexi's father, the Rev. Asher Kent, stood in the center of the aisle. Everyone had turned. All eyes were on her.

Yet all that mattered was Yani, standing at the front of the chapel, at the foot of the steps, smiling at her. Even now, there was a catch in her throat whenever she saw him. When she came home from a day's work and walked into the kitchen to see him pulling out pita bread and opening hummus, she had to pretend everything was normal. But how could it ever truly be normal? Sword 23—Yani—William Jonathan Burton, according to his Terris birth certificate—was in her kitchen.

In her living room.

In her bedroom. In her bed.

Like it was a normal thing.

Holy crap.

She would marry him fifty times, if she had to, and she would pretend he was just another groom, every time she did it.

By the time Jaime reached the rows of her family and friends, her mood had lifted considerably. It had finally become real to her that after the reception, she and Yani would have a week away, just to themselves. A whole week! That had never happened Terris-side.

The bride glanced to her left and saw activist and rock star Mark Shepard sitting on the aisle. Seated next to him was Chaplain Sherer, an old boss and mentor of Jaime's, who'd met Mark at Jaime's small wedding reception in Hochspeyer. The two of them got along well.

As Jaime passed their row, she saw that Mark was distracted. He smiled at her as she passed, but kept glancing down. As she moved on up the aisle, she saw him lose his battle with himself and thrust his hand into his pocket to dig out his phone.

Really? I know you're a rock star, but you can't turn your phone off at a wedding? What could be so important that it couldn't wait fifteen minutes? She smiled to see Chaplain Sherer giving him a "really?" look, as well.

Then they were in the front of the chapel, and Abe had handed her off to her husband. Together they followed Reverend Kent past the choir stalls and up the five marble steps to the altar. Yani's jet-black hair was cut just below his ears, and his dark eyes flashed fire. His face was nearly perfectly oval above a square jaw that could be set at a dangerous angle. But now his whole face was smiling.

As they turned to face each other, to join hands to take their vows, it happened.

Jaime saw Yani's watch, his top-secret watch, buzz, nearly silently, just once. For the merest split second, the watch face glowed blue. Probably no one but Jaime and Yani noticed it.

That never happened. It meant something was up—an emergency of international significance.

Now. Of course.

Frigging now.

SATURDAY, NOVEMBER 10, 2007, 1:38 P.M.
CADET CHAPEL, UNITED STATES MILITARY ACADEMY
WEST POINT, NEW YORK

THANK GOD THERE WAS A CRISIS.

Mark Shepard had been one of the first to slip out of Cadet Chapel when the ceremony was over. His driver had gotten his message and was waiting just where the driveway curved down the hill.

If the head of BeCause, his charitable foundation, hadn't called, he would have exited the church with everyone else, and been awash in the midst of the joy of the marriage, watching Jaime Richards, smiling—glowing, probably—holding the hand of her husband, who was not Shepard.

Yes, she had married Not Him, and Mark seemed incapable of not jetting around the world to watch her do it yet again.

So, thank God there was a terrible crisis.

When things in his life went wrong, Mark wrote songs. They were his psalms, his cries of anguish and of joy. It was what had made Borderland, his band, successful for two decades.

Given his upbringing, Mark had known life was hard for a very long time. Even after he became an internationally-renowned musician, he never, for one minute, presumed life would throw him any extra breaks. Who was he to have his young wife snatched away, killed by cancer? Who was he not to? He was the same as anyone who has lost someone he or she can't live without: a spouse, child, dear friend.

But then, the relentless assaults kept coming, and he'd lost not only his ability to compose, but his ability to be alive. It had taken him a long time to emerge from that dark, dark place.

Finally, one day, he awakened at the bottom of the pit of Can't Care, and felt the sun on his face. Nothing more, nothing better than that. But he felt the sun, and recognized the warmth. And he climbed, a little, each day.

Slowly, meaning crept in. Not joy, not careless happiness, but small fragments of meaning. He let it be enough.

He stayed at their place in Lac-Argent, France, and finished redoing their house, making the acreage and town self-sustaining. He lived a circumscribed life, finding contentment in small things. He started playing with lyrics again, and found that his band members had been writing songs while he was grieving. They recorded the best of them, and put out their first album in five years. It was good. It became a hit.

Mark became interested in economics, and began studying poverty and its causes and possible solutions. He was attending the World Economic Forum in Switzerland when he'd run into Jaime Richards. Jaime, who'd been married to Paul Atwood, Mark's best friend, who had been killed.

Jaime, who knew Mark. The real Mark.

A part of him long dead began to stir. When she agreed to come back to France, a quiet, deep joy swept through him—not the kind that was overwhelming and transient, but the kind that was sturdy and grounded, that gave birth to hope.

For the first time, he felt alive again—wanted to be alive.

He wrote a song in his head on the plane with her to Lac-Argent. The beginnings of another overtook him as he sat in the hot tub with Jaime, sipping wine and watching the Champagne sunset.

When he'd gone through the private living room off his bedroom that evening, lighting the fire in the centuries-old fireplace, and then dotting the room with small votive candles, he felt the return of possibility. Being with Jaime, kissing her, feeling her kinship as well as her body, he'd felt like the breath of life had filled him again, finally.

And then the panic button mounted on the wall had gone off. Mark had gone to investigate, only to be brutally attacked. Jaime had disappeared.

And yet, as he recovered in the hospital, he'd had a feeling, bordering on certainty, that she had survived. She was all right. Songs poured out from the depth of his being. Words and phrases swirled, chasing each other, as they had in the old days. Then, three days later, Jaime called. She was alive. She was also married.

He didn't believe it.

He went to the reception at her place in Hochspeyer, Germany, near where she'd been stationed. He met her husband, this Bill Burton fellow. Shepard felt that, indeed, there was some kind of quiet greatness about him.

But still, he couldn't believe it. He and Jaime had been so in sync. That night in France, her spirit—and her flesh—had responded with such passion. It made no sense.

He suspected that God was toying with him once again. God had brought him alive enough that he was able to feel the pain of loss. Thanks so much.

Why, after Hochspeyer, Mark felt he had to come and watch Jaime's church wedding, he wasn't sure. To torture himself? To prove that he could still feel something, even if it was pain?

Jaime didn't look like one of those rail-thin supermodels that used to frequent the cocaine-fueled parties after concerts. She looked like a real person, moderately tall, naturally blonde, fit but not *va-va-voom*. She was smart as anything, and she could see right through him, to his soul.

Still, he could have the supermodel of his choice. Why was he torturing himself?

Now there was a crisis. One that would set back BeCause's work in Darfur, and probably cost a million dollars. And, honestly,

Shepard counted it the kindest thing God had done for him in a long time. It got him the hell out of there.

Good-bye, Jaime Richards, he thought, as the car rolled out onto Stony Lonesome Road, continuing down the hilly road toward the Hudson River.

He decided he'd trust God, just this once more, to bring Shepard work with meaning, and break his petulant, self-destructive fixation on Jaime Richards.

That was worth a million dollars.

Seriously, it was.

SATURDAY, NOVEMBER 10, 2007, 7:12 P.M.
CASTEL DEL MONTE
ANDRIA, ITALY

IT HAD BEEN A GLORIOUS DAY.

Savi stood just inside the Castel del Monte, the thirteenth century citadel beneath which Bradley had outfitted one of the most tech-savvy headquarters in history. Savi liked the feel of the place. It was an octagon rimmed with eight turrets. It was truly still a citadel—just, now, of a different kind. It was closed for repairs this week, as it often was.

Savi also owned the repair company, keeping the coffers of the nearby town healthy.

A car pulled up just outside where he waited. From the adjacent room, Bradley's friend Ben, the genius code-writer, approached nervously. "You wanted to see me?" he asked.

"Yes. You had ideas about how to contain collateral damage?" Savino asked.

The young man relaxed visibly. "Well, if we could postpone the next two plagues, I'm sure we could contain the damage to innocent humans." As he spoke, he reached into his pocket for his cellphone, which had the calculations already run.

They walked outside together, and down the left hand side of the steps to the sedan.

The code writer continued talking. In the second it took him to look down and scroll back into his messages, Savi took out his Springfield Armory Enhanced Micro Pistol and put a bullet into the base of the young man's skull. He collapsed just behind the trunk of the sedan.

The driver and assistant had the trunk open and the body inside before the second sedan, this one Savi's ride, pulled up.

Savi climbed into the backseat and tried to be less annoyed. The plagues were happening. The two trails of breadcrumbs had been left. One for Analucia, one for the troublesome Sword 23. Would he take the bait? Follow the markers? Yes. Almost certainly. Sword 23 was just full of himself enough to think that only he could find Savi and save the world. Savino counted on it.

Within days, Sword 23 would simply disappear in much the same manner as had this programmer.

Simply disappear.

SATURDAY, NOVEMBER 10, 2007, 2:20 P.M.
CHAPLAIN'S RESIDENCE, CADET CHAPEL
WEST POINT, NEW YORK

THEY'D FINISHED THE CEREMONY.

Yani didn't know why he got such a kick out of it—except that he thought he'd never again be this visible. Never again be an Eden Operative or have a genuine Terris identity: William Burton, weapons inspector for the United Nations.

For years, Yani had been a Sword, one of only twelve living men who knew the way in and out of the place known as Eden, a hidden, altruistic society whose citizens worked to help those in what they called the Terris world. He'd been invisible, without home or emotional attachments. He'd given that up for this singular woman. In fact, he'd given up being a Sword for her before he'd even known if she'd be his or not—and first she had chosen the not.

Jaime undoubtedly thought he was goading her by going along with the ceremonies, the photos. But he wanted those photos to prove that this moment had existed in time and space. He wanted to claim it.

He wanted to claim her and be claimed by her. This intrepid female who somehow had never been intimidated by him, even when he'd kidnapped her in the ruins of Ur, in Iraq. He could have killed her, easily. She didn't care. She was still ticked off.

And once she heard about the terrible timing of this new assignment, she'd have every right to be ticked off yet again.

Jaime found him on the second floor landing of the quarters that had been lent to them by Chaplain (Colonel) Jim Thomsen and his wife Carol, who were away on two weeks' leave and knew that Jaime and Yani needed someplace to stay while her quarters were being redone. It was more than handy that these particular quarters were in a Gothic/Tudor style addition to the Cadet Chapel, complete with a concealed entrance to the chapel through a moveable bookshelf.

Yani had taken the opportunity to slip into the upstairs guest bathroom to call in; he was putting his phone back into his pocket as they met.

Below, talk and laughter swirled, with the string quartet's version of Pachelbel's "Canon" cascading from the enclosed back porch.

"What time did you say you'd be there?" was all she asked.

"Five," he answered.

"Five," she repeated.

He put a hand on her shoulder. "It's what we do," he said. "It's who we are."

"I know," she said, "but now? Now?"

More laughter, and the sound of footfalls on the stairs below them.

Yani grabbed her arm and pulled her into the nearest bedroom, which their hosts used as a workout room. As he did so, they heard guests approaching from below. As the explorers rounded the first turn on the staircase, Yani locked the door and led her back to another door that seemed like it would open into a closet. Instead, it opened to a short, secret hallway.

Yani led her in and closed the door behind them. The hidden room was square, with a shuttered secret window that overlooked the chancel with the choir stalls and altar in the Chapel below. He led her instead to another window in the wall across from the first.

"So, what's going on?" she asked. "What were they alerting you about? What's so important that it can't wait?"

"I don't know. But it's important enough that they're calling in the big guns. My love, I know you have a week's leave, and I know how hard it is to arrange that. I'll get back as soon as I can. We'll still have time together, I promise."

"You can't know that for sure."

"I'll move heaven and earth."

Jaime smiled, if slightly. "I do remember what you promised me, the first time we were married, in the cave in the Judean wilderness..."

"The time we first said it and meant it," Yani whispered.

"You said we would work together to bring about the Kingdom of God on this earth, whatever that meant."

"And you agreed."

Jaime sighed. "But, now?"

"Now?" he said. "I'm not going now. For the next hour, I'm here. And look at you." He couldn't keep the grin off his face. "A wedding dress becomes you." He took her hand, and stepped back, to get the full effect. He motioned, and she spun, letting him behold the back. "I love seeing you as a Terris bride," he said. "As my bride." He paused to consider. "But this jacket thing, I'm not sure we need this."

He tugged on the end of the sleeve and she let him pull it off. He ran his hands under her hair, over her bare shoulders.

A shaft of afternoon sunlight broke through the clouds. Jaime turned and looked out the window, then pushed it open, and drank the autumn air. Because the back of the house sat on the hill, she saw nothing but trees. "It almost reminds me of Eden," she said, wistfully. "When I had you, and you stayed put."

"When we looked together toward the future, and relished the present moment," he said. He came and stood behind her. He had a vial in his hands, a small vial, and he opened it. "This seems a fitting time." He poured a dab of oil on his finger and ran it softly against each side of her neck.

"Copper bell," she said. One of the delights of Eden was the plants that grew there and nowhere else, and the colors that morphed into bright new shades, and how sometimes even the air shimmered gold. This one scent was a passage back into that world.

Yani was still behind her. He unzipped the top of the back of her gown and the slip beneath. And then he was kissing her back, kissing the contours of the scars left by the lashing Frank McMillan had given her, which had eventually become infected and had nearly killed her.

"Your scars speak to me of your bravery," he breathed, kissing her again, "and what you were willing to risk to get to me."

"At the time," she said, not able to stop herself, "it certainly seemed you didn't care. You were angry I was there. You were angry I'd come to you for help."

He continued to peel down the top of her silken sheath. "When I saw these, when I saw what Frank had done to you…never in my life have I wanted so badly to kill a man with my bare hands."

His hands cupped her naked breasts. She was standing full at the window, but it was at such an angle that it was hidden from view of anyone and anything but the stark autumn branches, the billowing clouds, and the cool November sunlight playing behind.

Her gown and slip had fallen to her waist. Instead of guiding it the rest of the way off her hips, Yani lifted the hem from the floor, and let his hands travel up her thighs, until he found her panties. He dropped them to the ground.

"Now, I am here." He was kissing behind her shoulder blades and up her neck. "We are here, in this Terris realm, for this moment, this brief golden moment. Look, Jaime, look at the bark, the leaves, the clouds, the sky. Smell the copper bell. It is here, it is now, but you can also see eternity—"

He was kissing her and stroking her and he could tell her whole body was alive and shimmering—partly here, in this secret place with him; partly in Eden; and partly in eternity. When he took her, hard and purposefully, again and again, he knew that all they had—all they were ever promised or needed—was now.

Now.

SATURDAY, NOVEMBER 10, 2007, 7:20 P.M.
CÔTE DE BEAUNE
BURGUNDY, FRANCE

WHY WERE THEY THREATENING HIM? Why? There was no one he could tell. No one who would understand.

Archard Tavel stooped and grabbed a handful of fertile earth. He inhaled the lime and marl. Maybe he should just concentrate on this. His own little corner of paradise. At least, it could be.

Thanks to France's Napoleonic inheritance laws, vineyards such as theirs were passed down in equal part to all surviving children. That meant, by now, these acres were owned by more than a dozen cousins on his mother's side, many of whom he seldom met and didn't care for.

If he accepted the deal that he was being offered—being blackmailed to accept, really—if he sold the other business, the one his own father had overseen and grown, took the mounds of cash being shoved upon him, Archard could easily buy out most of his cousins, who at this point had much more interest in cold hard cash than their share of the glory and headaches of being a *vigneron* in this day and age.

Once, this had been his dream. To own one of the most prestigious Grand Cru vineyards in Burgundy. To nurture and protect the *terroir*, the combination of soil, climate, vineyard, grape and expertise that created the true character of the Pinot Noir that had been cultivated in Burgundy for centuries. To have a leggy, blonde wife who would have fit onto any of the catwalks of Paris or New York.

To have a son who was his spitting image.

To be handsomely rewarded for the work he'd done in expanding and consolidating the business his father's family had started three hundred years ago, when his grandfather, several greats back, had paid a handsome price for a parcel of land with a natural spring rumored to have curative powers.

But none of it felt like it was supposed to.

The cousins who owned the vineyard were argumentative and claimed to know more about wine than they really did. The leggy wife was off spending his money, likely some of it on grand hotel rooms in which he was not her partner in bed. And the son…he sighed. His son, Leal, was "on the autism spectrum." Which made it sound like he was enjoying an amusement park ride.

But worst, the selling of the family company wasn't a sale, but a ruthless buyout.

An "or else."

What did he have anymore that mattered? Who did he have that mattered? He crushed the soil in his fist.

At that moment, a flock of birds—useless birds, starlings flying south—rose as one from the vineyard floor, wheeled, and headed the direction he knew to be southwest.

Take me with you, Archard thought. *Let me fly away.*

SATURDAY, NOVEMBER 10, 2007, 7:40 P.M.
CÔTE DE BEAUNE
BURGUNDY, FRANCE

DOTS. BLACK DOTS. Starlings. Magnificent starlings. Flying. Painting against the clouds.

Leal squealed with joy and collapsed onto his back to watch the sky.

Starlings. Magnificent architects. Flying. Wheeling. Creating.

Apart. Together. In circles. Making a turret. A hole in the center. A castle turret. Round. Tall. High. Thirty feet across. It would need one hundred stairs to reach the sky.

And then, they came apart! And together! A different turret! Twenty feet across! Stairs. 120 stairs. Round and round. Starlings round and round.

Building. Flying apart.

Metz, the Porte des Allemands. The two towers in Angers.

Magnificent. In the sky.

The Chateau de Chinonceau.

Castles. In the sky.

Starlings. Magnificent architects. Flying. Wheeling. Creating.

Usually, things didn't spin. Usually, Leal had to spin.

The starlings pulled apart and wheeled together, forming yet another tall circle, another castle turret. He could gauge the dimensions. He could render the architectural drawings in his mind.

Leal felt the ground. He felt the sky. He counted the castles. Turret. Turret. Turret.

He laughed and laughed.

And then, the iron cuff.

SATURDAY, NOVEMBER 10, 2007, 2:30 P.M.
CHAPLAIN'S RESIDENCE, CADET CHAPEL
WEST POINT, NEW YORK

AFTERWARDS, THEY SLIPPED DOWN THE HALL to their bedroom to change. Jaime had a going away outfit laid out on the bed. She paused briefly, hand on hanger, as she hung it back up in the closet. There was something in that one action that spoke of the culmination of her life choices.

Some things, even important things, were out of her hands.

Instead, she chose pants, a top, and a light jacket, and sat down to pull on shoes. The young lieutenant's wedding had apparently gone as scheduled, as it was now letting out and guests outside were streaming toward their cars. She remembered their earlier conversation.

"You know, we haven't talked about this lately, but you weren't thinking you wanted to have children again, were you?" she asked Yani, who was stepping into black loafers.

He looked thoughtful. "I never thought I'd say this, but sometimes, I think yes. You know very well that after what happened, I've been hesitant, but I think I'd very much like to have a child with you. Maybe two. "

Jaime was stunned. "You would?" was all she could bring herself to say.

"We don't need to talk about it now. But maybe, we could think about it? In the meantime, I think perhaps we'd best go join our guests."

"Do you think maybe they've noticed we're missing?"

"I'll tell them I was just helping you with a zipper," he said, as he stood, kissed her like he meant it, and headed out into the hall.

"I'll be right down," she said.

Whoa. A child, maybe two? This was not what they'd talked about.

She heard laughter from downstairs, and knew she had to go join her guests.

Lord, lead me, she prayed.

No sooner had the prayer left her than her cell phone, charging across the room, began to ring.

Should she?

She went over, looked at the caller ID—and answered.

"Hello, Jaime," said the Operative Coordinator who oversaw her assignments as an agent of Eden. "I realize this is unfortunate timing, but I hear you have a week's leave. And you may, perhaps, have some unexpected free time. I wouldn't bother you, but something urgent has come up."

SATURDAY, NOVEMBER 10, 2007, 3:20 P.M.
THAYER HOTEL
WEST POINT, NEW YORK

THIS WAS A BIG MOMENT for every best man. Very shortly, Cadet Bak would make the traditional toast to the bride and groom. He whispered to his girlfriend, Shelby, that he was slipping out to use the restroom, but the truth was, he just wanted a moment to himself.

There was a lot he could say in the toast: that he was glad Rick Pellman had gone ahead and married Melissa, even though he was freaked out about her future plans with bomb disposal, and had gotten drunk as a skunk before the ceremony. That he was glad Melissa had married Rick even though he'd gotten drunk as a skunk.

The truth was, Djoko Bak was envious of Rick and Melissa. They had things far easier than he and Shelby did. Rick and Melissa could get married if they decided to, and both of their families were happy about it.

Djoko hadn't even figured out how to tell his parents he was dating an American cadet. He wasn't sure Shelby had figured out how to tell her mother about him, either.

But something else was going on. Djoko checked his most recent text from his father again. *Are you safe there at West Point?* his father had asked. *Is it hard for outsiders to get onto the base?*

Djoko had answered, *Yes, I'm very safe.*

But what did that mean?

As he thought that, he looked out onto the terrace beyond the reception room. A man was there, smoking. At first it looked like he was talking to himself, but when Bak looked more closely he could see the faint electronic glow of a Bluetooth earpiece. Likely a hotel guest. No one of consequence. But what if he was?

Why wouldn't his father tell him what he was worried about?

Or did being a government official in Indonesia mean being on edge all the time? And, if so, was that the life in store for Djoko? If so, how could he ever ask Shelby to join him?

Weddings made him think too much.

He had his toast written. His friends had helped, assuring him it was funny without being too insulting.

He headed back toward the reception. His lovely Shelby was standing at the doorway in her full dress greys with red sash. Djoko wished for a moment that, since this was a weekend wedding, she'd chosen to wear something other than a uniform, something flowing and feminine.

Djoko loved Shelby, and he was fairly sure she loved him. But he had an ominous feeling about the text from his father, and about this week in general.

"Everything all right?" Shelby asked.

"Yes," he said.

"Good." And she gave his hand a brief squeeze as they returned to the party.

SATURDAY, NOVEMBER 10, 2007, 4:20 P.M.
ROUTE 32
VAILS GATE, NEW YORK

JAIME'S CAR LEFT WEST POINT through Washington Gate. Shortly thereafter, the driver put up the soundproof window between the front and rear seats, and Jaime put on her glasses and earpiece.

"Hello, Jaime," said her OC. "Sorry to grab you on such a momentous day, but we need someone with your skills, right away. I take it you've seen the situation on the television?"

"Four satellites fell from the sky?" she said.

"Yes. But rather than focus on the why, our attention has been drawn to an obscure website. Well, obscure until now. Others are sure to find it quickly."

"What is it?" Jaime asked.

"WheelofPlagues.com," said her OC. As she spoke, the website bounced into view on the sides of the smart glasses. On the front page of the website was a large wheel, with pie-shaped slices of different colors. She read them with fascination: Water to Blood; Frogs; Gnats or Lice; Flies; Livestock Diseased; Boils; Burning Hail; Locusts; Darkness; Death of the Firstborn.

In other words, the plagues God had visited on the Pharaoh of Egypt when the Pharaoh had refused to free the Israelite slaves.

Three of the slices were grayed out to the point that you could barely read the labels.

Below the wheel was a bar of large numbers. It was a clock, ticking backwards, counting down. TIME TO NEXT SPIN, it read.

Currently, it stood at 26:14:55. As she watched, the seconds tumbled quickly backwards.

On the bottom of the page lettering proclaimed, DEATH OF THE FIRSTBORN. Underneath was a clock with its numbers counting down. It was currently at seventy hours and change.

Up in the left corner were screen shots of three smaller versions of the Plague Wheel. Jaime clicked through to them. Wheel One had landed on FLIES. Wheel Two was stopped on LIVESTOCK DISEASED. The third wheel had landed on BURNING HAIL.

Holy crap.

"What do you notice?" asked the OC.

"That according to the website, this is the third time they've done this—that fire from the sky is the third plague," said Jaime.

"Yes, and we're working right now to put together possible recent catastrophes with this crazy lottery."

"Also that there are only seventy hours until the Death of the Firstborn—but there will be other plagues before that one."

"So, we have a limited timeframe to divert further disaster," said her OC. "Death of the Firstborn—firstborn of whom? World leaders? Financiers? Normal people? We don't know. And whatever the next plague will be, it is sure to be as catastrophic as those that have already taken place. Now." She paused, and went on. "Now, read the paragraph underneath. Some of it seems gobbledy-gook. But see if any words jump out at you."

"Yes, of course," Jaime said after the second viewing. "It mentions the Terris world and the Steppe and the Six Sisters. It can't get much plainer than that." Each of those phrases related very specifically to the hidden world of Eden. "You think those words were purposeful—left as a message for us?"

"Seems very likely. Something else of note has been going on. It turns out that the four satellites that came down in Egypt all crashed within five miles of an interesting archeological dig. A source on the ground tells us that the archeologist in charge, Dr. Samuel Golding, has been finding some strange objects. We want to get you over there right away to talk to him. Thing is, many scientists and astrophysicists will be descending to sift through the remains of the satellites. We can't have you show up by yourself asking archeological questions without raising questions about who you are and why you're asking, so we got you a ride over with someone who is involved in the satellite part of the situation. That plane will be leaving within the half hour—as soon as we can get you to Stewart Airport in Newburgh."

"What kinds of question do I ask at the dig?"

"Speak only to Dr. Golding. Ask about the unusual things unearthed there. We'll be in touch as new information surfaces."

"It seems likely that all this somehow has a connection with the Steppe." The Steppe was how the residents of Eden referred to their home.

"A little too likely."

"How have I been explained to the satellite person with whom I'm hitching a ride?"

"Free Winds has been helping finance his own efforts to use satellites to monitor and diffuse violent situations. Unfortunately, his satellite was one that came down. He's been told you're with Free Winds."

"Got it."

Free Winds was the nongovernmental organization under which many Gardener enterprises were financed in the Terris world.

Even as Jaime spoke, the sedan followed a sign toward the airport. It pulled around to the small private plane terminal. And indeed, as she got out, she saw a large private jet waiting with its front steps down. It was a Gulfstream 500, long enough to have seven windows. It seemed Eden was serious about getting them to Egypt quickly. Jaime grabbed her duffel. This wasn't at all the way she'd envisioned the end of this day.

As she strode toward the plane, her OC's voice came again over her headphone. "Jaime, keep in touch. Things are happening quickly," she said.

"I'm about to board the plane," Jaime answered. "Is it all right for my host to see me using the glasses?"

There was an intake of air. “Try to excuse yourself to the restroom or other part of the plane,” she said. “The best way to avoid lying is to avoid questions being asked.”

“Yes, ma’am,” said Jaime, more out of habit than from protocol.

As she approached the stairs, her host appeared at the top, framed by the open door.

“Hello,” he said, and then he stopped.

Jaime, now on the third step, also stopped dead. Above her stood Mark Shepard.

“Hello, Mark,” she finally said.

“Strange way to begin a honeymoon,” he replied.

SATURDAY, NOVEMBER 10, 2007, 10:45 P.M.
VIGNETI PARADISO RITROVATO
MINERVINO MERGE, ITALY

A TINY, ROUND, ORANGE-COATED PILL.

Savino sat by the fireplace in his spacious master bedroom and contemplated the medicine he held in his hand. He had been taking Thorazine for the last five years. He hated the idea of being chained to a drug, but when mood swings and sudden episodes of deep sadness had threatened to overtake his life, this little pill had made all the difference.

He reached for the glass of red wine on the coffee table. He knew he wasn't supposed to take the drug with alcohol. But wine was his life. He couldn't stop drinking because of a stupid pill. And besides, his body seemed to have so acclimatized to this medicine that he felt no ill effects when he took the pills. No side effects was a good thing.

Savi gently swirled the deep red liquid around the walls of the goblet. He waved his hand across the wide opening of the glass, smiling as the exquisite mixture of scents reached his nose. How would he explain the aromas to Terris-dwellers? He might tease them with "butterscotch" or "earthy." But it wasn't. They could do their best to describe it, but it would be a fool's exercise, like trying to describe a color you'd never seen. He lifted the glass to his lips, taking only a small mouthful, which he rolled around his tongue. He suddenly swallowed, threw the orange pill to the back of his throat, and took a larger gulp of wine.

Returning his glass to the coffee table, Savi leaned back into his chair and gazed into the fire. His mind went immediately to his lovely Analucia. Her beautiful face floated before him. She was right there. He reached out and felt himself caress her cheek.

"My darling. Soon all impediments will be removed. Your captors will no longer keep us apart. I have laid the trail. You will know how to find me. Just follow your heart. In the end you will discover me with open arms."

The fire was beginning to cool, flames receding and replaced by glowing coals. Savi reached for the poker and began to move the logs about to reinvigorate the fire.

"Impediments removed!" He imagined the face of Sword 23, whom he despised. Savi jabbed the poker deep into the fire, letting loose a flurry of sparks. One ember landed, burning, on the carpet next to him. Slowly, deliberately, he crushed it, ignoring the burn-mark it left.

Savi looked up from the carpet to see a face floating in the darkness of the adjoining bathroom. He started, then calmed as he realized it was only his housekeeper, who was probably waiting for the right moment to turn down his bed.

He reached for his wine goblet, finished the last of his drink, and stood to walk about his estate before retiring to bed.

SATURDAY, NOVEMBER 10, 2007, 4:52 P.M.
STEWART AIRPORT
NEWBURGH, NEW YORK

MARK SHEPARD GRABBED JAIME'S DUFFEL and stepped back to allow her to board the plane.

"We're ready for takeoff as soon as you're seated," said Ken, their pilot, who stood at the door to the cockpit.

"Thanks," said Jaime.

She followed Mark into the cabin, where they settled into two large, cream-colored leather easy chairs that sat side by side, an aisle in between; each had its own large table and circular window. They buckled in. Mark, fit and tan, his thick black hair worn long, had also changed clothes. He was wearing khaki pants and a polo shirt—the shirt clinging to his sculpted torso and his rakishly-styled hair adding more than a hint of wildness.

Mark was American, but now mostly lived in France. He'd come to the reception after her wedding in Germany. He certainly didn't have the time to go jaunting around the world to yet another of her nuptials. As the plane began to taxi, she asked, more brusquely than she meant to, "So, why are you here?"

He barely looked at her. "You invited me."

"No, I didn't."

"Yes, you did."

"Well, I was only being polite."

"Well then, so was I."

The noise of the engines and the rushing air filled the air between them. Conversation stopped as they took off.

Once the plane reached cruising altitude, a male flight attendant appeared. He was in his late twenties, introduced himself as Luke, and amiably told them their flight to Port Said Airport in Egypt would take approximately eleven hours; they'd be landing close to 1:30 p.m. local time. He added that he would be in charge of preparing their meals while in the air, and to please let him know whenever they'd like something to eat or drink. He brought in a basket of fruits, crackers, and cheeses, and put it down on the table by the two couches behind them.

Once he left, Jaime leaned over to Mark. "Hey. I'm sorry. I didn't mean to be rude. What you said on the steps was correct. This isn't exactly how I'd pictured this day ending." The musician was looking out the window. He didn't move. Jaime went on. "I'm guessing, from the fact that you're also on a plane to a satellite crash site in Egypt, that this isn't how you'd hoped it would end, either."

"You've got that right," he said.

Jaime looked back out her window. Small cities and yacht harbors were disappearing as they started over the seemingly endless expanse of the Atlantic Ocean.

"Is this your plane?" she asked. At first she'd assumed it was, but now, looking around, she realized it was much larger than the private plane on which he'd flown her from Switzerland to France. Also, he didn't seem to know the flight attendant.

"No. This is a get-to-Egypt-without-stopping plane."

Mark stood and stretched. He walked back to where the two couches faced each other and picked up a red and yellow apple from the basket.

Jaime unbuckled and stood as well. "Can we start again?"

"Whatever," he said.

She walked back, looked at the fruit, and realized she hadn't actually eaten at their reception. There were two small plates. She put grapes onto one, then added crackers and small slices of several white-to-orange cheeses.

"Hi, I'm Jaime Richards," she said. "Why are *you* heading for Egypt?"

Mark looked at her, and she could see the decision-making synapses flashing through his brain. He expelled a sigh. "Because my satellite crashed," he said.

Jaime looked at him, confused. "*Your* satellite?"

"One that was gathering information for BeCause, yes," he said.

Jaime knew that BeCause was the charitable foundation that funneled some of his money to good causes. "Can you explain?"

He sat down on one of the two facing sofas. Jaime sat on the other end of the same couch, a cushion-length between them. "You're no doubt aware of the humanitarian crisis in Darfur," he said. "The Sudan government, funding the Janjaweed militia, has systemically been surrounding villages, raping and killing inhabitants, taking land. Hundreds of thousands have been killed, hundreds of thousands more have been relocated into camps. Land has systematically been stolen and ethnic cleansing has wiped out entire populations. International peacekeepers have been rebuffed, and workers for aid organizations have been shot. It's grim.

"Since the end of the Cold War and the break-up of the Soviet Union, many satellites in orbit aren't needed as they once were. So, the satellites' owners lease out time. We've been trying to watch the movements of the Janjaweed, hoping to warn villages, or at least document the atrocities."

"Really? Civilians can do that?"

"Often, according to international law, we're the only ones who can."

"Did it help?"

Shepard sighed. "Seemingly not at all. Part of it was that we didn't have the resources to monitor and interpret the data in real time. It's a huge undertaking. I still believe it's a good idea; there just need to be more of us, and with more resources. The thing that scares me now is the idea that somehow the Sudan government in Darfur had the wherewithal to put an end to the satellite, the same way they've been attacking UN workers and aid groups." He shook his head. "But how did they pull this off?"

Mark looked so angry and sad at the same time that Jaime felt even worse about being rude to him earlier. "Are you sure they did pull this off?" she asked. "Yours wasn't the only satellite brought down."

"True," he said. "And I hate to say it, but I am hoping the Sudan government doesn't have this kind of power. That this isn't a personal attack against our satellite."

Luke appeared again, to ask what they wanted to drink. Jaime asked for seltzer. Shepard ordered Scotch.

Then he turned to Jaime. "So. What are you doing here? Don't tell me you have a satellite, too?"

"Nope. I did ask for one on the wedding gift registry, but so far, no go." She didn't mean to make light, but he was sitting there looking so…knight-erranty.

"So, why are you here? After what happened in Lac-Argent, it seems pretty clear you're not simply a chaplain in the US Army."

Darn. Why did they put her on this plane, with the one person who could call her bluff? What was she supposed to say?

"I think I need to use the restroom," she answered. "I'll be right back."

SATURDAY, NOVEMBER 11, 2007, 10:31 P.M.
VIGNETI PARADISO RITROVATO
MINERVINO MERGE, ITALY

HE HAD RETURNED.

Xiaofan pulled her red and white hanfu robe around her and stood silently across the master bedroom, waiting for Savino Latorre to notice and acknowledge her. Xiaofan would have been willing to wear Western dress, but it became clear that Savino appreciated her more when she wore striking Chinese apparel. He encouraged her to buy the best. She knew all the current designers of note, and most of them now knew of her.

She didn't mind wearing the lovely hanfu silk robes or the brocaded cheongsams. They made her feel and move elegantly. Back in China, she never would have spent that much on traditional clothing—or taken such care with her appearance. The hanfu was a red and white print, with flowing bell sleeves. It was triple belted in bright red.

There were many facets to the job Xiaofan did for Savino. But her main duty was a silent one—to remind him from whence she came, and whom she represented. For this purpose, the traditional clothing was a good fit.

"Shăguā." He had seen her.

"Yes, Guī dàn?" She was sure he had been told the Chinese names he used for her were sweet diminutives and not outright insults. A game two could play.

"It has been a successful day."

"Yes." She approached him silently, and knelt beside the bed where he was now reading.

"May I give you massage?"

"You always know. My neck is killing me."

He sat up and she came beside him. She ran her hands up his neck and easily felt the knots that were stemming clear blood flow and causing him pain. She began to gently massage the muscles that led to them.

"So it was a good day?" she prompted again.

"Yes. Very good. You have seen the news?"

"Not often," she said.

"The satellites are down."

"I'm glad, if this is good thing."

"Ow, ow—no, don't stop, it's good," he said of her kneading hands. "Sometimes I think you know me better than anyone."

"You know I only keep you until She arrives," Xiaofan answered quietly.

"It should be soon now," he said. "But don't worry. Don't worry. You will always have an honored place."

"Is my place in your bed tonight?" she breathed softly.

In response, he turned to her and met her lips gently with his own.

He was a surprising and complex man, this erstwhile Guī dàn of hers.

SATURDAY, NOVEMBER 10, 2007, 5:32 P.M.
OVER THE ATLANTIC OCEAN

JAIME RETURNED TO FIND MARK READING a copy of *Rolling Stone*. The cover photo, as always, was arresting. In this one, Mark himself was in the center foreground, with the other members of Borderland, his band, fanning back on each side.

"Wow, Mark, cover of the *Rolling Stone*!" she said. "I mean, I'm sure you're used to it by now—but, wow! What's the occasion? Or just your general greatness?"

"New album drops this week," he said.

"A new Borderland album? Cool. And the story—can I see it?" she asked.

"No," he responded, "This is an advance copy, not on stands yet." He put it back into his case. "You were gone a long time."

"I was also checking in," she said. "I've gotten permission to share some information with you that I hope you'll find useful."

In fact, in the time she'd been gone, she had spoken to both her OC and Yani.

"Permission from whom, Jaime?" he asked. "What is going on? Who are you really, and who are you working for?"

"I'm really me, Jaime, and I'm really a full-time, active duty chaplain in the US Army. But times like this, when I'm on leave… sometimes I go on fact-finding missions for Free Winds. Times such as now."

Shepard sat there, scrutinizing her; she saw questions forming and being dismissed before he spoke them.

"Okay," she said, "I'm going to show you two things. Here's the first."

She took out her Eden glasses, and handed them to Mark. He took them and put them on. Jaime couldn't help but remember the first time Yani had handed her a similar pair of glasses, in a hidden room under the ruins of Ur in Southern Iraq.

"There should be a screen to the side," she said.

"Yup," he said.

"Do you see a website?"

"Yes," he said, "what the heck is it?"

"It's called the Wheel of Plagues—as in the Biblical plagues visited on the Egyptians in the book of Exodus. We don't know who's behind it. But we do know that whoever—or whatever organization—it is, is taking responsibility for downing the satellites."

"Whoa," he said. "And this is *good* news?"

"Good news only in that it likely isn't personally about you or BeCause's use of the satellite."

"How do I scroll around the website?" Mark asked, fascinated by the technology, in spite of himself.

Jaime showed him.

"So, I'm guessing that, if the good news is that it isn't about BeCause and Janjaweed, the bad news is that plagues are never good."

"Pretty much," she said. "Nor is it good news that, according to the website's clock, there are less than twenty-four hours until the next 'plague.' These plagues are killing people and animals and doing irreparable harm to countries and ecosystems. Not to mention that there are fewer than sixty hours until the ultimate catastrophe—Death of the Firstborn. We don't even know what that means—or how many 'firstborn' will be killed. It also likely means a lot of other destruction will happen in the next three days if someone doesn't stop it."

"What can we do?" Mark asked.

"Let's get to Egypt, and see if there are any clues about just who has decided to play God."

SATURDAY, NOVEMBER 10, 2007, 10:32 P.M.
TAVEL APARTMENT, 7TH ARRONDISSMENT
PARIS, FRANCE

FURY. HIS FATHER YELLING. PULLING. So angry.

Why? Why did Leal do things to make him so angry? So troubled? His mother had gone away. Always away. And his father, Archard, angry. Leal didn't mean to, he didn't mean to.

"Meltdown?" Leal asked Danièle.

"Yes," she said.

"I'm sorry."

"He doesn't understand."

"Stairs were there. 120 stairs."

"Leal, stairs were where? Can you find the words? Are they hiding in your mind?"

Leal remembered the birds. The turrets. The dimensions.

"Stairs were there." Those were good words. Words to say. "Stairs were there. Stairs were there." In the sky. Stars. Stair stars. "Stairs were there."

Danièle Coralie Guillory had filled his pool. His floating pool. It was a water hug. In it, he was safe. All the little fish swam by. The primordial fish. He was back. He had gone back. Everything was all right now.

Stairs were there. Stairs were there.

SATURDAY, NOVEMBER 10, 2007, 6:02 P.M.
UNDISCLOSED LOCATION
MIDTOWN EAST, MANHATTAN, NEW YORK

YANI SAT IN THE OFFICE assigned him in the nondescript building on Manhattan's Midtown East, near the United Nations. Not quite Del Floria's tailor shop, but the same idea.

He had just briefed his United Nations team supervisor on the existence of the Wheel of Plagues website, to which he had been alerted by his wife, who was also an agent—though as an Eden operative—on this mission. Obviously, both the government of the Terris world and the Gardeners had taken note of the destructive things that were happening. This time, the Gardeners were a step ahead.

Yani knew he needed to click into mission mode—and he had, 99.9%. Just the fact that he was cognizant that his wife was on her own trajectory—that he was thinking of Jaime as his wife, not simply an Agent of Eden, frightened him.

His last wife had also been involved in missions. And 99.9% of the time, it had been all right.

"Bill—Bill, you there? What are you thinking?" His team supervisor asked.

"Just trying to put the pieces together," he said.

"The website to which you've called our attention changes everything," she said.

"Yes, it does."

She didn't ask where he'd gotten the information. The sources he couldn't disclose were too important to jeopardize.

"We'll still keep working on finding out how and who brought down the satellites, but now we'll also start fitting the pieces together about the other plagues. Just when you hope there are no more madmen, or madwomen..."

"There always are," Yani said. "The Time Between."

The Time Between was a code phrase for the epoch in between humankind's discovery of weapons of mass destruction and the moment some scientists felt would inevitably arrive when madmen or extremists would make use of them to destroy humanity. This particular UN task force, though technically under Weapons Inspection, had as their unofficial purpose to prolong the length of The Time Between.

"Let's extend it as long as we can."

"So, is there somewhere different you need to go, now?" she asked.

"Yes. There's a string I need to pull to see if I can get closer to our mastermind. And the clock is ticking down."

Again, no questions. She stood, nodded briefly, and left the small office.

Yani looked again at the WheelofPlagues.com website. His life as an Eden Operative was always a dance: who to tell what, and when. He couldn't tell the United Nations task force about the markers that led him to believe that the mastermind was a former Gardener. And he wasn't going to tell Jaime that there seemed to be a coded, personal message at the bottom of the home-page.

A small photo of a wine glass charm ring. It was a tall tree in full green leaf, with one leaf of shining gold.

The Tree of Life.

A code that only three people in Eden and two here, in the Terris world, would understand. It was a message for Yani, likely from the only one of four others Yani would just as soon not cross paths with again in this lifetime, a man named Yacov Wester. Wester was a Gardener who had chosen to leave Eden and come to reside here in the Terris world.

When Yani had reported this, his Eden Operative Coordinator had told him that they had lost all contact with Wester back in the late 1950s. He had vanished without a trace. His last known location had been a winery on the California coast.

Yani sighed. He wasn't enthused about tracking down this guy. And yet, Wester seemed to be somehow involved in this current plagues debacle. Not only that, he had left a personal message for Yani. For the first time, Yani briefly wished he'd declined requests for help and had simply gone on his damn honeymoon.

SUNDAY

SUNDAY, NOVEMBER 11, 2007
ARGENTINA
IN THE DARK

ALEJANDRA CRUZ *WAS.*

Darkness enfolded and welcomed her.

She floated alone and naked in an endless universe.

Some part of her knew she was floating, buoyant, beyond the pull of gravity, in salt water at exactly body temperature. But after the first few minutes in her float tank, boundaries ceased to exist. The universe and the space inside her was one.

This is what a return to her home country meant. Time at home. In her own pod.

Renewal.

Many people, when using a float pod, found their minds emptied. Meditation states were reached and surpassed.

Being was all, and it was enough.

Alejandra would reach that state, and purposefully move past it.

Into chaos.

Golden bursts of light. Meteors streaking all around. Inside. Outside.

Human beings tried so hard to create order, systems, laws, straight lines, boxes.

But the universe was chaos. Life was chaos. Chaos was beauty.

It was also, currently, her job.

Alejandra, with her Castilian bronze skin, long oval face, perfectly sculpted Greek nose, and wide full lips, was considered by many to be a beauty, but she had less than no interest in such things. She could have worked as a model, but would rather slit her own throat than primp in front of a mirror.

The only external augmentation she had chosen for her body was a Barnsley Fern, tattooed across her right shoulder, which represented the fractal work of a British chaos theorist. She also sported an emerald stud nose ring in her right nostril and had chosen to dye her long brunette hair a burgundy color.

Although Alejandra chose to downplay her natural beauty, she was not beyond using it to distract someone while she and Bradley Kluge accomplished one of their chaos raids. The thing she loved most in life was to introduce unpredictable change into a system: ecological, political, economic—it didn't matter. Then, sit back and see what type of major ripples might develop.

She knew that personality trait drove her father crazy. As a senior leader in the Argentinean military, he liked things in perfect order, predictable, by the book. In retaliation, Alejandra loved to bring confusion and disorder to people's lives.

Her recent raids had brought deep personal satisfaction. When the street kids she hired had left animal corpses infested with blow fly maggots all over the central Buda district of Budapest, the big fat flies that emerged found their way into every restaurant across a four-mile radius. The area was now quarantined while the authorities attempted to clean up the mess. This stunt had devastated both the tourism and overall economy of Hungary. No doubt heads would roll during their next election.

The second chaos raid had been much more complicated to effect, and so was even more satisfying. Spreading anthrax microbes throughout the food sources of cattle in Tasmania had required a lot more planning and stealth. Australia had such pride in their disease-free food supply, it was fun to bring their cattle industry to its knees.

Where her source had obtained the highly weaponized anthrax microbes she didn't need to know, but they had been extremely effective.

While Bradley's rain of satellite parts had been truly spectacular, she could not claim any credit for that one.

It was thanks to Savino Latorre they had such wonderful opportunities to wreak havoc. Releasing his plagues had been a challenge she and Bradley could not resist. Of course, Savino was certifiable, but that made him all the more appealing.

Psychotic = unpredictable = chaos, the perfect equation.

A gentle hum alerted her that her session was over. Time once again to bring the beauty of chaos to the everyday lives of Earth dwellers. She stretched and smiled and slowly rose.

SUNDAY, NOVEMBER 11, 2007, 1:35 P.M.
TEL EL-BALAMUN, EGYPT

SAM GOLDING WAS ANGRY. As he had tried to assign some meaning to the crazy events of the previous twenty-four hours, his emotions had ranged from intense sadness, through confusion, and on to total numbness. But underneath, grounding it all, Sam was just plain angry.

Tromping all over his dig, *his dig*, were countless experts in electronic whatever, treating the ancient grounds like a bloody crime scene. But the crime in which they were interested had nothing to do with the death of his close friend and co-workers, Ibrahim and Enoch. Instead they were obsessed with all the damn pieces of space junk that had rained down upon the camp the night before.

It was fortunate that in his efforts to clear his head after the firestorm, Sam had walked through the temple, checking the status of the ruins. Because once the satellite people had arrived and interviewed his team, they were denied access to the site while the "experts" did their thing. He could not access any spot even close to where a piece of space debris had landed.

For hours, Sam had planted himself on his makeshift porch under a large canvas tent flap, drinking first water, then juice, followed by tea. He was just about ready to move on to the hard stuff when he noted a dust cloud on the horizon. Another vehicle! More investigators. When would it stop?

It was a car, approaching from the direction of Port Said. Sam expected to see one of the rattletraps that the locals used as taxis to cart foreigners around. But as it drew closer, he could see that it was a very well kept olive green Mercedes. Not new, by any means, but it was obvious the owner loved that car.

Who around here would have access to a car like that?

The car slowed to a stop. A tall man, probably in his mid-thirties, jumped out and headed immediately to the largest group of investigators. A rather intense discussion ensued. As Sam watched, he had a nagging feeling that he should recognize the guy, but couldn't quite place him.

The second person to emerge from the car was a woman somewhere in her thirties, he guessed. Medium height, blonde hair in a French braid, she moved with a sense of determination. Then she paused and looked around, taking it all in. This woman intrigued him. She slowly, calmly, surveyed the entire site, as if not interested at all in the satellite investigation.

When her gaze fell upon his makeshift porch, the woman made eye contact with him. She smiled and began to walk his way.

"I'm looking for Dr. Samuel Golding," she said.

Sam stood, suddenly wishing he were not dressed in torn khaki shorts and a sweat-stained t-shirt.

"That would be me."

"Jaime Richards." She held out her hand in greeting and he grasped it. "I'm with Free Winds. My colleague is busy looking for parts of our satellite. I'm interested in your dig."

"Please, have a seat. Can I get you something to drink? It's not quite tea time, but I think you Yanks don't worry about that." He poured lukewarm tea from a pot on a small Coleman stove and offered her a cup, which she gladly received.

"How long have you been here?"

Sam considered the question, and pondered whether she meant the dig or him personally. He chose the latter as his answer.

"I've been involved in the dig here at Tel el-Balamun for the last three years, primarily as Assistant Project Leader. But when this off-cycle opportunity to dig came up, the museum gave me the opportunity to be lead for three weeks." He looked across the damage to the ancient ruins and remembered Ibrahim's smiling face. His anger surged. "And now, *this* is my legacy!" His hand jabbed toward the investigators crawling around the ruins.

"But it's certainly not your fault."

"Whether it is or not, my name will always be associated with death and destruction here at the dig. And, even if no one else remembers, *I* can never forget." He paused, unable to speak further.

The young woman looked thoughtful and spoke, almost too softly for Sam to hear, "They said two of your team died last night. I'm so sorry."

And that was all she said. Sam appreciated that she did not try to give some cosmic reason for it all or suggest that she understood his grief.

This moment brought him closer to pain than he had been yet during the last twenty-four hours. Seeming to recognize this, his visitor aided him by moving the conversation onto a different subject.

She took a sip of tea and set her cup down on a crate, which served as a makeshift end table. "What did you mean when you said, 'off-cycle?' You wouldn't normally be here?"

"No, we come in the spring. But a special donor gave enough money for us to open the dig up for a few weeks this fall."

"Is that usual? Who was the donor?"

"I don't know. I heard rumors it was an anonymous donation."

"So, has it been worthwhile?" The archeologist flinched at the question. "At least until the space junk came raining down?"

"We have unearthed a number of interesting pottery pieces," Sam turned on his tour guide mode. "We also began to clear the temple steps, and..."

He hesitated, about to say more than he had planned. Few people knew about the strange piece he had unearthed near the temple steps. Of course, now that the dig was littered with satellite pieces, he was not sure it mattered.

"You were about to say something?" The woman encouraged Sam to continue.

There was something about this woman that made him trust her. Was it her calm demeanor? Her caring support for a stranger trying to deal with loss? Sam didn't know, but he made a split second decision.

"I found a brick that was totally out of place. It was the wrong type of clay for the area, and situated as if it were buried here recently."

"Odd."

"Yes." Sam was almost relieved to tell the story that he had been keeping bottled up. "And what's stranger, the brick looks old but there's etching on it that seems quite fresh. It isn't Egyptian. It's some sort of cuneiform. I'm more of an Egyptian language specialist, so I'm not one hundred percent sure."

Sam noticed his guest's eyes widen at the use of the term "cuneiform." To his surprise, she seemed to understand the implications of his words.

"Cuneiform? Here? You're right. It makes no sense. But I would love to see it!"

"I have it right here. I'm not really sure what to do with it." He disappeared into the tent and returned with a reddish-brown brick. The edges were rounded and worn, and there were markings carved into one side.

The visitor weighed the brick in her hands and turned it over, examining all sides.

Strange, Sam thought as he watched her. Her eyes moved almost as if she were reading. Maybe she was an artist. They tend to notice detail in things that others miss.

"Cool," she piped up after examining the brick. "Do you mind if I take a picture…?" She pulled out her cell phone and snapped a shot before he could object.

The archeologist didn't like the thought of stray pictures leaving the site. He reached over and secured the brick from his guest.

"I'd prefer," he said with irritation, "that this brick not be publicly displayed on the Internet or elsewhere."

"Not to worry!" She smiled that engaging smile, which put him back at ease. "I'll keep it in house. In fact, I think we can say with some certainty that this was planted on the site. I'm not sure you need to mention it as part of the dig at all."

He started to ask what she meant by "in house" when her travelling companion broke off his conversation with the investigators and approached them.

"Dr. Golding, this is Mark Shepard," said Jaime.

Ah, that was how he recognized her companion. Musician type so famous that even he had heard of the fellow.

"Sam, please," he said, shaking hands once more.

The musician held a piece of the space debris in one hand, and transferred it to the other.

"And call me Mark," said the musician. "Bizarre thing. No one can figure out what brought the satellites down. No sign of anything launched from Earth. No sign of anything hitting them from space; and the fact that they detonated—or whatever—in such an order as to all land here—well, it's got everyone puzzled. Most they can figure is that it was either someone who works programming the satellites, or that it was an act of God. And, apparently, these satellites all have different owners, so it couldn't be one programmer, it would have to be massive collusion. They're talking to each and every person with access to the satellites and orbits, but so far, it seems not only unlikely, but impossible, that so many people could work together without discovery."

"So, are they looking into who was using these particular satellites?" Jaime asked. "Any common threads there?"

"So far, absolutely no link between owners or users. In fact, nothing but dead ends."

"Could it be a hacker?"

"Again, the different systems that would have to be hacked without anyone noticing makes that unlikely. But they're trying not to rule anything out."

"So we've landed on act of God?" Jaime asked, with an ironic smile.

"The ancient Egyptians would know it was magic," Sam said.

"At the moment, magic seems like the most plausible explanation," agreed Mark. "And it seems like we came all this way to know less than we did before."

SUNDAY, NOVEMBER 11, 2007, 1:35 P.M.
CASTEL DEL MONTE
ANDRIA, ITALY

BRADLEY KLUGE SAT AT HIS CONSOLE, facing the wall of television screens. He took another bite of the flakey Italian pastry known as a lobster tail. This one was chocolate cream. It was heaven.

It was almost too much fun to watch the experts flail around for explanations about the satellites.

In fact, no one could just decide to hack into satellites to bring them down. As with any good magic trick, the stage had to be preset. And someone had to have the wads of cash to take control.

In this case, the four satellites in question had been launched with chips containing malware, which had been inserted at the factory. In an effort to control costs—i.e., cut corners—the corporations that had commissioned these satellites had each purchased chips from a certain manufacturer.

For a substantial price, this manufacturer had embedded a malware program in the chips, allowing anyone with the right password to access the satellite flight controls.

Savino Latorre, billionaire wine maker and grape grower, had paid that very large price.

The result was that his computer expert/astrophysicist had been able to access the flight controls.

Since these satellites had low earth orbits, they didn't have to be nudged too far to begin tumbling toward the earth. The crash sequence had been placed in motion only about eight hours before the crash. It would take months to discover all the links between the four downed crafts. Likely, they shared parts from a dozen other purveyors. It was also likely that other satellites still orbiting had perfectly normal chips from the same Chinese factory.

Meanwhile, the telling evidence had been destroyed in—well, can you say, "fiery hail?"

However, as Ben had noted, bring down the satellites hadn't simply brought chaos to a country's industry and finance; they'd killed someone. Two someones.

Collateral damage, he supposed. It upset Ben, but hey, sometimes it couldn't be helped. Where was Ben, anyway? He couldn't just slink off and stew. That's not what they were paying him for. And Bradley could use help finishing this code.

Perhaps Ben had been a bit too "normal" for this position. Ben was truly a nerd, an egghead, whatever you wanted to call the super-braniacs, while Bradley had always known himself to be a little "off." He'd prided himself on it. Bradley had found his fellow geniuses a little too black-and-white in their thinking.

He'd even considered starting PsychoCon, just to do it. Not for board game players, for actual psychotic individuals. He probably would have, except he was becoming serious about chaos and Chaos Theory and didn't want to attract the attention of law enforcement. He was also a stickler for correct use of language, and he knew he wasn't actually a psychopath.

ChaosCon; *that's* the gathering he should start. Except that, if he did it right, it would be too chaotic. No predicable start time, no obvious location. He smiled. He did amuse himself, sometimes.

Bradley finished his pastry and poured a fresh cup of joe. On to the next. The text was coming in now. Buenos Aires was a go. Good. Both he and Alejandra would have been sorry to cancel that one. It would show off some of their best work.

SUNDAY, NOVEMBER 11, 2007, 4:22 P.M.
ROAD FROM TEL EL-BALAMUN TO PORT SAID AIRPORT
EGYPT

"SO, IT SAYS SOMETHING," Mark Shepard said, looking over Jaime's shoulder at the odd cuneiform in the photo Jaime had taken at the dig.

"Problem is, I speak it more fluently than I read it," she said, frustrated. She then looked up, realizing she'd given away more than she should have in that one statement.

"You speak cuneiform," said Mark.

"No. Of course not. Cuneiform is a method of writing using symbols rather than an alphabet."

He continued to stare at her.

"I speak a modern form of Sumerian," she said. "It's often transcribed with symbols."

"Nothing odd about that," he said.

She was saved by the tick of an incoming message. Jaime had immediately sent the photo in, and before they reached the airport, she got back a translation, which was very close to her own:

Where the Malbec grape is loved
Find a river of silver,
Though a Conquistador sailed away in shame,
His visage remains in a place of honor.

"*Conquistador*," she said to her Operative Coordinator, who came on at the same time the text of the translation was sent. "I got 'conqueror,' but I didn't understand the notation afterwards."

"So. This alone tells us several things," said her OC. "First, that whoever wrote it speaks modern Sumerian, and is likely a Gardener. Or former Gardener. Fact is, Sword 23 thinks he knows who it is."

"Really. This is good news, certainly? We can find the perpetrator and stop him?" Jaime hoped she sounded professional. Sword 23 was Yani. If she were just another agent, she'd be delighted that he was "on it." That could mean nothing but successful resolution, no?

Now, though, it nearly took her breath away to know Yani was yet again on the front lines. She knew it also meant she likely wouldn't be able to speak to him again until this was all over.

"Find him and stop him. Two things more easily said than done. But we're on it."

"And the clock is ticking."

"It is indeed. Only fifty hours remain until the Death of the Firstborn. And less than eighteen as countdown to whatever the next plague will be."

"So what is this marker about? Where does it lead? And why?"

"We're hoping it will lead to the location of the next plague."

"And, do you get a location from it? I was getting either France or Argentina, but then you add in the conquistador, and the River of Silver..."

"Very good. Yes. Argentina. And there aren't that many statues of conquistadors in Argentina, let alone on the Plata de Oro. So it seems you're headed for Buenos Aires. Specifically to the Parque Lezama."

"And what am I looking for there?"

"He wants us to come there...or some Gardener to come there. Sword 23 thinks these might be markers for a woman from the Steppe with whom he has fallen in love. It may be one way of heading off the 'plagues.' Or another way to find him. And, as we said, we don't have much time."

"Does 'he' have a name?"

"His name in the Steppe was Yacov Wester. Are you willing to stick with this? We'd like to have one person . . . preferably a woman . . . visibly following the markers. Each 'plague' has wreaked some kind of ecological and financial disaster on the country where it's been perpetrated. We'll have people on the ground trying to head it off, or help control it. What do you think? Are you willing to go forward? These people are obviously very dangerous."

Jaime thought only a moment. She remembered the look on Sam Golding's face, and thought of the families the two men had left behind. "I'm in it now," she said. "Let's bring it to resolution. So the pilot knows where we're headed?"

"Yes. Another long flight, I'm afraid. Flight plans have already been filed. The plane should be ready for takeoff. And this time, you'll need to stop to refuel. You can tell Mark Shepard that his pilot has already flown back to France from New York. He is awaiting word and will pick up Mark wherever you stop to refuel before crossing back over the Atlantic. Probably Portugal. Your pilot should have that airport location shortly."

"All right. We'll speak soon."

There was a sense of both relief and sadness when she thought about losing Mark's companionship.

Jaime looked up to find they were reaching the outskirts of the airport. Both she and Mark produced their papers, passports, and identification to the well-armed guards, and the car proceeded to the hangars for the private planes.

"So," said Mark finally, "what's up? It seems you have some idea who's doing this."

"Yes," said Jaime. "Now the problem is finding where in the world he is. I'm headed for Argentina. Your plane is back in France already. The plan is for us to get out of Egypt, then for your pilot to pick you up where we stop to refuel before leaving Europe and crossing the Atlantic. Our pilot should know that location before we board, so your pilot can meet us there. I think they mentioned Portugal."

Their driver pulled up beside the Gulfstream that had brought them this far.

They got out of the car. Mark came around to Jaime. It struck her that he looked like he belonged here, in Egypt, trying to solve international problems. His intellect, his charisma, not to mention the dashing cut of his hair, worked together to make him nearly spellbinding. She was glad he was on their side.

"Thanks for everything," she said.

He stood there, staring at her. The intensity of his focus bound her to the spot. She understood how thousands of concertgoers could each feel they had a personal connection to him. So the only-her, laser-focus thing was…uncomfortable.

"What? Let's ask Ken where we're going to refuel, and you can make arrangements."

"You're serious," Mark said.

"What?"

"That I'm getting off the plane and sending you off to stop a madman by yourself."

"It's my job, Mark. It's your job to figure out what is going on with the satellites and run BeCause and launch your new album. You have a new album, remember? And likely a band who's ticked off that you've been MIA."

"Priorities," he said.

"It's not your job," she said. "But thanks for the help, so far."

"You can fly to Portugal," he said. "But I'm not getting off."

"Come on," she said. "We don't have time for this."

"Look. If you don't have to drop me off, we don't have to go to Portugal. You can refuel in South Africa, and save hours. The route would be much more direct."

"Mark!"

"What?"

"You have a worldwide album release in four days! I'm sure you've already missed two dozen interviews already! You're not in this!"

He took her arm. "How could I be any more in this? Talk to whomever you need to talk to. I won't get in the way. I won't ask questions. Okay, so I'll ask questions, but if you can't answer, I won't push it. You need backup."

She stood, trying her best to stare him down.

"I'm not getting off the plane. So I may as well not get off in Capetown as in Portugal."

SUNDAY, NOVEMBER 11, 2007, 4:30 P.M.
TIME ZONE 1

SHANLEI HAD DISCOVERED YEARS AGO there are three secrets to working with the Chinese government: bribe the right people in ways that aren't considered bribes; keep the government in the loop so they feel they know what you're doing; set up holdings and companies in other countries that the Chinese government can't see or control.

Before Shanlei could make a final push to actually control crucial natural resources, companies had to be in place to appear to own and control them regionally and locally. That is why the mini-pharaohs represented every continent and many economies and governments.

It would be a risk, afterwards, to take on other corporate giants. Shanlei knew that would be more of a gamble than picking off individuals who had the right company or political office in the right places.

With the proper finesse, the link between these companies would be invisible to all but those who needed to know. Anyone else who figured it out would simply disappear.

In the meantime, it was a perk that one of the best ways to control what needed to be controlled and hide what needed to be hidden was through wineries.

Shanlei raised a glass, and took a sip. A perk, indeed.

SUNDAY, NOVEMBER 11, 2007, 9:35 A.M.
SCOUT VINEYARDS
SONOMA COAST, CALIFORNIA

YANI STOOD IN THE CHILLY MORNING AIR, surveying the dense fog that cloaked the Pacific Ocean like a living shroud. The stately mansion before him was built in 1888 by Renee and Ernst Scout, who had come from Switzerland to follow their love of the grape. The four-story Victorian with cupolas and outdoor porches framed in gingerbread fretwork was surrounded by vineyards. The Scouts had chosen the Sonoma coast, west of the Russian River valley, for its unique cold-climate growing area.

The current owners, Renee and Ernst's grandson Leonard and his wife, Ruth, had added fifty more acres of cultivation. Their grapes were garnering worldwide attention. Their 2006 Pinot Noir had won numerous medals. They now shared the house with their daughter, son-in-law, and grandchildren.

Small wooden trail markers pointed the way to the caves that had been hewn from the loam of the local hills and noted that the first tour started at 9:30 a.m. There were perhaps a dozen cars in the parking lot. Late-arrivers headed quickly down the path.

Yani was not interested in a tour. He waited until Frederic, the son-in-law, exited the rear of the house and headed back to convene the guests. His wife had gone ahead of him to unlock the caves and turn on the lights. Their children had already boarded the local yellow and black school bus at the end of the long driveway. That meant there was a good chance that Leonard and Ruth would be alone in the house.

Yani veered from the path and walked around to the kitchen door. Stucco pots with bright red geraniums and marigolds sat at the top of the four concrete steps. In the old days, when the house was first built, this would have been the door to welcome friends of the family.

He knocked.

There was a moment of hesitation, as if someone was rising from the breakfast table, then a soft shuffling. The gingham curtain that framed the window in the door was pulled back, and a silver-haired woman looked out at him.

He smiled and doffed his cap.

She opened the door a crack. "Yes?"

"Hello," he said. "I'm Bill Burton. I'm looking for Leonard Scout. I'm hoping he might have some information on an older relative of mine."

"What'd you say your name was?" she asked. Before he could answer, they both heard movement, and her husband joined her at the door.

"What'd you say your name was?" he asked. He was mid-seventies, with a rim of white hair around his otherwise balding head. He wore black glasses, a light blue turtleneck, and a sand colored sweater. He looked vaguely like he should write science fiction.

"Bill Burton. Pleased to meet you, Mr. Scout. This may seem odd, I realize, but I'm looking for information on a fellow who stayed here a long time ago. More than fifty years. You would have only been a boy, yourself, but I wondered if you might remember him."

Yani fished the photo of Yacov Wester from his pocket and proffered it.

Leonard Scout took it, and squinted. "No need to stand out there," he said. "Come on in. Let me get my glasses."

Yani entered. Len's wife Ruth took this as a cue that he was all right and offered him coffee. Len led him to the breakfast table.

"This is a fellow...?"

"Who stayed here for a while. He might have worked for your parents."

Len took off his glasses, wiped each lens with a breakfast napkin, put them on, and looked again. "Hmm," he said. Then, "Wait. There was a fellow like this. He came over from Europe, like my folks. Wanted to become a vintner himself, he said, was willing to work for them for free, for the experience. Had read about how the extreme conditions here on the coast let us produce a fully ripened grape at a lower brix, or sugar content, along with a high-acid profile, which made for an exceptional balance. Smart fellow, finding his way here."

Yani nodded.

"He stayed on for three or four years. Came just before I finished high school, and left when I was off at college."

"Do you remember his name?"

"Certainly I do. And funny you should come around asking for him. His name was Vino...something having to do with wine."

"Savino," said Ruth, bringing over a plate of croissants and sitting down across from him. "That's what it says on the envelope."

"Envelope?"

Len looked at her like she'd given up the big secret. "Yeah, Savino Latorre. Hadn't heard from him—or thought of him—for decades, and then, two weeks ago, a package arrived from him. On the front, it asked us to pass it along when the addressee showed up."

Blood surged through Yani's veins. Yet he sat, calm, and asked, "Oh?"

"A woman's name, though. Maybe you'd know her?"

The way they both looked at him, he realized this was a test. "Was it addressed to our mutual friend, Analucia?"

"Analucia?"

They wanted a last name. What version of her Eden last name had Wester used? There were several possible variations.

"Analucia Sarai."

Len headed out toward the front hall and returned with a padded manila envelope. He set it down in front of Yani. It hadn't been opened.

The addressee was Analucia Sarai. He'd guessed correctly.

And the name at the top of the return address was Savino Latorre. The envelope was covered with customs stamps. It had been mailed from mainland China.

"So you know her?" asked Ruth. "This Analucia?"

"Yes," said Yani. "She is a close friend."

"You could get the envelope to her?"

"Yes," said Yani. "And thank you. This is very helpful."

"Are you interested in wine?" asked Len. "Would you like a personal tour? Or, better yet, to taste our Pinot Noir?"

"Not today. But if it's all right, I might return with my wife to see the place."

"We'd like that," said Len. "And if you find this Savino fellow, tell him I said hello."

SUNDAY, NOVEMBER 11, 2007, 6:35 P.M.
VIGNETI PARADISO RITROVATO
MINERVINO MERGE, ITALY

SAVINO LATORRE KNEW he needed to get back over to headquarters to make certain everything was in place for the next day.

But his thoughts were a little fuzzy. It worried him. This cloud came over him sometimes, and, when he could, he stayed by himself until it lifted.

He hadn't had any drugs, or even any wine, yet today.

He didn't want Bradley to worry, and he certainly didn't need Shanlei to know. Sometimes, to get things done, one must make a pact with the devil. He sometimes did consider Shanlei to be the devil, although they'd never met in person. The man was ruthless. He didn't mind killing or "collateral damage." Or ecological damage. In fact, that was the point.

But there were upsides to doing business with him. Billions of green paper upsides. And, of course, Xiaofan. He would make sure she could stay on, even after Shanlei got what he wanted. Even if he had to buy her, or trade for her—whatever was appropriate in their culture.

Would Ana mind?

No. Analucia was perfect. She would know she was the center of his world. The grape was named for her. The grape that would change the world.

It was all starting to happen. Yani and Analucia were probably finding their "breadcrumbs" even now. Following them to certain death, and certain happiness, respectively.

He had to get a grip.

He had to retain his single-mindedness. His ruthlessness.

When he was well, it all came so naturally. When he was under the fog, as he was just now…he would stay away, by himself. Hidden away.

SUNDAY, NOVEMBER 11, 2007, 10:29 A.M.
SCOUT VINEYARDS
SONOMA COAST, CALIFORNIA

YANI WALKED TO THE BLUFF that halted the churning sea. The morning fog still hovered as a silent blanket; only the sound of the crashing waves below assured him he was on the precipice. A wind circled and played; soon enough it would clear the coast and bring the day bright November sunshine.

As of yet, however, he was the only one who had walked the serpentine path to the cliffs. He knew that the case supervisor at the UN task force would be anxious to hear from him.

Not yet.

He held the manila envelope, as yet unopened, in one hand. The fact that it was addressed to Analucia from Savino Latorre and had been posted in the Terris world plunged the investigation into a tangle of possible motives and emotions.

He knew he would be instructed to open it, but he wanted to play this one by the book—if only situations like this came with a "book." The impenetrable fog and powerful swells felt like warnings from the past; the roiling surf echoed inside his chest like the boom of a bass drum. As yet, he was on the edge. But if Savino—or Wester—was really behind these insane "plagues," there was nothing to do but step off the cliff.

Yani put on his interactive glasses and flipped the small switch that allowed sound.

"Anything?" It was his Operative Coordinator. "I'm here, also, Sword 23," said TC4. Each of the Operative Coordinators worldwide reported to one of four Terris Coordinators. You knew when a Terris Coordinator became involved that the case was of high importance.

"Hello, TC4," said Yani. "I was able to speak to Leonard Scout. He remembered Wester from the photo and said he did stay there, learning about winemaking. Wester is now going by the name Savino Latorre."

"We'll trace that name immediately. You mentioned Wester in connection with the Wheel of Plagues website, and some sort of inside message to two or three people. The history there?"

"Long ago. First thirty. Our Vintner's Cup wine appreciation group in Eden was small—there were only six of us. Yacov, Analucia, and I were the younger ones. We all got along well."

As Yani spoke, it was as if he was wrapped in tactile memories. The vineyards in Eden—the Steppe—were terraced. From the wine presses at the summit, you could see the valley below, hear the bird song, smell the rich earth.

Fine wines were among the most cherished legacies of Eden. Perhaps it was that the soil and the water were so unspoiled or that the range of fruits and grapes at their disposal was unparalleled, but the varietals were complex and outstanding. Cultivating and appreciation of wine was taught and treasured. In time, each Gardener participated in the Vintner's Cup, during which time they learned winemaking from the experts who oversaw those terraced vineyards. It was during his time in the Vintner's Cup that Yani had found his first footing.

Yani's mother, Mara, had died suddenly the year before. Death wasn't viewed the same way in Eden that it was in the Terris world. The veil between the now and the to come was much more gossamer—the knowledge of the eternal, assured. Because of this, Gardeners did not mourn death the same way.

Yani had understood this and had gone along with it—until his mother was gone—snatched away. As deep as relationships ran with his father, his sister, his friends and mentors, his mother was the sun around which all their other planets revolved. She was laughter and understanding, wisdom and seeking.

He was devastated. Even though he knew the rending was not permanent, that she would not want him to mourn, that she was close by, he couldn't find his way past the sorrow.

What made it worse was that the Steppe was infused with infectious curiosity. People loved life. They were fascinated by everything. But after his mother died, nothing interested him, not creating, nor discovery, not invention, nor growing and tending, not relationship.

The six months he participated in the Vintner's Cup was the first time he found companionship worth the time and effort. It was due, in large part, to the fact that neither of his peers, Yacov and Analucia, treated him like Yani the Bereft. The rapport amongst them was easy and instantly familiar. Yakov was fine, a friendly young man. But it was really Analucia who set the tone. She was caring and lovely, interested and interesting. She could pose questions about the process of growing the grapes and the marrying of the wines that had sparks of intuition. She could also sink into the enjoyment of the moment.

He remembered one particular sunkissed afternoon, after they had helped trim the vines, when the three of them sat together overlooking the verdant valley. As Yani had sipped the earthy wine with incredible top notes of Amal, a grape known only to Eden, he was bathed in the glow of pure presence, being fully alive and fully in the moment; completely content.

That was the gift of Eden, and of the Eden wines; utter contentment.

"Did any romantic attachments develop?" It was TC4.

"As time went by, it did seem like Yakov began to fancy Analucia. But she never showed romantic interest in either of us," Yani answered.

The Steppe was an extraordinarily egalitarian society. During its earliest centuries, though, it had been a matriarchy, and some vestiges of that still existed, however subconsciously. For one thing, the women were comfortable with power and had an inbred sense of worth—as did the men. However, still, the women usually made the first move in terms of a romantic relationship.

Yani had been happy not to have the added complexities of romantic attachments. He didn't know if it was because what he responded to in Analucia were some of the same sensibilities he'd cherished in his mother, but he found the three times each week they were together to be an oasis for him, a reprieve from both grief and thoughts of the future. Thus, Yani found it annoying that Yacov seemed not to take Analucia's lead in regard to remaining platonic friends.

"It made things tense, toward the end, as he was so obviously smitten," Yani continued. "Analucia was never rude, but she never encouraged his attentions, either."

"And how did it affect your own relationship with Yacov?"

"It irritated me. As time went by, perhaps more than it should have. Yacov and I both chose to come Topside. About the same time I became an Agent of Eden, he decided to make his fortune in the Terris world. He and I came through together. He was bringing out vine cuttings from the Steppe. I called him on it, but it was hardly like he was going out of his way to disguise what he was doing. He knew full well it was forbidden, and that if he let me see, I would report it. Now I'm wondering if he had others hidden more carefully, and was misdirecting our attention.

"Then, just before I was…reassigned, he sent a message back, asking Analucia to join him. I was tasked with delivering her reply, which was a polite, 'not interested.'" Yani took a breath. "It might not have been the kindest of deliveries."

"I see."

It had been in Paris, a foggy day. Yani found Wester, as planned, on a bench in the Parc de Bellville, eating a sausage from a vendor.

"Yacov," he'd said. "I've brought news. Analucia sends her best regards, but feels her place is in the Steppe. She will not be coming."

Wester had simply stared at him. "I don't believe it."

Yani had sighed. "How hard is it to believe? Unless you two had something secret between you, I never saw any sign she was interested—in either you or me."

"You don't know everything," Wester had said.

"No. Of course not. The three of us had some nice times together. But they're in the past."

"You don't believe someone like her could love someone like me," Wester spat, accusingly.

"She could have. But she didn't. She doesn't," Yani said, annoyed. "I'm sorry."

"No, you're not."

"All right, I'm not. But this is all in your head. For all our sakes, give it up."

And Yani had left, shaking his head. Yacov Wester, who had once been an interesting fellow with whom to trade ideas and spend a sunny afternoon, now did nothing but annoy him.

"I'm fairly certain that, if he thinks of me now, it is not kindly," he said now to his Terris Coordinator. "Should I open the envelope addressed to her from him, as Savino?"

"Yes. Current events necessitate moving things along."

Yani did. "Hmm," he said. "It's a brochure, written in English, French, and Chinese. For the Golden Sun Winery in the Ningxia Province of China."

"Does it say anything? Any note to her, or instructions?"

He looked through the paper. "There is one note scrawled. It says, 'Ask for Tommy Liu.'"

"So he's asking her to come?"

"Somehow the crazy stuff he's doing is meant in part to catch her attention. Perhaps he wants to meet her there."

"Do you think it's worth pursuing?"

"Yes, I do. Why don't you go about tracing the whereabouts of Wester under his new identity as Latorre. If we assume this envelope can really have come from Wester to Analucia, it could be a way in. Let me pursue it. It's the only clue we have at the moment about Yacov's whereabouts. Can you get me to Ningxia?"

"Okay. Be in touch when you reach the airport. But Yani—this guy's gone off the deep end. Not to mention, he's expecting Analucia but getting you. Be careful."

Yani put on his aviator sunglasses and turned back toward the car. He hardly noticed the old farm truck, its cab and open back laden with boxes of spinach and arugula, pulled over so the driver could talk on his cell phone.

"Yes," said the driver. "He left Scout Vineyards twenty minutes ago. Heading south. His plane is at Sonoma International. Give it a while and check the flight plans."

The old farmer in the overalls, with a salt-and-pepper beard, gave a smile, and a friendly two finger wave to Yani as he got into his own car and proceeded on his way.

SUNDAY, NOVEMBER 11, 2007, 7:44 P.M.
VIGNETI PARADISO RITROVATO
MINERVINO MERGE, ITALY

THEY CONCERNED HER, the times Savino stayed by himself now. At first, he took these mini-retreats in the middle of the day for only ten or fifteen minutes at a time. Now, they lasted an hour or more.

At first, Xiaofan had been worried that he was doing more dealings, this time behind the back of Shanlei. But now she knew that he was hiding himself because things didn't add up.

These were times when Savino lost his moorings, his focus.

What he was pulling off was truly amazing; it had required a decade of stellar preparations. How would it change when *she* arrived? Undoubtedly, his concentration would improve.

And his focus would change.

Perhaps that was the best that could happen, all around.

SUNDAY, NOVEMBER 11, 2007, 10:45 P.M.
TAVEL APARTMENT, 7TH ARRONDISSEMENT
PARIS, FRANCE

THE FIRE HAD TURNED TO EMBERS. When the final log fell, spitting gold green sparks, Archard started from his sleep. His glass of 2006 Riesling (Grand cru, of course) sat, half drunk, on the table before him.

Time for bed. He stood and stretched.

His favorite pieces of art—paintings and sculptures—were here, in his library. Before turning to leave the room, he stopped and studied his favorite, *View of Auvers-sur-Oise* by Paul Cezanne.

Archard knew that view in Auvers-sur-Oise. They had stopped there often when he was a child, on the drive between Paris and Côte de Beaune. The town had once been a collective for painters. Van Gogh died in a home that was now a restaurant. When Archard was younger, he had fantasized that he'd lived there among those creative, sometimes temperamental, dangerously brilliant minds. That he had set down an easel beside theirs. In his mind, he had friendly arguments with Theo and Vincent Van Gogh, and Cezanne as well. They accepted Archard as one of them.

Archard's father had urged him to become "an artist of the business world," and so he had.

Oddly, the person who was demanding to take over control of the Tavel businesses did not want Archard to disappear. To the contrary, he would be required to stay on as a figurehead or puppet, still seemingly in the driver's seat. But his will would not be his own.

And if he did not agree? The terms had been made quite clear. If he did not agree, that which was of most value to him would be removed. Usually, one might think that meant kidnapping a loved one, a wife or child. But surely the blackmailers would have seen, through Archard's actions, that was not where his heart—or his time—was spent.

So what would they guess to be that which meant the most to him? One might see how often he travelled to Burgundy and guess it was the vineyard. He would be sad to lose that, surely. What frightened him most was that somehow they might have discovered the truth. That he loved his art collection with a degree of feeling he knew nowhere else. So much so that he'd even dabbled in the black market when a purchase called out to him. How could they know such a thing? Through a connection with his broker? Surely not from banking transfers. He always used sideline funds for those purchases.

And, even if they did know he was an avid collector, how would they guess which painting spoke to him in a way that none of the others did? How would anyone know he even owned *View of Auvers-sur-Oise*, let alone gain access to it?

Even though the painting was only valued at five million dollars, he'd taken every precaution. The walls of his Paris apartment were reinforced. All the doors and windows were alarmed, and there was a motion detector. The painting itself was bolted to the wall and alarmed. It was as theft-proof as a painting could be. All of the art in his library was.

As of yet, he had neither agreed to nor declined the offer. And the painting remained.

They'd told him he had the weekend to decide.

Archard took another swig of the Riesling, remembered how good it was, and picked up the glass. He carried it with him down the long hallway, past the room where his son watched a DVD of the series *Arthur of Camelot.* Even Archard, who did not watch television, could recite the scene from memory. The damn kid. Every time they had to come home, he threw a tantrum. Damn kid and his damn drawing pads and his freaking *Arthur of Camelot.*

Alone in his bedroom, Archard pulled on a pair of pajama pants and kept on his t-shirt. Then he sank into the inviting cocoon of his bed.

SUNDAY, NOVEMBER 11, 2007, 11:45 P.M.
RIO DE LA PLATA
ISLA LUCA, ARGENTINA

ALEJANDRA CRUZADO SLOWLY IDLED a small, powerful speedboat along an inlet of the Rio de la Plata. She loved this part perhaps best of all.

The night before, when the world still proceeded apace, with no idea of the fate that awaited, the chaos already set into motion.

Once the sun rose, the results of months of her handiwork would be spectacular.

Alejandra was passing Isla Luca, directly north of Buenos Aires, as she dumped her last bucket. She was just preparing to rev the engine up to full power and motor back to the dock when she noticed running lights in the distance. It looked to be a boat about twice the size of Alejandra's, and was moving too fast to be a fishing boat.

Probably the *Prefectura Naval Argentina*, or PNA, Argentina's version of the coast guard. Whether they were trying to catch drug smugglers or stop illegal fishing, Alejandra did not want an encounter with them that might be registered in their logbooks. Tomorrow, when all hell broke loose, they might recall a woman out on the water, by herself, at midnight.

She quickly cut her engine and the running lights, drifting silently toward the larger boat. Had they seen her? She could barely make out the outline of the other vessel. It was a twin engine, might be a Zodiac, definitely had a cabin. It was looking more and more like the PNA every minute.

Alejandra held her breath. Should she make a run for it? She was fast, but their engines could outrun her in a heartbeat. And two men she could probably handle, especially if they weren't expecting resistance, but this boat could have a crew of four. Not good.

The searchlights of the other vessel suddenly illuminated the water, and both engines roared to full power. Alejandra's eyes hardened and she reached for the semi-automatic pistol she had hidden under the dashboard. She laid one hand upon the cool metal of the weapon and held it there, calmly awaiting the approach of the coast guard.

The other boat sped off in a wide arc away from Alejandra, heading north up the coast with sirens blaring. She released the breath she had been holding for at least one minute and pulled her hand away from the hidden weapon.

Chaos, the unexpected, that's what she loved about life. Maybe some poor sod had gotten drunk and fallen overboard. You couldn't plan for it. If she had tried to create a diversion it would not have been as effective.

After giving the patrol boat a few minutes leeway, she started her engine and turned toward port, ready for one final chore before leaving Argentina.

MONDAY

MONDAY NOVEMBER 12, 2007, EARLY MORNING
OVER THE ATLANTIC

JAIME PULLED HERSELF TO WAKEFULNESS, lying still for a moment to discern what had called her from sleep. She opened her eyes to find she was stretched out on one of the sofas in the Gulfstream 550. The cabin had been darkened, except for the running lights.

Mark Shepard slept on the sofa across from hers.

Her Free Winds phone was vibrating.

She closed her eyes for another moment, then slowly sat up and waited for her head to clear. When it had, she got up, staggered back past the table to the private conference area, and pulled the door shut. She'd been glad to discover she didn't have to go into the restroom to talk to her OC.

"What's up?" she asked.

"Sorry to wake you," the OC said, sounding rather recently-awakened herself, "but the Wheel of Plagues has spun again."

"And the lucky pie slice?"

"Water to blood."

"Great."

"Yes. Not sure what to make of it. If he means literal blood, well, it would take millions of gallons to make a river or coastline actually change color. But so far, he's been willing to make modern interpretations. Our one hope is that he is starting to leave markers so that Gardeners might find him. Whether he means for us to find him before these 'plagues' occur is unclear."

"Okay."

"We've got people on the ground in Argentina, looking for anything out of the ordinary."

"Or any sign that blood banks have been burgled, or cattle drained?" Jaime asked.

"Nothing like that so far. But listen, do keep an eye out. Like many murderers, whoever is doing this may well be there—or have an accomplice there—at the marker drop. So keep a keen eye. We've really got to figure out where Wester is. We've got to get ahead of this. Only thirty-six hours until Death of the Firstborn."

"Shoot, " Jaime muttered. "Any intel on Sword 23?"

There was a pause. "Nothing that would affect your current assignment."

Jaime sighed. "Okay. Thanks."

"Again, sorry to wake you, but it seemed important. Get more sleep if you can. Always crucial for good judgment."

"Yes, ma'am," she said. And she thought, *Not bloody likely.*

MONDAY, NOVEMBER 12, 2007, 2:05 A.M.
PARQUE LEZAMA
BUENOS AIRES, ARGENTINA

ALEJANDRA CRUZADO STROLLED SLOWLY but confidently along Avenida Martin Garcia, making her second pass around the perimeter of Parque Lezama.

Dressed in a white, fur-collared waistcoat jacket, short black skirt, and black high-heeled boots that reached above the knee, she knew most passers-by would take her for a hooker. In fact, one car had slowed to check her out. A dull-faced man with flabby cheeks and a five o'clock shadow rolled down his window and beckoned toward her.

Alejandra waved haughtily for him to drive on, saying, "*Sigue adelante! No tienes lo que quiero.*" (Move on! You don't have what I want.)

The man spat out an obscenity and drove off.

She turned right on Avenida Defensa and made her way past the Historical Museum. In the daytime the park had a quiet, restful feeling to it, but at night the lights from the streetlamps playing through the trees danced with an eerie glow. Alejandra preferred the night.

For the second time she approached the life-sized marble relief of a conquistador, foot on the bow of a boat, *El sueno del la sierra de la plata* (the dream of the mountain of silver). Behind him was the massive relief of a bare-breasted native with arms raised. The entire statue was shaped like a giant chair, with the conquistador, Pedro

Mendoza, standing on the seat. Surrounding the statue was a black wrought-iron fence with padlocked gate.

The fence would be easy. Alejandra could hurdle that. The base of the statue, however, was taller than she could reach, so she had dropped a small step stool behind the bushes on her first pass around the perimeter.

Seeing no one in the area, she grabbed the stool and threw it over the fence. Then, with a running start, she caught the top of the fence with her hands and kicked her feet high over the fence, doing a half twist and landing perfectly in her high-heeled boots.

I haven't lost it! She thought, tugging her skirt, which had ridden half way up her butt, back down into place.

Too bad Bradley isn't here, she thought with a laugh, *he would have enjoyed the view.*

Taking one last quick glance to ensure there was no one to observe her movements, she placed the step stool at the base of the statue and reached up. She placed a scroll wrapped in plastic behind the feet of the conquistador. The base was high enough that no one would see the scroll unless they were lifted up, or standing on a small ladder.

Alejandra climbed back down, wiped her fingerprints off the step stool, and dropped it behind a nearby bush. *Why make it any harder for someone looking for the markers?*

She was glad to head back to her apartment to change.

It was nearly showtime.

MONDAY, NOVEMBER 12, 2007, 5:30 P.M.
AN HOUR EAST OF YINCHUAN AIRPORT
NINGXIA AUTONOMOUS REGION, CHINA

YANI SIPPED HIS SMALL CUP OF TEA and looked out the window over the Helan Mountains. The topography of the Ningxia Region was stunning—mostly uninhabitable, but stunning.

"The joke is that the Chinese have been slow to acquire a taste for wine," said a young American female wine critic to the small circle of three adoring males. "However, the better and more expensive the wine, the faster it sold. It was prized as a bribe to officials, who would then use it as a bribe of their own. How many bottles of fine wine have been appreciated in China, but never drunk!"

Yani was not an expert on Asia. He had trained twice as an agent: once, specializing in Europe, and the next time in the Middle East. Of course, all agents were given primers on all areas—to the degree that most Terris folks would consider them experts. But this adjunct training, to Yani's mind, served to underscore how very much he didn't know.

Usually, he wouldn't be pursuing a mission into mainland China. But Wester—or Savino Latorre—had become very dangerous. Why Wester had posted the wine rings the three of them had used during their stint in Vintner's Cup he didn't know, but he meant to find out.

Now that they had the Terris name Wester was going by, TC4 had told Yani, they'd found his extensive vineyards in Italy. The vineyard wasn't yet shipping wine or open to the public, and Savino himself was seldom sighted there.

He had, however, taken frequent trips to China.

Eden had trained operatives in place all over the world. However, they also had a larger network of friends upon whom they could call to help them integrate areas or situations.

Robert Zhu was one such friend. In the struggle for international recognition for Chinese wines, Zhu was bringing a group of food and wine critics—including the well known Nancy Moore—to his own vineyards and winery, which was not far from Golden Sun. Yani had come into the country travelling as one of his French advisors.

The plan was for Yani to enter Golden Sun as soon as possible—first, as an innocent tourist. He would meet up with another friend of Eden, a Mr. Shěn, who would be acting as a tour guide. With Bruce Shěn's help, he would get the lie of the land. They would then make a plan to find out who Tommy Liu was, and why Analucia was being advised to ask for him.

"So." Ms. Moore, the most important wine critic aboard, sat down in the camel-colored chair next to Yani's. "You haven't been joining the conversation."

"Sorry," he said. "Lost in my own thoughts."

She was slim, with salt-and-pepper hair in a shoulder-length bob. She wore glasses that complemented her face but didn't scream designer. That gave her points in his book.

It was clear she'd tired of the conversation behind her. It was likely that she travelled the world so often that trips such as this had become humdrum for her. And she had to be tired of the sycophantic nature of the fawning newbies behind her.

"So," she started again, "what do *you* find interesting or ironic about wine production here in the Ningxia Autonomous Region?"

Yani had the feeling she was desperate for new blood or a different spin on a tired conversation. "Hmm, ironic?" he responded. "Probably that this area is known for its population of Hui, who are predominantly Muslim."

"And therefore, don't drink wine."

"Exactly."

Ms. Moore slid into a discussion of wines she'd had made by Chinese vintners currently living in France. Yani found he enjoyed the discussion that followed. It took him back to the happier days of wine cultivation.

The flight from Beijing to Yinchuan took only a couple of hours. As they came in for landing, Nancy returned to her seat. The other critics furtively studied the tall, dark-haired man who had kept her interested for so long.

As they did, Robert slid into the seat she'd vacated.

"The Golden Sun has evening tours. We will drop you there as we pass. But I must tell you—I'm not sure how much help we can be should anything go wrong. Do you know when you will need to be leaving China again?"

"I don't," he said.

"This group flies out again in two days. We will expect you to depart with them."

"And you'll worry if I don't?"

"Worry might be all I can do." Robert gave a curt nod, and went back to his own seat.

Two days. What could possibly go wrong in two days deep inside mainland China, pursuing a madman with a vendetta and a very large pocket book?

At the rate things were happening with the Wheel of Plagues' website, two days might be too long to prevent another disaster.

Yani sat back, enjoying the freedom of not piloting this particular flight. Two days, plus crossing the International Date Line. He sighed as he saw his honeymoon forever slipping away.

MONDAY, NOVEMBER 12, 2007, 10:15 A.M.
TAVEL CORPORATE OFFICES, AVENUE HOCHE
PARIS, FRANCE

ARCHARD STOOD AT HIS OFFICE WINDOW, looking down at traffic on the Avenue Hoche below.

The new Tavel corporate offices had been completed only two years earlier. Building in Paris was highly regulated, and their world-renowned architect had to work hand in glove with the Architect of Paris to come up with a design that would be modern and green, yet fit in with the older facades along the avenue. The good news was that the building was stunning, built around a soaring atrium with circular staircases, rounded hallways of glass, and a green roof.

The bad news was that the building was five stories tall. Not a guaranteed death, even if you jumped from the roof.

That would be the final horror. To become injured and paralyzed, yet forced to watch as his company was run without him, passed down to Leal and overseen by the next of his wife's young lovers while she sold off his art collection.

Shoot me now.

Oh, God, that would be so appreciated. Anyone.

Anyone?

For in less than two hours, the call would come and he'd have to agree to become a figurehead in his family's company. Thank God his father was not alive to see this day.

They'd somehow survived the 1990s when Nestlé had come into France and had taken over Perrier, Carola, Contrex, and half a dozen other French water companies—not to mention San Pellegrino, Arrowhead, Deer Park, Poland Spring, and twenty others around the world. They'd survived the mass acquisition; in fact, his father had led the charge for the larger of the remaining French spring water companies to band together as protection.

Now, apparently, they'd all go down together on his watch.

Speaking of watches, he looked at his.

An hour and a half before the phone would ring. He would accept an offer of nearly a billion dollars; his own net worth would skyrocket.

Perhaps he was the only near-multi-millionaire in the world who was wondering how he'd make himself live another day.

MONDAY, NOVEMBER 12, 2007, 10:30 A.M.
VIGNETI PARADISO RITROVATO
MINERVINO MERGE, ITALY

"SO, HAVE YOU CHOSEN A DATE?"

"December first. Saturday. At noon."

Savino watched Donato Giordano, the manager of the Vigneti Paradiso Ritrovato, as he held his white Borsolino hat in his hands, figuring things out quickly in his head.

"All will be ready? It is enough time." It was a statement, not a question.

"*Si, signore.* It is both enough time, and not near enough. We will make the announcement. Everyone will protest they don't have enough time to clear their schedules, but everyone will. Talk of the new Paradiso Ritrovato varietal has reached fever pitch. No one will pass up the opportunity to be among the first to taste it."

Although Savino Latorre had lived and worked this land for forty years, he was still considered a newcomer in Puglia. He was first generation here, and he was not Italian. He smiled, knowing none of his fellow vintners, or his neighbors, had any idea where he was from. Although Giordano had worked for him, painstakingly overseeing his vineyards for thirty-five years, Latorre knew he was still an enigma to the man. And he meant to keep it that way.

He knew that to his Italian neighbors the oddest thing was that the Vigneti Paradiso Ritrovato had sold no wine.

Usually, even when nurturing new strains, a vineyard will sell older, more common varieties of wine. It is their business, after all.

But not Vigneti Paradiso Ritrovato. He had the funds to wait, for forty years: summer, winter, spring, fall. Years with no rain and years with plenty. Nurturing and nudging this one new grape, and then the wine that came from it, to maturity.

And, after all those decades, all those years, he was giving Giordano two weeks to arrange the unveiling.

Of course, Donato Giordano had known this day would come; in fact, he had to have suspected they were growing close. Preparations had been in the final stages for years, and the wines were now all perfectly aged and ready.

He nodded, pretending to be annoyed by the short amount of time, but they both knew the time could not come soon enough. Donato left, muttering under his breath and shaking his head. But he was also smiling.

Analucia—she would need a new dress. A new wardrobe for the occasion.

They would get to work on it the moment she arrived.

MONDAY, NOVEMBER 12, 2007, 5:45 A.M.
BUS HEADING INTO NEW YORK CITY FROM WEST POINT, NY

"I HOPE IT'S GOING TO WARM UP," Cadet Djoko Bak said, wrapping his fingers around his travel mug as he sat on the bus with his girlfriend, Cadet Shelby Fairfield. Together they watched the skyline of Manhattan draw closer across the expanse of the George Washington Bridge. They were sitting together, maintaining the maximum closeness allowed between two cadets in public. In other words, the only body contact took place when Shelby briefly leaned across him to snap a photo of the Empire State Building.

"C'mon, Joke!" The young woman laughed as she punched him playfully on the arm. "The temperature during the parade is supposed to be in the forties. I can't believe that, after more than three years in this country, you think that is cold!" The two were preparing to march in the Veterans Day Parade with their fellow cadets.

The young man smiled at the use of his nickname. It had been conferred upon him by upperclassmen during his first hours at West Point, the dreaded Reception Day, after they'd spent thirty seconds trying to wrap their minds around "Djoko," and had followed him throughout his academy days.

"That's not fair!" Bak tried to look hurt but it wasn't working. "I spent the first eighteen years of my life where the temperature never goes below seventy, and the only two seasons of the year are the wet and dry. You grew up skiing the Rocky Mountains, and you think it's hot when the temperature goes into the eighties!"

"Hey," said Shelby, "On the ride back, maybe we could talk for a little bit about my branch choices. If I go aviation, the chances of deploying are pretty strong. Tom Pellman is having a hard time accepting Melissa's branch choice of EOD, so I thought we might avoid some of those issues by talking about it ahead of time."

"Okay." He tried to clear his head. "But I feel like, really, the bigger question is whether I'm going to accept my commission in the Indonesian Army next summer. My family would probably disown me if I didn't. As the firstborn son I am expected to follow my father's path: service in the military followed by a political position in the government."

"Why does your father have to be a cabinet minister? It makes everything so difficult!"

"It is what it is, Shelby. I can't change it anymore than you can change the fact that your mother is in public office. We just have to deal with it."

As he spoke, he remembered the recent text from his father. The cadets marched in the parade every year, yet this was the first time Djoko was uneasy. He wished his father had been more specific. There were crowds of people in New York City. Anyone who was watching him could easily blend into the crowd.

Their conversation was interrupted by instructions as the bus stopped at their assigned discharge point. As they climbed off and went their separate ways, Shelby was momentarily distracted by a ringing cell phone. The tone was "Party Like a Rock Star." She turned to see which one of her idiot classmates had downloaded that song to their phone and was surprised to see the back of a middle-aged male with thinning light brown hair. He stood in the middle of the crowd of their friends and other marchers.

Shelby was struck by the man's hands as he quickly put his hand up to a Bluetooth earpiece to shut off the phone. His nails were well manicured, which didn't seem to jibe with the wrinkled denim shirt he wore or the stubble visible on his chin.

Weird, she thought.

And then they were called into formation, and the occurrence went completely out of her mind.

MONDAY, NOVEMBER 12, 2007
AN HOUR EAST OF BUENOS AIRES, ARGENTINA

MARK SHEPARD SAT UP on the long couch where he'd been sleeping and felt the familiar vibrations of a plane in flight. When he was a kid growing up outside Chicago, it would have tickled him to think that one day he'd complain about waking up on private planes far too often.

One glance reminded him that this one wasn't his.

Jaime was no longer on the sofa across from him. He stretched and leaned over to slide open the window cover. It was beginning to be light. Dawn had followed them across the Atlantic. It was about to overtake them.

Mark had no idea of where or when he was. But he knew he was on a mission to stop a madman. Everything else, he declined to think about.

He used the fore restroom, splashed his face with water, and ran a comb through his hair, to little effect.

Then he went back through the fore cabin with its four loungers, past the middle cabin with the identical sofas where he and Jaime had slept, and through the galley with the table and four chairs. He saw that there was a light on in the last, most private section of the plane's interior. She'd probably come back here to keep from waking him.

Mark walked back, knocking softly on the partition to alert her that he was awake; he was here. They could make a plan.

What he saw stopped him short. The breath left his body as surely as if someone had landed a punch to his solar plexus.

She was reading the damn *Rolling Stone*.

His immediate reaction was to be furious: *I freaking told you not to look at it!*

But even as his adrenaline surged, he knew he was angry at himself. It happened very seldom, but sometimes…when you were talking to a reporter who was knowledgeable or well known, who wrote for a prestigious publication…and you wanted your interview to be as cool as Bono's or Springsteen's, you talked too much. About personal things.

Shit.

Jaime sat in the single chair by the window. A halo of soft white from the reading light encompassed her head and shoulders and the magazine; the effect was a cameo brooch.

Shepard took a deep breath. He sat down on the sofa across from her. She didn't acknowledge his presence. It gave him time to think. *Maybe it's best that it's out. Maybe it's best that it's now. Secrets have power. Truth can be healing.*

Or, it can freaking ruin everything.

It was a long article. She had already reached the part that had been continued toward the back of the issue.

Silence filled the space between them. When Jaime finally finished reading, she didn't look up. She closed the magazine, and looked at the cover again for a brief moment, without really seeing it.

When she turned to face him, she said nothing. She looked at him, and he finally met her eyes.

"I'm sorry," she said. "Sorry you went through so much. It must have been painful when your wife and your closest friend died so tragically, and in such a short space of time. That you went so long, not being able to write music. I know that's who you are. And then, on top of everything, to lose your voice for half a year, out of the blue? Deeply painful."

He didn't say anything. He'd done his talking through the

article. Now it was over to her. It didn't help that her first response was one of compassion. He wanted a reason not to love her. He'd take anything at this point.

She took a breath. It was obvious what she'd read had affected her. "And I'm sorry for any part I played. Dear God, Mark, I brought that monster to your home! Because of that, Derek is dead. I am so sorry."

Again, he had so much to say. And nothing.

Jaime looked down at the issue, again. "It mentions me by name. There's a photo."

"I know! I can't believe it. I never gave your name. Not once."

How stupid was I? I know the media. I understand how things work. Jaime had been identified as the woman kidnapped from Lac-Argent. Any journalist worth his salt could have put two and two together. Was I being stupid? Or did I want her to be identified? Did I want this all to come out? Did I want to force her hand?

"Shit, Mark. I mean, really. Shit."

"I'm sorry. At least you live on a military base. The press can't get to you there."

She closed her eyes, undoubtedly thinking about the havoc this would wreak on her private life, and possibly her career. How had he been such a jackass?

"So what now?" she asked, out loud. "What happens now?"

Seriously? It's over to you. If it was up to me, what? You'd say, if only I'd known. *Then we'd fuck like rabbits, right here on the sofa. You'd quit everything and come and live with me in France and we'd get married and have incredible sex multiple times a day for the rest of our lives.*

"You tell me."

Jaime took a breath. "If it's too hard for us to work together right now, we can easily get you home from Argentina. We can work this all out later. Probably that's best."

She reached over and put a hand on his arm. Her left hand. The one with the wedding ring on it.

"I'm glad you're writing again," she said. "That's wonderful. And I'd like to meet your mentor, Silas, some day. He sounds like quite a guy."

A scratch from the plane's public address system made them both jump.

"Good morning, Ms. Richards and Mr. Shepard. We've begun our descent into Buenos Aires. Luke has some coffee and breakfast in the fore cabin if you'd like to sit there for landing. We should be on the ground in twenty minutes or so."

Mark and Jaime stood to head toward the front of the plane.

Before they left the aft cabin, Jaime gave Mark a hug. "Thanks," she said. "I'm flattered. But I think you need to head home. We'll deal with all this later."

"No. I'm in this. I can handle it. I have to handle it. If I go back home without any kind of resolution, it will eat me alive. It would—"

But the last word was never spoken. Because he saw something over her shoulder, outside the rounded window of the plane.

"Jaime—what's that? What the hell is that?"

She turned. They both sat on the couch and looked out separate windows.

Below, they were approaching the coast of Argentina, circling the city of Buenos Aires, preparing to land at Aeroparque Jorge Newbery. There was a large inlet where the Rio de la Plata ran into the Atlantic. Buenos Aires was on its southern shore.

As the rays of the morning sun hit the water of the inlet, it began to sparkle—and run red. Brilliant red.

"Water to Blood," said Jaime.

"Water to Blood," said Shepard. "Holy shit."

MONDAY, NOVEMBER 12, 2007, 8:12 P.M.
GOLDEN SUN VINEYARDS
NINGXIA AUTONOMOUS REGION, CHINA

THE GOLDEN SUN WINERY was nothing like he'd expected.

Yani sat in the seat directly behind the driver of the small luxury bus that was taking the critics to the Zhu winery, so he could quickly jump off at his stop. He'd been slightly surprised when critic Nancy Moore had taken the seat next to his.

"You're making a stop?" she asked.

"Checking out the competition," he said.

Then, they reached Golden Sun. At least, the outside of it. There was a huge wrought-iron fence, with molded pillars and golden shields. It must have been fifteen feet high. It looked like it could surround Buckingham Palace.

It obviously was made for show, not safety, because the huge gate in the middle sat wide open. Above the gate, in carved iron, were lions holding a shield.

The bus signaled and turned in. Both Yani and Nancy inhaled, then laughed.

They were driving up to Versailles. The avenue before them was wide and well-paved. Ornate fountains flanked the drive and ran the entire length of the approach, which must have been nearly a quarter of a mile. Behind the fountains were manicured lawns, complete with topiary trees in the shapes of wild animals.

The avenue ended in a huge rectangular fountain, water cascading from four levels. Now, as darkness fell, it sparkled with lights. It wasn't the Bellagio, but the lights did change colors, and the waters did "dance."

Not what Yani had expected in the Ningxia Autonomous Region of China.

The bus pulled around the main fountain, and came to a stop. The chateau before them was huge. Versailles-huge. It was French in every aspect; the mansard roof, the rounded towers, the crème colored stone and rounded windows. It stood four stories tall.

"Well," said Nancy, "if this is your competition, good luck."

He chuckled and shook her hand on his way past her. "I hope to see you for the return trip," he said. He disembarked and headed toward the broad steps that led to the main entrance.

"English?" asked the steward, making a quick appraisal of the newcomer. He wore a well-pressed tuxedo.

"Yes," Yani responded. "I'm afraid I'm late."

"You're here for the tour?"

"Yes. They said eight p.m."

"It's just leaving now. May I ask, do you have a ticket?"

"I don't. Is that a problem?"

"No, no. I'm sure there is room for you to join them."

Yani exhaled. If he'd missed the last tour, he wouldn't be able to join up with his partner, Bruce Shěn.

Thankfully, he'd arrived on time, and he was more than curious about the Golden Sun winery and its connections. Was this it? Was he going to catch up with the elusive Mr. Latorre/Wester? Was he going to find out what all this was about?

There were twelve people on the eight p.m. tour; Yani joined as number thirteen. They were in the process of exiting the main reception room, a long room with forty-foot ceilings, which were painted with frescos—but instead of dancing cherubs, they depicted great moments in the Chinese wine industry. To Yani's surprise, their guide wasn't a Mr. Shěn, but a lovely twenty-something Chinese woman.

Where was his colleague? He looked around at the others on the tour, but none of them looked anything like the photo of the lean man with the high cheekbones that had been shown him by his TC. He decided his best bet was to continue on, hoping that there was a simple explanation for why he wasn't here, hoping they would catch up after the tour, without having raised suspicion.

The tour's next stop further underscored the grandeur of the vineyard's past. They filed onto a circular platform, ringed by a railing at hand-height, which looked very much like the holodeck of the Enterprise. The lights went out, and all around them played the history of the Golden Sun, using film clips and photographs, music and interviews.

Savino Latorre was not mentioned once, although Yani thought he might have spied him in one of the early photos, when the vineyards were being laid out and planted.

"Follow me, please," said the guide. She was pleasant and prepared and showed no extra interest in him whatsoever. Even so, his senses were on alert.

Even without his colleague here, it was imperative to gain a working knowledge of the layout of the vineyard. And yet...had something gone wrong?

They walked into the next room—the smallest yet, and also circular, with a circumference of about ten feet. Once they were all inside, the door closed and the entire room began to descend.

"The world's largest elevator!" whispered a woman next to him to her husband. It was a stage whisper, loud, in an American accent. Without lowering her voice, she added, "Can we just get to the wine tasting?"

"One more stop only before the tasting," said the guide perkily.

The room elevator proceeded down two levels.

When the door opened, it was to a rectangular room with a large model in the center. They gathered around to find that it was a topographical model of the Ningxia Autonomous Region, with Golden Sun Winery highlighted in the center. The yellow river ran large and blue along the back of the fifteen-foot model.

"This demonstration shows why this region was chosen as one of the world's best for growing grapes," she said. "We think you will soon understand." She repeated the words in French and in Mandarin.

The lights went out. The room was plunged into total darkness. Then, slowly, "sunlight" rose over the model. The demonstration continued with thunder and lightning, rain and hail, and even a sandstorm. Even the reluctant woman seemed impressed.

"That is why this region, and these 5,000 acres of land, have been chosen for our fine wines," intoned a deep male voice as the demonstration ended. There was a smattering of applause, and the room was once again plunged into total darkness.

Immediately, in the total darkness, came the dramatic sound of wind and rain.

And Yani felt a strong arm placed across his chest, and the sharp sting of a needle into the back of his shoulder. A final crash of thunder masked any sound of person thirteen being quickly removed from the room.

MONDAY, NOVEMBER 12, 2007, 12:10 P.M.
VIGNETI PARADISO RITROVATO
MINERVINO MERGE, ITALY

SAVINO BARRELED THROUGH THE WIDE MARBLE HALLS of his estate.

Final meetings with Giordano had put him behind. He had no intention of missing this moment of moments, on this day of days.

Xiaofan appeared as he reached the central courtyard on the top floor of the palatial centerpiece of the estate. She stood where three floor-to-ceiling windows with curved tops boasted views of the rolling hills. His rolling hills.

"Has it happened?" she asked.

"I don't know. She should be there, or at least on her way. And he has walked into the trap."

"The plague, master," she said. "Has the plague struck, as planned?"

She had dared put a hand on his arm. He shook it off.

"Of course. We would have heard otherwise. Of course."

His words were brusque, his demeanor thunderous at the idea of her stopping him, even for a moment.

He started down the circular stairs toward the waiting car, not looking back.

MONDAY, NOVEMBER 12, 2007, 8:00 A.M.
RIO DE LA PLATA
BUENOS AIRES, ARGENTINA

"WE'RE PULLING UP TO THE RESERVE NOW," Jaime alerted TC4 and her Operative Coordinator together. She had been updating her supervisors from the back seat of a Citroën as a local driver brought her and Mark from the airport to the river. It was clear that the stakes were rising quickly in their race to avert further catastrophes.

They'd been sent directly to the Costanera Sur Ecological Reserve. Not only was it directly on the Rio de la Plata, but Teodozia Turczan, a microbiologist who often worked with Free Winds, was working on site. She would be their introduction to the local scientists.

From her car window Jaime noted the manic activity on the boardwalk of the Costanera Sur Ecological Reserve. Police were setting up barricades to prevent onlookers from walking to the waterfront. An ambulance had pulled to the curb and two EMTs were wheeling a stretcher with a small body strapped on it. Following the EMTs was a woman who seemed to be in some distress.

"Leave your glasses on," said her OC. "I'm going to listen in, along with one of our scientists."

Jaime touched her right earpiece and the glasses went into reflective mode, resembling a pair of mirrored sunglasses.

"What's that smell?" Jaime's nose was assaulted by a foul odor as she opened her door.

Mark, who had been silent the entire ride, said in a low voice, "Dead fish."

Before exiting the vehicle, Jaime leaned forward to speak to the driver. "*Treinta minutos aquí?*"

"*Sí, señora.*" The driver nodded. Jaime stepped out and closed the door behind her. Their attention was drawn to the scene at the ambulance nearby.

The woman was clinging to one of the medics, shaking him as he tried to load the stretcher into the ambulance.

"*Mi hija, ¿qué le pasa a mi hija? ¿Por qué no se mueve?*" she yelled, almost in hysterics.

"Do you understand what she's saying?" said Mark quietly in her ear.

"Mostly," responded Jaime. "It's her daughter. She wants to know what is wrong with her." *Why is it the innocent who always suffer? We must put an end to this.*

"We have to stop these people!" Mark said angrily. "Can Free Winds—the driver—"

Before Jaime could talk to her OC, a slight but determined woman exited the perimeter of the park. She spoke to the ambulance attendants, and then turned to the distraught mother. Putting her arm around her, she walked the woman to the ambulance and helped her into the passenger seat. She gave the woman a card, which the woman read before looking at her with gratitude. The ambulance lights came on and the vehicle pulled away.

As Jaime and Mark watched the action, a man in a black short-sleeved shirt with "Policia" on a sleeve emblem barred their way to the beach path.

"*Lo siento, prohibida la entrada.*"

Just as Jaime was trying to decide how to explain, with her high-school-level Spanish, that she was there on official business, the woman who'd helped with the ambulance came back to them. She was slight, maybe five feet four, with striking shades of silver interspersed in her short jet-black hair.

"Are you Jaime?" she asked.

Jaime nodded. "And this is Mark."

"Dozia," she said, shaking hands briskly.

"Will the child be all right?" Mark asked.

"I've got the name of the hospital," Teodozia said. "We'll see to it that the family is cared for. The mother says they were newly arrived here, and were staying in the park while she looked for a job. We'll make sure the girl gets the best care."

"If they need anything else—" Mark said, bringing out a BeCause business card.

"Thank you," she said, walking back toward the park. "Come on back. Let's see if we can figure this out."

She signaled to the officer, who waved them past. Just beyond the barrier, a man in his late forties awaited them. Of medium build and about five feet nine, his face had the swarthy, wrinkled look of one who spends most of his time in the sun. He had a scruffy goatee of brown mixed with grey, and sported a well-worn light-blue ball cap bearing the symbol of Argentina soccer. A blue bandana tied around his neck looked as though it had just been pulled down from his face.

"This is the team from Free Winds," said Dozia.

"Glad you're here." His words were accented, but he spoke excellent English.

"Yes, my name is Jaime Richards, and this is my colleague, Mark…"

"…Shepard. Yes, I recognize you from my daughter's wall." He chuckled. "I am Dr. Eduardo Lasla, of the *Instituto Nacional de Investigación y Desarrollo Pesquero*." It rolled off his tongue so quickly that Jaime couldn't catch all the words, and Mark had that deer in the headlights look.

Seeing their puzzled looks, Dozia translated, "National Institute for Fisheries Research and Development." She smiled. "Spanish is my third language," she said as they headed back into the park. "Ukranian is my first. And my second…is New York. I speak fluent lower East Side." She smiled. "I'm on loan from Beekman Hospital."

Jaime and Mark fell into step with the scientists as they walked briskly into the park. "I appreciate the visit, but I'm not sure what your organization will be able to do to help. We are still trying to figure out what is happening," said Dr. Lasla.

"Please tell us what you know and we can go from there."

"Let me show you. First, you will need to cover your face. I don't have any masks, so these bandanas will have to do for now." He threw them each a cloth pulled from his back pocket.

Mark tied his bandana, covering his nose and mouth. "Yes, this smell is awful."

"We're not so concerned about the smell," said Dozia. "The gases off the water have been causing some people severe respiratory distress."

As the four walked toward the shore, they approached a marshy area where a group of people were trying to drag a large dolphin out of the water onto land. There were hundreds of dead fish floating belly-up around them in the water.

"La Plata dolphin, indigenous to this area," said Dr. Lasla as they paused to watch the group at work. "We found a pair of them here in the water. The other is already dead, this one barely alive. But pulling it out of this fetid water is just the first challenge. We have to figure a way to keep it soaked with clean water until we can somehow transport it to a safe place. Also, a small pod of penguins beached about 500 meters further up the estuary."

"So, what do you know about the cause?" Jaime marveled at the extent of devastation caused by this plague.

"About ninety minutes after the sun hit the water, it bloomed. Which tells me it is a photosynthetic process," said Dozia Turczan. "With the color and the dead sea life, I am thinking dinoflagellates, and somewhere there was a nitrogen spill that fed them."

Red Tide. Jaime heard in her ear, from a male voice she did not recognize. She almost jumped, because she had forgotten she was transmitting the conversation to TC4.

"Red tide," she said matter-of-factly.

"Yes," Lasla was pleased with her understanding.

Mark cocked his head and looked at her suspiciously.

Have they identified the species? Jaime repeated the question from the Eden scientist out loud.

"Our team has rushed water samples back to the lab. Should know soon. But I am certain we have never seen this on our coast before," said Lasla.

Walk over to the shore and slowly scan the water. Jaime walked closer to the water and Shepard followed. As she slowly panned the view of the water, she heard the voice once again. *Ask more about the human symptoms.*

"You said there are people who've suffered bad reactions?"

"Breathing the air off the waves has caused coughing, vomiting, and even paralysis in some cases. It seems to be especially dangerous for those who already have some sort of respiratory problem. We found that young girl paralyzed here on the shore," answered Dozia.

"Was that the girl they were placing in the ambulance when we arrived?" Shepard pointed back toward the street.

Suddenly a stream of text appeared on Jaime's viewscreen. *Most likely a species from the Florida Coast, Karenia brevis. Produces nasty brevetoxins that cause neurotoxic shellfish poisoning. Disastrous for fishing industry. Suggest he contact MOTE Marine Laboratory in Sarasota, Florida, for expert advice. We will mobilize a team to assist with cleanup.*

"Dr. Lasla, as you probably know, red tides are pretty common on the Florida Gulf Coast. As Dozia may know, Free Winds has a long-standing relationship with MOTE Marine Laboratory in Sarasota, Florida, and it would be well worth your time to contact them for support." Jaime turned and spoke directly to the woman. "This could be Karenia brevis, a strain they are experienced in dealing with."

The microbiologist nodded, not surprised at the breadth of Jaime's knowledge.

"That would make sense," was all she said.

"Thank you," added Dr. Lasla. He nodded at an assistant. "We're aware of MOTE. We'll get in touch with them immediately."

"Also, Free Winds will send a team to assist with clean up." *Twenty-four hours.* "They are mobilizing now and should arrive within twenty-four hours."

Jaime was aware that the Wheel of Plagues clock was ticking, and began to move back toward the road to meet their ride. "One last thing," she said as they walked toward the waiting Citroën. "As you search for a trigger, keep an eye out for something that was not natural. Something someone may have planted on purpose."

Eduardo nodded. "I've been wondering about that. The tide bloomed so suddenly, and we have no reports of chemical spills anywhere along the river."

Jaime and Mark shook hands with the scientist and parted ways. As they walked along, Shepard whispered to Jaime. "Impressive, Richards. I gotta get a pair of those glasses!"

"Meanwhile, on to the statue of our disgraced conquistador."

MONDAY, NOVEMBER 12, 2007, 12:15 P.M.
TAVEL CORPORATE OFFICES, AVENUE HOCHE
PARIS, FRANCE

THE TELEPHONE RANG in the Office of the Director.

Archard Tavel looked at it.

No one had miraculously appeared to shoot him and put him out of his misery.

But he also didn't believe they could gain entrance to his apartment, to his library and steal his beloved art. And the vineyards—they weren't even his yet. He'd sold his yacht a year ago. No, he felt he had safely barricaded what meant most to him.

He picked up the receiver.

"Good afternoon, Monsieur Tavel," said the voice on the other end, the proxy for whoever was making this move. "We would like confirmation that you've found the terms acceptable. Our attorneys can meet with your attorneys as soon as tomorrow."

"*Non*," he said. "You will not need to trouble your attorneys."

There was silence on the other end.

"I did not find the terms acceptable," he said.

And he hung up.

MONDAY, NOVEMBER 12, 2007, 12:30 P.M.
TIME ZONE 1

INTERESTING.

Shanlei looked at the text just in concerning the small pharaoh in France.

He'd said no. That was unexpected.

After the magnificent showing of "Water to Blood," Señora Buenos Aires had finally seen reason. The powerful men behind two more "squares" had also capitulated and had been sewn into the quilt.

Therefore, neither the plague of locusts nor the plague of boils would be necessary. They had been cancelled.

Only four holdouts remained, including Monsieur le France—now, two Monsieurs de France.

Two splendid plagues.

Shanlei's father, who went by the Western name of Robert Lei, had also been a "captain of industry." Robert and his brother owned twenty factories in China. From the beginning, Robert had found Shanlei wanting. Due to the country's restrictive one-child policy, no other siblings had appeared. Robert had instead anointed his brother's son as heir.

Robert had thought that being a factory owner was a grand achievement—even if most of those factories had been handed down. *Well, Father, if that's the size of your vision. Just stay alive for another decade and see what you could have had. What you passed up. Wait and see what real power looks like.*

Shanlei was certain the quilt would be completely stitched together by evening the next night.

MONDAY, NOVEMBER 12, 2007, 12:42 P.M.
CASTEL DEL MONTE
ANDRIA, ITALY

I AM THE KEYMASTER, thought Bradley Kluge as he managed multiple actions from his console in the operations center. Between texts and chats he was simultaneously in contact with agents around the world, as well as with Alejandra in Buenos Aires and an electronics expert who was helping work through some tricky calculations for the next phase of the operation.

He wished Alejandra could witness the power he held, the importance of what he was doing and the nonchalance with which he was pulling it off.

She was sitting in a little café called the Bar Británico, with a perfect window view of the statue of Lezama.

Anything happening? he texted her.

Quiet right now. Enjoying a Catena Malbec.

Sucks to be you!

A chat on his computer screen re-energized. His contact in Europe.

Here are the schematics you need, with exact placement for explosives.

Bradley downloaded the attached file, then shot back. *Got it. Payment transferred within the hour.*

BTW, he texted back to Alejandra, *your dinoflagellates were a big hit! Argentina has never seen a red tide from that species, so they are falling all over themselves trying to figure out how to clean it up.*

Your dinoflagellates, he texted with a grin. *Talk sexy to me.*

With all he'd accomplished, all he'd done, the chaos he'd created, without a doubt the best day of his life had been the first time he'd bedded Alejandra. Not only was she drop-dead gorgeous, with her toned body and sinewy thighs…sinewy, that was good—sinewy thighs...but she *got* him. More than got him, *was* him. With her Barnsley Fern and her dyed magenta hair and her nose ring—she was him with more courage and more of an f.u. attitude.

The fact she had let him take her—repeatedly—signaled to him that his transformation from invisible nerd to genius world-changer was complete.

God, he loved her.

And he understood her enough to know he could never, ever say as much.

How did you get enough fertilizer to send them into that fantastic bloom?

Amazing how many vagrants are willing to make a few bucks by buying a bag of fertilizer.

Bradley smiled, imagining her bribing homeless men on the street in Buenos Aires. If she'd bought that many bags herself, someone might have thought she was building a bomb. And she had been—just not the traditional kind.

Tell me about the Malbec, he shot back. *I want to imagine I am with you.*

Only she would be drinking wine at this time of morning. But she'd undoubtedly been up for hours, if not all night.

Deep purple, dark fruity aroma, a hint of vanilla, my hand on your…

The text suddenly cut off.

Don't stop now!

Hold on, she sent back after a few moments silence. *I think it's show time.*

Someone's approaching the statue?

Very interested.

While Bradley waited, staring at his phone, for the story to unfold before him, he sensed a presence behind him. Turning, he discovered Savi, reading over his shoulder.

"It looks like someone is about to take the next marker," Bradley said.

"So I see," said Savi, with an undertone of both excitement and trepidation. He pulled up a stool next to Bradley and waited for further info. "Is it a woman?"

By this time, Bradley fully understood that there was a double mission unfolding in Buenos Aires. One involved the red tide and the other involved Savi's ladylove finding the markers they had left and being drawn back in to Savi's life.

It annoyed Bradley that Savi seemed to be assigning equal importance to his personal agenda. As hot as Alejandra was, he would never let their relationship endanger the missions they'd been working toward for well over two years.

Yet this woman was Analucia, the muse for whom Savi had named his grape. The woman for whom Savi had left inexplicable clues on the Wheel of Plagues website. The woman for whom he had had an ancient brick planted at an Egyptian dig, and a scroll placed on a statue in Buenos Aires.

Had she found, and followed, the trail?

A man and a woman, came the next text.

Savi looked confused, then concerned.

Both older than me, guessing thirties.

Then, *The guy looks familiar. Need a closer look.*

"Tell her to get a picture of them!" Savi snapped.

Send photo, typed Bradley.

NP.

Don't let them make you.

NP. I am the wind.

He smiled. Somehow, everything with her was NP: *no problem.*

The two men waited for five minutes before another text arrived.

The man had to boost the woman on his shoulders. Humorous. She pulled down the scroll. Bag lady shouted at them, threatened to call police.

"The picture, did she get a picture!?" Savi jabbed his finger strongly at the screen.

Got pic as they ran by, said her next text. This one was accompanied by a multimedia message.

Bradley tapped on the photo. He heard Savi's labored breathing as he sat on the edge of his seat waiting for the image to appear larger.

This was it. The moment he'd been waiting for.

Bradley clicked on the image to make it full screen.

What they saw was a slightly blurred photo of a man and a woman. The faces were clear enough for Bradley to think he had seen the man in the photo somewhere before. But just as he was starting to put a name to it, he heard Savi yell, "No!"

MONDAY, NOVEMBER 12, 8:48 A.M.
BAR BRITÁNICO
BUENOS AIRES, ARGENTINA

JAIME AND MARK CROSSED THE STREET from the statue of the conquistador that held the next marker. Jaime had allowed herself to open the scroll briefly, just long enough to see it was written in modern Sumerian.

Thank God. What if they'd come this far, and it hadn't been there?

They'd spotted the café across the street and decided to take refuge there. It was an old-fashioned café in a building whose rounded corner jutted between two streets. Tables filled the outdoor sidewalk, and many locals from the San Telmo district sat, drinking coffee, chatting, or having an early lunch.

Also, today, they were inevitably discussing the catastrophe on the waterfront.

Jaime's first thought would have been to grab an outdoor table, but Mark headed inside without conferring. The black and white floor tiles, along with the wooden tables and ceiling fans gave the place an old world feeling. Not many of the tables were occupied, but Mark headed for one farthest from the windows. Of course. She was beginning to catch on to his celebrity self-preservation techniques.

Unlike gunslingers in the old West, he sat with his back to the door. Jaime sat across from him, and quickly scanned the area. No one seemed interested in them on any account.

The first thing she did was to unroll the scroll on the table and study it with her glasses on.

"Got it," said her OC.

"*Buenos días*," said the waitress. "*Café?*"

"*Te*," answered Jaime, and Shepard nodded as well. "*Y medialunes, por favor.*" She'd passed patrons eating the Argentinean version of the croissant. They looked homemade. Mark ordered coffee.

Once the waitress had gone, Jaime took her napkin off the scroll and copied the symbols into the small notebook she always carried. She was aware that Mark was watching her transcribe. One unusual thing about agents and operatives from Eden: they were taught to put as much trust in people as they could; to assume people were on their side and would assist them, until proven otherwise. They didn't go around giving out inside information, of course, but Jaime knew they'd trusted Mark Shepard and had been working with him, through Free Winds, for years. They'd gotten him on the fastest plane to Egypt, for starters.

Then she sat silently working, wanting to see how much she could translate before her Operative Coordinator got back to her with the official version.

She'd gotten pretty far when the drinks and medialunes arrived. By the time the waitress had brought them half and half, butter, and jam, the translation had come through from headquarters, via the glasses.

Once they were alone, Jaime added the final words to her own translation:

Come find a black pine that sparkles
Atop the Lady of Iron
Ask for the Widow's drink and
Your way will be lit
To the seat of an ancient brotherhood

She turned the page sideways so that both she and Shepard could look at it.

"The Lady of Iron?" she asked, mostly to her OC.

"Remember, the hard part of these markers is that they're written in modern Sumerian," came the voice. "If you can find them and read them, the instructions themselves have been kept simple."

"So what, or who, is the Iron Lady? I thought that was Margaret Thatcher. So, London? Or—would you call the Statue of Liberty the Iron Lady? Maybe it's leading us to New York Harbor?"

"No, no, no," interrupted Shepard. "*La dame de fer*—the Lady of Iron—that's what the French call the Eiffel Tower."

"The Eiffel Tower?" Jaime asked.

Mark had grabbed the marker. "Yes. Yes! Look here—a black pine. A black pine! The whole marker is referring to words in French."

"Black pine?"

"*Pinot noir*," said Shepard. "The grape that's the basis of most Champagnes."

"That's what we're getting on this side, also, Jaime," said her OC.

"So, we're headed for France."

"We're already swapping out pilots, so yours will be fresh for the return flight across the Atlantic. By the time you get back to the airport, flight plans should be filed. The driver will be out front shortly."

"Got it," said Jaime, glancing reluctantly at the uneaten pastries.

Malbec, Pinot Noir—there was certainly a theme drawing them on.

"And, oh, Jaime, more news," said her Operative Coordinator, "about the time you picked up that last marker—in fact, almost to the minute—the clock on the website started counting down to the next 'plague.'"

"How much time have we got?"

"Put it this way. It should happen just after eleven p.m., local Paris time."

"Does it say which plague is next?"

"Negative."

"What's left?"

"Gnats, Frogs, Boils, Locusts, and Darkness. We assume the next one won't be Death of the Firstborn, since that one already has a ticking clock. And the Death of the Firstborn will happen less than eighteen hours after the next plague."

"We've got to get in front of this! We've got to stop them," Jaime said through clenched teeth. As she spoke, a picture of Sam Golding, and the naked pain of loss on his face flashed through her consciousness, and the stark pain on the face of the mother whose daughter had been poisoned by the red tide.

"Right there with you," said her OC. "So you're okay continuing to be the 'seen' on this one?"

"Try to stop me," Jaime said, and she meant it.

By the time their driver pulled up in front of the restaurant, they'd paid the bill and were headed to the street.

MONDAY, NOVEMBER 12, 2007, 1:28 P.M.
CASTEL DEL MONTE
ANDRIA, ITALY

IT WASN'T HER.

Savino's anger burned white hot. After all these years, they were still standing between him and his precious Analucia.

He was standing between them. Again.

1955, Paris. The war had been over for ten years and France was once again a center for fashion, racing, art, literature. A younger Yacov Wester sat expectantly at a small table along a quiet tree-lined park. The previous day he had received a message to meet an Eden Operative for an answer to the important question he had posed weeks before. He was certain the answer would include the schedule for the door opening that would bring his Analucia to his arms.

As he waited, Yacov had been observing another patron of the park who sat at a nearby table. He was an older Parisian man in a suit and tie, highly buffed shoes, and black fedora. The man had a glass of wine before him, a cigarette in his mouth, and was quietly stroking a large, shaggy black dog, which lay beside him on the walkway. As he smiled at the fellow's dog-walking attire, the one man he wished not to see plopped down in the chair across from him.

Yani. With his thick dark hair and athletic physique he looked like a movie star. Of all people, why did they send him?

Yani's cruel smile hinted at the answer to Wester's request before he even opened his mouth.

"I'm sorry, Yacov." He didn't sound sorry. "But I have been asked to inform you that Analucia politely declines your invitation to join you in the Terris world."

Yani didn't even try to hide his smirk.

"This can't be. I'm sure the message was not relayed correctly."

"Wake up, Yacov. She doesn't love you. She never loved you. Be serious, how could a classy lady like her ever have any interest in someone like you?" His voice dripped with disdain.

And then, something even worse. Yacov saw a hint of pity in the young operative's eyes. Pity! He preferred the disdain.

It was devastating that this man, this totally self-absorbed, unfeeling son-of-a-bitch, should witness Yacov's rejection. That he should revel in it, even.

I don't want your pity. I want you out of my life. I want Eden out of my life.

Yacov quickly stood, knocking his chair backwards and stumbling away into the park, wanting to be as far away from this place as his feet would take him.

"You have done this, Sword 23!" Savi screamed into the air. "You've blocked every attempt for my Analucia to be free. You send your minions in her place, thinking I will not know. Thinking you can fool me.

"Wait and see what you have unleashed. The next plague will be beyond your comprehension. And you, *you* will be to blame."

Bradley sat quietly on his stool, watching with a quizzical look.

"The two in the picture. Get rid of them."

"Get rid of them?" Bradley asked, startled. "You mean, kill them?"

"Yes. They must be stopped."

"I'll put one of the hit men on it."

"There is no time. They're already focused on other targets. Get your girlfriend on it."

"But, no. That isn't what we were hired for!"

"You are being so handsomely paid to do what needs to be done!" Savi yelled. "Alejandra is creative. She can figure a way."

Then he turned to the woman standing beside him, the beautiful woman with thick black hair falling just below her shoulders, and skin the color of sun-kissed sand, whom only he could see. "I shall release you from your bondage, my lovely Analucia. You shall be free."

At that moment all of the angry energy drained from him, and all that was left was a deep sadness and total exhaustion.

MONDAY, NOVEMBER 12, 2007, 9:30 A.M.
AEROPARQUE JORGE NEWBERY
BUENOS AIRES, ARGENTINA

IT TURNED OUT THAT FREE WINDS had not only swapped out the pilot, they'd swapped out the plane. The new one was both shorter and leaner, with two sets of four luxurious seats facing each other, but no private compartments other than the galley up front and the head in the back.

"This one is faster," explained Jaime's OC. "It will cut off a third of the time it would take a regular commercial flight. We're serious about getting on the other side of this. We've got to start preventing the plagues."

Their concierge Luke was back, having showered and shaved. Jaime and Mark happily accepted Luke's offer of soup and crusty bread to be served for lunch after they were airborne.

Then they both sat, silent, in the forward facing seats toward the back of the plane as the pilot prepared for takeoff.

Jaime remembered clearly the first time she'd met Mark Shepard. She'd known for a while that Paul, her professor-turned-peer-turned-significant other, was tight with Shepard and his wife, Ondine. Paul and Mark had met working together for a non-governmental agency created to promote peace in the Middle East. Together they'd taken fact-finding missions to Israel, Jordan, Egypt, and the lands that had been Palestine. The experiences the two men shared honed a deep kinship and camaraderie as well as a sense of urgency and purpose.

Jaime knew that while Paul truly enjoyed Shepard's music, he didn't give a rip about his rock star status. So when Paul had brought Jaime to meet Mark and Ondine, who were staying with friends in Southampton on Long Island's south shore, Jaime had done her best to be casual about it.

In fact, part of what made Jaime an effective chaplain was her ability to look past surface distinctions—rich, poor, young, old, waitress, rock star, private, general—and see the person. The spiritual being.

However, once they'd reached the multi-million dollar shingle-style beach house where Mark and Ondine were staying as guests, all she could think was, holy shit, don't stare, don't trip, don't spill whatever drink they put into your hand.

It's Mark Freaking Shepard.

Ondine had saved her.

Jaime had liked Mark's wife immediately. The tall, willowy Frenchwoman with the chestnut brown hair and the ready laugh was the opposite of pretentious. She talked to people, she listened when they talked, she was curious about the world. It was clear she was a grounding presence for the rock star.

She shared his concern for the troubled areas of the world—in fact, for any troubles—and was interested in what others thought and did.

During that first visit, Jaime spent nearly all her time with Ondine. She had been introduced to Shepard, and had been polite. But she'd needed time to regulate her breathing in his company. He was tall—six feet three—and had a full, semi-curly mop of hair that he often ran his hand through when he was talking, for emphasis. Not to mention, there was something about his voice, even his speaking voice, that hinted at the magnificent instrument that could soar and tease and quietly lure the listener into an intimate space with the musician.

Mostly, there was an uncanny magnetism.

Jaime suspected that Ondine knew her husband had this effect on people, and did her best to help them negotiate the process.

Ondine could read someone's motives in a nanosecond. If she perceived you were authentic, and at least trying not to stare, open-mouthed, at her mega-famous husband, she helped you out.

Three years later, Ondine had orchestrated Jaime and Paul's wedding. For that alone, Jaime would be always in her debt. If she hadn't, Jaime and Paul would never have married that quickly—which meant not at all, since Paul had died so soon after.

When Ondine died, Jaime had been shattered, as Shepard had been. He had known all too well what he had in Ondine, and had appreciated it.

Ondine, help me here, Jaime thought to herself with an "if only" wistfulness.

Her Operative Coordinator interrupted her thoughts. "Good news," she said. "They were able to stabilize Dominica, the young girl from the Reserve. With time, she should make a full recovery. And we have a Gardener there to help the mother negotiate the process. We'll find her a job and an apartment, if they want to stay in Buenos Aires."

Jaime reported this to Mark as they took off. She got a quiet smile in response.

"So, we're heading to France," Shepard said, once they were aloft.

"We can't be of much help with the red tide," answered Jaime. "Teodozia is on top of it."

"How do you think we can be of help in Paris?"

"I don't know," Jaime said. "Somehow these markers have all been planted—or led to—wherever the next plague was going to be released, where the next catastrophe was going to happen. The objective is to get on the other side of the events—to stop them before they take place. Especially the Death of the Firstborn. Depending on who is being targeted, something like that could have serious world-wide repercussions."

"And how do your miraculous glasses think we're going to be able to do this?"

"There are others working on it besides us. There are teams in Paris already."

"So *we're* heading there, because?"

"We've become 'boots on the ground.' We're the ones who have been visibly tugging on this thread. Since we don't know what the next plague will be, the objective is to interact with someone who does. For better or worse, you and I are the ones who have been picking up the markers. We're the ones who have been following the leads. No one else will be seen. The person or persons planting markers may not choose to interact with us, but we have become that visible point of contact."

Mark took a sip from the mug of coffee Luke had provided. "What you're saying is, although we're likely not the intended recipients of these markers, we are being put out there as the bait."

Jaime had gotten a cinnamon spice tea. The aroma alone was comforting.

She looked Mark in the eye. "You say that as if being 'bait' is a negative thing," she said.

He stared at her.

She started to laugh. "Oh, for God's sake. Yes. We can only hope someone will take the frigging bait. How else are we going to communicate with these people? As I said, there will be protection teams in place. But Mark—I'm in this. You're not in this. You're not bait. For your next birthday I will get you a t-shirt that says, 'I'm with Minnow' with one of those arrows pointing in my direction. So don't worry about it. We're heading for France. Your home base. You're outta here. Relax."

"Don't tell me. Here we go again."

"What?"

"We've just walked into a catastrophe of international proportions. We've found the cause, helped mobilize help and cleanup efforts, gone to find some crazy marker on a statue to a loser of a conquistador, figured out where it leads, and, once again, you're ready to toss me on the rubbish heap. Thanks but no thanks."

"But you live in France. It's perfect. And in the very near future, you and I will get together and hammer things out."

"Just stop. I mean it." Shepard's voice was hard. He was a man used to getting his way. Instead of feeling intimidated, Jaime enjoyed rising to the challenge. She had, in fact, chosen to marry a man very used to getting his way. A man who specialized in finessing people into thinking they were getting their own way even while their way morphed into service of Yani's objective. This had, in fact, been brought up during their marriage counseling at Mountaintop in Eden. Seems there were very specific challenges, should one choose to marry an agent, let alone, God help you, a Sword.

Mark's demeanor softened as Luke served their carrot ginger soup. Jaime admired the fact that, unlike many celebrities, Mark purposely surrounded himself with truth-tellers. He wasn't interested in sycophants. He didn't like to hear "no," but he would hear it. Only, apparently, not about this.

Once Luke left, Mark continued, "If you and I part when we get to France, you'll go back to your life and your honeymoon and I'll release the album and go on tour and neither one of us will want to sit in a room and look at each other while you say, 'you poor idiot, I'm married to somebody else.' This will be it, Jaime. Not to mention, there seems to be some sort of terrorist madman waiting for one or both of us at the Eiffel Tower. Put the two things together, and it seems there's a bit more we need to work out, you and I.

"So, here's a question I said I might ask. It's clear your version of Free Winds is more proactive than the one that supports BeCause. Can you tell me any more about it? Just exactly who is talking to you when you wear those glasses?"

"And, the answer you knew I might give: I can't say any more. Sorry."

"But you will admit I'm not crazy thinking there's more to Free Winds than making charitable contributions."

"Admitting there's more to Free Winds does not necessarily mean I don't think you're crazy." Jaime smiled.

For a few minutes, they concentrated on their food.

Jaime had thought that being honest with Mark about her unavailability—being *married*, stating her firm disinterest—would create and solidify the wall around her own heart, harden her inappropriate emotions. She was surprised that she still felt the tug of his charisma.

"Look. I just have to say this," Jaime said. "You are an aggressively wonderful human being. That's not even counting the 'fame and fortune and plain old genius' card. There are currently more than two billion women in the world whose greatest dream would come true, were you to sweep them off their feet. I've seen supermodels and A-list actresses throw themselves in your direction. I am, obviously, not a supermodel." Jaime took a deep breath. "Let's be honest here. I'm guessing the most attractive thing about me, as far as you're concerned, is that I'm not available. One of the very few who isn't. You want me because you can't have me. You need a challenge."

"That insults me. Which is all right. But in saying that, you also insult yourself—which really pisses me off. Really? Supermodels? You think that's what I'm interested in? Looks?"

"Okay, sorry. I'm assuming supermodels can also be brilliant."

"Point taken. But I don't care. You're asking if there's a reason I'd like you, other than that us being together would impose a challenge. You're seriously asking me that? Okay, here's my partial, off-the-top-of-my-head list. We have history. We've been friends for over a decade. You knew my wife. I knew your husband. That gives us a certain level of understanding. Also, we can be real with each other. We don't have to put on an act, or pretend to be something we're not. We're also not looking for the other person to be something he or she isn't. I kind of assume, when you're climbing up onto my shoulders trying to get at a marker that will help save a portion of the world, that you don't care if I'm a rock musician.

"Also, we've both been through tough times. Very tough times. Not only the death of our spouses, but what we went through in France. And other things. That tends to give people a shorthand.

"But mostly—mostly—you're awake. You see the world around you. You see its people, and their loves and desires and needs. You see the hungry and the lonely and the displaced. You see what God is asking us to do, and you're willing to step up and do it."

He dipped his bread into the soup, and gestured above the bowl. "You find me someone else like that, and I'll happily do my best to fall out of love with you."

He took a bite. "And, apparently, you have two billion choices, so you'd best get to it."

"Mark. I hear what you're saying. You know what? It's true that Yani didn't know Paul. But he knows me. Really knows me. In ways that only people like you, whom I've known forever and have true kinship with, do. And because of that, it's like, in a very real way, he did know Paul. And I did know his wife, who died. Soul mates are like that. And I have no doubt whatsoever that yours is waiting."

Mark finished his soup and used the remaining crust to clean the bowl.

"Good soup," he said.

"You're not buying this, are you?"

"Not for a minute. But I appreciate what you're trying to do."

MONDAY, NOVEMBER 12, 2007, 3:30 P.M.
VIGNETI PARADISO RITROVATO
MINERVINO MERGE, ITALY

"HOW CAN IT BE?"

Savino burst back into the soaring welcome hall of his mansion. He picked up a vase—from her vantage point around the corner upstairs, she couldn't see specifically which one, but she knew it was over 2000 years old, from ancient Greece. With a deep thunk it smashed to the floor.

The maggiordomo took Savino's coat and signaled for help. His assistant was barely up the stairs when Xiaofan stepped forward to meet him. Together they descended quickly.

"The markers have all been left for her—but it wasn't her!"

Xiaofan took Savi's arm, and spoke soothingly. "Guī dàn, she's not here *yet*. That's all. Come, let's talk."

"Would you like lunch sent up?" asked the chef.

"Yes, in an hour," replied Xiaofan. "Now, come, sir, we have much to discuss."

Alone in his suite, Xiaofan closed the door. "Are you all right?" she asked, when he was seated. The concern in her voice calmed him. She went into his bathroom.

Alone and out of sight, she allowed herself a moment to lean against the wall to catch her breath.

Savi had *erotomanic delusional disorder*, she knew that. Among other symptoms, he was living a grand love with a real person, entirely in his mind. At least, Xiaofan assumed this Analucia was real. The meds had been able to control the more dangerous and troubling indicators of his disorder. But for the last few months, the plan had been for her to slowly decrease—and finally stop—his medications altogether.

For a week now, she'd been giving him nothing but placebos.

It was obviously too much, too soon. They needed him to be rational until the plagues were played out, which would be days from now. At least, rational enough to bring the project to glorious resolution.

Could she get him back again? At least, back enough that he could finish the final two plagues?

Xiaofan exited the bathroom with a pill, a small crystal glass of water, and a reassuring smile. Savi didn't ask. He took it.

"Where is she?" he keened.

"I don't know. How were you expecting her to find you, to find *here*?"

"I put markers. On the website. And, after the last plague—the one in Egypt—someone, a woman, someone, was picking them up. Was coming."

"Why did you think only your Analucia could read the markers?"

He looked up at her, and she could tell he was trying to decide how much to trust her. "They were in an ancient language. A modern one."

"That only she can read?"

"Well, no, there are others…but they would tell her!"

"How do you know? Why do you think so?"

"They just…would."

"This is simple. You must speak to them. Ask for her by name."

"How? How? I don't want to put her name on the website. It is not for the world to know!"

"A way will present itself, Guī dàn. It always does." She had him sitting on the bed; she knelt to take off his shoes, and she swung his legs up to the bed. "Rest now. You are a great man. And you always think better after a rest."

"I do," he said, his eyes heavy with fatigue and pharmaceuticals. Just before he nodded off, he opened his eyes suddenly and looked straight at her.

"I'm going to kill them, you know," he said. "The false Analucia and her accomplice."

"Yes, Guī dàn," she said.

MONDAY, NOVEMBER 12, 2007, 9:40 A.M.
AEROPARQUE JORGE NEWBERY
BUENOS AIRES, ARGENTINA

WELL, THAT ANSWERS THAT QUESTION! Alejandra flicked shut her phone after reading her text message.

The private jet sitting across the runway had just cleared a flight plan for Paris. It pays to know people in the right places, and her contact in Buenos Aires Air Traffic Control had just come through big time.

So, they had successfully deciphered the next marker.

Sucks to be them. If they weren't so smart they would live longer...

One part of Alejandra had hoped the man and woman would misread the marker and be diverted to another place. Then she wouldn't have to bother with them.

But another part of her was looking forward to this assignment. This was something new. Something she had never tried before.

She was stretched out on a couch in the private rear cabin of the jet that had been her transport the last few days. It was a really nice craft by the French company Dassault, and as soon as she had boarded the first time, she had wondered about this "Mr. Big" who was backing their mission. According to Bradley, Savino said his name meant Mountain Thunder in Chinese, but between themselves, they referred to him as Thunder Mountain, after the amusement park ride. To the point: Savi had a lot of dough, and he didn't mind spreading it around, but this plane was beyond even his resources. This Falcon 900EX was bigger, faster, and more luxurious than any other private jet she had seen.

Even more telling was the crew. Four pilots, so you could literally fly anywhere in the world without crew change. The two female flight attendants were Asian. Probably Chinese, but Alejandra didn't ask. Their English, which was the preferred language on the aircraft, was perfect.

Thunder Mountain, whom they had never seen nor heard, must have very deep pockets. He also seemed to know *everything*. He must have eyes everywhere. His messages often had details they had not yet reported to him. Bradley had looked for spyware on his computers, searched the war room for hidden devices, but had found nothing he had not put there himself. It drove him crazy that he couldn't figure out how the information was being passed.

Her mind came back to the problem at hand. How to remove these two bothersome people quickly, cleanly, and preferably before they reached the next marker? Alejandra had caused a lot of chaos in life, but she had never killed someone in cold blood. Interesting phrase, "kill in cold blood." Blood ran hot.

Alejandra stared up at the ceiling and tried to visualize the act of killing. Squeeze the trigger, don't jerk it. Once. Twice. The weapon bucks lightly with each round. Impact. Momentary look of surprise. Then the spark of awareness is gone and their brain waves enter the cosmic flow.

Bradley was much more concerned about this mission than she was. It wasn't because of any moralistic crap. He, like her, was decidedly amoral. But Bradley did seem concerned about the danger to her. How sweet. But misguided.

"Don't sound like an old woman," Alejandra had told him a few minutes earlier as they argued on the phone. "I can do this. They have gone through two stops undisturbed. They have no reason to expect an ambush in Paris. The plague is already set into motion, and can't change. So I simply need to stop them. They're getting much too close."

"C'mon, Alejandra, just be smart." Bradley was not giving in easily. "We haven't had a chance to study this thing. We don't know much about these two. I think I've figured out who the guy is. He's a well-known musician. Which means the woman could be some sort of body guard or undercover police."

"Well, then I need to take her out first, after which the rock star should be a breeze!"

Bradley had shut up at that point, but she could tell he wasn't happy.

Alejandra sat up and looked out the window. The sleek private jet across the tarmac, the one that belonged to Free Winds, had begun to taxi. No worries, her aircraft was faster. She should reach Paris first, and have time to arrange a surprise for the intruders before they found the next marker.

A female voice spoke over the intercom. "Take off in five minutes. Please prepare."

Alejandra moved to the executive chair in the center of her cabin and buckled in. As the jet began to taxi, she tapped on the computer screen embedded in the table before her to find a weather forecast for Paris. It looked like temperatures would run between two and nine Celsius.

Back to the Northern Hemisphere. She sighed. It was tough to leave her native Argentina at the height of spring, but it couldn't be helped.

As soon as the plane lifted off she washed up in her private lavatory, unfolded the divan to a bed, and took an Ambien. Hopefully, she would sleep for about six hours. This would put her on an opposite sleep cycle from the sun, but that was to her advantage. The darkness was her friend, and she needed to be ready for night action when she arrived.

As the jet settled into cruising altitude, Alejandra pulled a blanket over her and let the darkness take her.

TUESDAY, NOVEMBER 13, 2007, 12:12 A.M.
GOLDEN SUN VINEYARDS
NINGXIA AUTONOMOUS REGION, CHINA

HIS FIRST CONSCIOUS THOUGHT was that he had no idea where he was. When he was. Why he was wherever and whenever he was.

His second thought was that he'd had this experience too often in his life.

His third was a reminder to himself that it often wasn't helpful to broadcast his return to consciousness.

Instead, Yani remained as still as possible, purposefully keeping his breathing shallow, and took stock of his physical situation slowly, without opening his eyes, as categorical thought returned.

He was lying prone on his stomach. On something cold.

There was a band of pressure across his back. Another across his shoulders. And across his thighs and calves. He thought there was something around his wrists, but didn't dare move them to try to ascertain what or how tight.

Okay, I'm going to try to solve the puzzle, he said to an imaginary game show host. *I'm restrained. And, by how cold I feel, I've likely been stripped of my clothing.*

He opened his left eye slightly to see walls of cream-colored brick. Which meant he wasn't in a prison, or a hospital. Instead of a door, there was a wrought-iron gate. A man wearing black creased trousers walked past him. A different man was talking, being answered by a woman.

A mechanical sound. Someone had plugged in a machine, or turned one on.

The conversation between the three other people was pointed and specific. They weren't friends or even friendly co-workers. They were getting something done. He wished he understood Chinese.

The woman, who was standing to his right, said something, and he felt some sort of goo land on his right hip. Then he felt something with pressure, perhaps two inches wide, running up and down his buttock. What were they doing?

They continued talking. She went over the entire area of his hip, very thoroughly, at least twice. The pressure stopped. Someone took a cloth and removed most of the goo.

The woman moved to his other side. Again, the sticky substance applied, this time to his left hip. And as the pressure was applied, he suddenly knew exactly what was happening.

A happy exhalation from the woman and the other man. They'd found what they were looking for. His Eden locator. Nestled by the iliac crest.

Damn.

"Are you starting to wake up, Sword 23?" The man in the creased pants leaned down to smile at him. "You should be, just about now. And if you're not quite awake, we'll help you the rest of the way."

It was obvious that admitting he was conscious was the only way he'd gather any information in English. It was equally obvious there was no point in pretending to be a hapless tourist.

"What's going on?" he asked. "I'm only looking for Mr. Latorre."

"Don't worry. Mr. Latorre was expecting you. He asked us to entertain you when you arrived. First, though, he wants you to disappear. So we'll be removing your locator device. Doesn't make much sense to me, as you'll likely be dead by morning. But it's likely best if your body is never found. And orders are orders."

A swift smell of alcohol, and a swab across the center of his hip. Then the swift sting of a needle, and again.

"What's that?" asked his host.

The second man answered.

A brief conversation ensued. Creased pants man was obviously in charge.

"Sorry. They were numbing the area. But international spies like you don't need to bother with such trivialities."

Yani wasn't technically a spy. But he thought arguing that point would probably take the conversation in the wrong direction. And if they'd been told not only that he had a locator device but where it was, there was probably no point in protesting his innocence, either.

The sonogram wand again, pressing down hard into his muscle.

Now the two medical personnel were conferring. The second one stretched his skin taut, and then a much larger needle was inserted. All the way down to bone.

It burned. But he was trained to deal with pain.

"Oops, sorry," said Creased Trouser Man. "Almost."

Needle withdrawn. Sonogram repositioned. Wand held firm, needle coming in, this time from an angle. Same needle, less sharp. Damn. It was all he could do to keep his breathing shallow and precise. He didn't want to give them the satisfaction of him admitting pain.

It took three tries before the huge needle hit the chip squarely and was able to aspirate and capture it. Yani had spent happier times.

The medical personnel were relieved. They cleaned off his hip, held a bandage down firmly, and when the bleeding had stopped, finally taped a clean one in place.

One of them reached down to unclasp the belt across his back, but was angrily stopped. The belt was retightened. Two more guards entered the room, and the medical duo and their portable sonogram machine were hustled from the room.

"Such a tiny nuisance," said the boss man, showing Yani the tiny transmitter that had so recently been residing deep inside his muscle. "Now you can disappear, like the friend who was meeting you here. And, I might add, the woman who was giving him a brief, part-time job."

What? Had he just told him that the man he'd been supposed to meet had been captured and killed?

Another needle punctured Yani's left shoulder, in the trapezius muscle, close to where the first knock-out drug had been administered.

Savino can't be wanting to kill me without talking to me first, he thought. Even if they wanted him to disappear, it would have been much simpler to remove the tracker once he was dead. They must need him for something, to keep him alive.

But who knew? Darkness closed in again.

Damn.

MONDAY, NOVEMBER 12, 2007, 9:06 P.M.
TIME ZONE 1

IT WAS ALL BEGINNING TO COME TOGETHER.

Shanlei sat, savoring the success that, in country after country, was bringing those who had not wished to co-operate to their knees. It had taken two billion dollars and much patience. But what was two billion dollars in the face of two hundred billion?

You thought you were so magnificent, Father, with your factories. You thought you were wealthy. Did you not see how small this planet is, and how limited our resources? What do we need? Fuel. Oil and gas, and wind. Why not seek control of those resources so limited and necessary?

One step at a time.

Twenty-one hours and counting down.

Ah. On to the next.

MONDAY, NOVEMBER 12, 2007, 10:02 P.M.
LE BOURGET AIRPORT
PARIS, FRANCE

IT WAS ONE THING TO BE CAVALIER about being bait when safely in an airplane, half a world away. It was something else completely when one was on the ground, getting into a minnow frame of mind.

Their lean Cessna landed at Le Bourget Airport outside of Paris. They had seen the City of Light, and the well-lit Eiffel Tower, spread like a fairy-tale jewelry box below them as they approached.

Jaime had flown out of this airport before, although she'd never been into Paris proper. She looked out the window to see if she could recognize the private hangar in which she'd met with the TC for the Middle East during a previous mission. She thought she could pick it out, but didn't have enough time to be sure.

It had been a traumatic time. When she had once again been caught between life and death. Between Mark Shepard and Yani.

"Wheels down at 10:03," Jaime's Operative Coordinator said as they rolled smoothly onto the runway. "You only have fifty-seven minutes to get there, and talk your way in. The Eiffel Tower closes at eleven o'clock. Tomorrow morning will be too late."

"How long will it take to get there?"

"Usually forty-five minutes, once you've left the airport. We have a driver waiting who knows an alternate route. Still iffy."

The minute the plane came to a stop, Luke had the door open and the steps down. Jaime and Mark were prepared to run.

A dark sedan awaited them. They each grabbed their bag and took a flying leap into the back seat of the car. Without a word, the driver headed out.

Fifty-one minutes remained.

The sedan came to a gate, and their driver showed credentials. From there, they followed a quick roundabout and accelerated onto the Route de Flandre.

"And now we're in the ballgame," whispered Mark.

"What?"

"However our driver got us through that gate, it cut ten minutes off our travel time. We're not there yet, but we've got a chance."

They merged onto the A1, Autoroute de Nord. As they exited onto the Boulevard Périphérique, then onto the Avenue de la Grand Armée, heading toward the Arc de Triomphe, Mark leaned over to her. "Welcome to Paris," he said. "I wish we were here under different circumstances. I'd love to show you around."

"Perhaps we should just find a small café and have some dinner," Jaime replied.

"Good idea. Kind of tired of this save-the-world stuff."

"Oh, let's save it just this one last time."

"All right. Once more, for the lady."

They both smiled. "Meanwhile," Jaime said, and looked again at the marker, now lit on her phone.

Come find a black pine that sparkles
Atop the Lady of Iron
Ask for the Widow's drink and
Your way will be lit
To the seat of an ancient brotherhood

10:39: It was obvious this wasn't their driver's first time in Paris. Jaime would have thrown up her hands in the craziness around the Arc de Triomphe, but he navigated it quickly and turned onto the Avenue d'Iéna.

As the Eiffel Tower came into view, Jaime checked her watch.

10:45: Her heart was accelerating madly. When Mark reached over and took her hand, she welcomed the gesture. At least they were in this together.

By 10:48, they were crossing the Seine, and the tower was square before them.

The driver screeched off of the Quai Branley onto the Avenue de Suffren.

"You have your plan?" asked the driver, for the first time.

Mark shrugged. "We're going up," he said. A statement of fact.

The car made the final turn onto the Avenue Gustav Eiffel.

10:51: The car slowed. Mark already had one hand on the door latch, and one hand on Jaime's wrist. Together they ran, headlong, past the knots of tourists who had just come down off the tower. They ran to the entrance, under the awning, where no lines waited. The glass doors were locked.

A man and a woman with official Eiffel Tower shirts stood inside, guiding remaining tourists from the final elevator rides down.

Jaime banged on the door.

"*Pardon*," said the man. "We are closed."

Mark came and stood in front of her, where he could plainly be seen. "Please," he said. "Can we talk to you?"

"*Non*," repeated the man, looking straight at them, but obviously more than ready to go home. "We are closed."

And he turned away.

MONDAY, NOVEMBER 12, 2007, 10:42 P.M.
CASTEL DEL MONTE
ANDRIA, ITALY

T MINUS EIGHTEEN.

Usually at this point, Bradley was sitting silently, enjoying the sprinting of adrenaline through his veins, the feral electricity that heightened his senses. Each plague was so specific, involving so many months of planning, calculation and so many moving parts, that it was both a triumph and a joy when each came to fruition.

Paris, this one, had required more hired hands—and greased palms—than any yet. It also had more built-in safeties. Short of the apocalypse, nothing could stop it. And Bradley would have seen an approaching apocalypse on one of his screens.

Then Savi had raised the stakes on this one. Unnecessarily.

Kill them, fine. There are people whose job it is to do that. People who were in Paris at this very moment with time on their hands.

Why was Savi insisting it be Alejandra?

Bradley knew he should relax. She was good at what she did. And she was perfect at being invisible. But damn Savi, anyway.

Not to mention, Bradley's college buddy Ben had disappeared shortly after complaining about collateral damage. Disappeared, as in, off the face of the Earth. His cell phone had even been cancelled. Bradley had asked Savi once, but the look he'd gotten in response had shut down any further inquiries. He was afraid to continue thinking about it.

The soft ping from his computer nearly made Bradley jump.

Alejandra was approaching the Eiffel Tower. In the intervening hours, he had verified that her male target was indeed the singer called Shepard, frontman of the band Borderline. Bradley had also successfully used facial recognition software to identify the female. She was Jaime Richards. American military: Army. A chaplain. Which made no sense. Why would a rock star be working with the Army? And did this mean the US military was involved? Doubtful. And they wouldn't send chaplains, who are non-combatants.

This ping alerted him to a new hit for the name "Jaime Richards."

When he searched, he'd found that "Jaime Richards" was not an uncommon name, although the spelling "Jamie" was far more common. Still, all he had found on *his* Jaime were photos of her, in uniform, usually standing with a bunch of other soldiers in uniform. Nothing that would explain why she was running around with Shepard.

Then, this ping. Someone had posted new photos, in an album labeled "Jaime Richards + Bill Burton Wedding."

Even if it was her, he didn't really care about her nuptials. He barely glanced to see if it was even the right Jaime. Then he glanced again. Then he pulled up the photos, full screen.

According to the photographer's caption, she had been married two days ago. And not to this Shepard fellow.

Instead, her groom, the man labeled Bill Burton, was the man for whom Savi had been searching for a decade. The one they had finally lured to China only hours before.

What did it mean?

For one thing, it meant she was part of a dangerous web.

What should Bradley do with this puzzling information? Perhaps, if he told Savino, his boss would see an advantage in bringing her in alive to question her. Perhaps he'd cancel Alejandra's kill order.

"Savino, I believe you'll want to see this," he said.

The well-dressed gentleman came over. "What have you got?"

"The woman picking up the markers. Turns out she's married to your friend."

Savino looked at the photo. He was confused for a moment, then a large smile spread across his face. "Perfect," he said.

"Shall we bring her in?" he asked.

"What? No! Kill her."

"But—"

"And be sure to get a photo. A nice close-up."

Savi took out a handkerchief to wipe his brow, and went to get a refill on his glass of wine.

Bradley looked again at the screen. The new information did nothing to allay the bad feeling he had about this.

Nothing at all.

MONDAY, NOVEMBER 12, 2007, 10:53 P.M.
THE EIFFEL TOWER
PARIS, FRANCE

FORTUNATELY, THE FEMALE EMPLOYEE kept staring at them.

Mark smiled at her. He used his most winning smile. He saw the moment recognition lit her eyes and that's when he took Jaime's hand and winked at the woman. He pulled something out of his far pocket.

"What?" asked Jaime under her breath.

"Go with it," came the barely-audible response. "Smile."

Jaime smiled.

The woman walked over and opened the door. "Are you Shepard?" she asked.

"Yes," he said. "And I need to go up. For ten minutes only. With my friend." He pronounced the word friend with heavy meaning.

"Ten minutes?" the woman asked. She was still gazing at Mark.

"I promise."

She opened the door. Her colleague glared.

"Thank you, *merci*," said Shepard, as he passed. "This is for you," he said to the woman and pressed something into her hand.

"Quickly, come on," she said, and led them back to the elevator.

They quickly walked onto the elevator. "*What*?" the elevator man said to her.

"Ten minutes. They'll come down with Daniel."

Mark and Jaime smiled. Mark continued to hold her hand.

"What did you give her?" she asked, once they started their ascent.

"A copy of the new Borderland CD, which doesn't come out until next week. Signed it on the plane, just in case."

"You have the CDs?"

"Sure."

She'd read the article. She wasn't sure how she'd handle listening to the CD.

"So she thinks we're going up so that you can propose?"

"Celebrities do things like that."

Unexpectedly, Jaime laughed. "How did I get here?" she asked under her breath.

The trip to the top of the tower required two elevator rides. After they disembarked the first elevator on the second floor with all its restaurants and shops, Jaime and Mark had to convince yet another elevator operator to take them up the central shaft to the very top. This employee, like the first one, had thought she would see no more tourists and was ready to go home for the evening. But since the two visitors had been allowed to take the first lift, she could not deny them the rest of the tour.

The bright red elevator car, which looked for all the world like a European phone booth, chugged its way to the upper level of the Eiffel Tower. As it slowed to a stop, its heavy doors slid open and Jaime and Mark stepped out onto the platform.

"*Cinq minutes!*" yelled the elevator operator, glaring at the two visitors as the door closed behind them.

"Wow," said Jaime, stopping to look back toward the descending car. "I'm glad to be done with that clickety-clack elevator. Not the sturdiest thing I have ever ridden."

Yet another sign that it's my life, Jaime thought. *On top of the Eiffel Tower without a second to take in the view.* She barely had time to glance down at the Louvre, a little up the river to Notre Dame.

"I think this is our place." Mark pointed to a large sign with giant orange letters that read "Bar A Champagne."

The bar's beige metal door was closed, but through the glass window they could see a young man inside scrubbing the countertop. Mark tapped lightly on the window, but the bartender studiously ignored the sound and kept cleaning. Mark rapped harder, using his knuckle, and the young man sighed visibly and walked to the window.

"*On est fermé,*" he said through the glass.

"This is really important," Mark pleaded.

"I know who you are. I don't care," said the young man in slightly accented English. "I just want to finish cleaning up and get out of here."

"Please, Daniel," Jaime stepped to the window, using the name she had overheard in the conversation on the elevator. "We just need to see if something was left for us up here. We were told to ask for the Widow's drink."

The bartender paused, nodded, and slid the door open. "Here." He reached under the counter and held up a large bottle of Champagne. "I've been holding onto this damn thing all night."

"Thank you!" Jaime couldn't believe, after all they had been through today, that they had actually made it in time.

"We really mean it," said Mark, handing Daniel a hundred-euro bill and taking the bottle of Champagne. "Thank you. I'm sorry we interrupted your closing."

Mark led Jaime away from the window. "Of course," he said. "Veuve Clicquot—the brand of Champagne. It means 'The Widow Clicquot.' She started the vineyard."

"So it's the Widow's drink," Jaime said, as she put on her glasses and scanned the bottle. "But how does that help?"

"Here. Look. There seems to be writing." At the bottom of the gold label, some symbols had been added in black.

Jaime immediately took out her phone and snapped a photo. It took her seconds to attach and send it in a text to her Operative Coordinator. As she did, the whole tower, which had been lit up like a golden torch, began to sparkle, with lights blinking on and off.

"The light show," said Mark. "It must be eleven p.m., on the dot." As the lights twinkled all around them, he looked at the cuneiform symbols and asked, "Do you know what it says?"

"Where the monks find…comfort? Solace? I think that's it. But I don't understand. How does it light our way to an ancient brotherhood?"

No sooner had she spoken than they heard a faint *boom* in the distance. Then a second *boom!* somewhat closer. A third *boom!* and they felt the structure vibrate slightly.

That's all it took for Jaime to be back in Iraq. *Incoming rockets! Must take cover!*

She dove under the counter just as a fourth *BOOM!* shook the tower. The tower swayed for a few seconds, and then the lights went out.

In the dark, Jaime suddenly realized where she was. Embarrassed by her dive to the floor, she was momentarily thankful for the darkness. Once she was sure the structure had stopped vibrating, she stood up slowly and brushed herself off.

"You okay?" came the voice of the bartender out of the now-opened door. "What's going on? Terrorists? Are we under attack?"

"I'm okay," Jaime said, a bit sheepish. "But what's happening?"

"Come look." It was Mark. She could barely see his silhouette against the night sky. She moved to his side and was greeted with a completely different view of the city from the one they had seen a few minutes earlier.

You could no longer see the Louvre or Notre Dame. The streets were marked by car headlights, stopped in place, but all the buildings and streetlamps were black. The City of Light had gone completely dark.

"The Plague of Darkness," whispered Jaime. "Holy crap."

"Plague? What?" asked Daniel.

"Except, look!" Mark pointed. "One neighborhood is still lit."

Just across the river to the west, one area still had electricity. It stood out against the blackness like an illuminated torch.

"What is that? Down there?" Jaime asked Daniel, who'd closed and locked the Champagne bar, and now stood beside them.

"The Trocadero Gardens is directly across the bridge. But the lights are nearly straight west of us, across the Seine. I think that's Charles Dickens Square, just above the train bridge. But why are there no lights anywhere else? Or electricity? What's going on?"

"I don't know," she said, snapping a photo of the light pattern on her phone, "but I don't want to be cornered up here. How do we get down?"

"We can't. We wait. Sooner or later, the lights will come on and we can go back down by elevator."

"Isn't there another way?"

"There was a spiral staircase originally built in the tower, but it was dismantled years ago. The only option is a metal staircase for emergencies and maintenance, but we aren't allowed to use it. Besides, it is totally open to the air, not safe even when the lights are on. And we're at a height of eighty-one stories up!"

"Eighty-one stories? It does seem wise to wait until the lights come on," said Mark. "There must be emergency generators. It can't take long."

"No." Jaime was adamant. "We need to get down. I have a bad feeling about all this. Daniel, please just show us the emergency stairs."

"Okay, but you're crazy."

"Oh, yes, we certainly are!" Mark muttered under his breath, as he glumly followed Jaime and the young Frenchman to the stairwell entrance.

MONDAY, NOVEMBER 12, 2007, 11:15 P.M.
TAVEL APARTMENT, 7TH ARRONDISSEMENT
PARIS, FRANCE

ARCHARD COULD ONLY SLEEP in complete darkness. So when he was awakened by sirens on the street below, he did not know what was wrong.

He took off his sleep mask and took a moment to lie there in the dark. He grabbed his phone by the bed. As it sprang to life, the small amount of light it emitted was enough to help him see his way across his bedroom to the tall doors that opened onto his terrace.

As he opened them, he was more curious than concerned.

Outside, he was greeted by a sight he'd never seen before.

All of Paris was dark.

Traditionally, Paris was not a city with "lights there shining just as bright as day," at all hours, as George M. Cohan had boasted about New York. It went fairly dark at night. But not black. Not block after block with no neighbors with lights on, or flickers of television, block after block with no street lights. No power.

No alarms?

Crap. This had to be a coincidence. No one would go to this trouble over his comparatively small company.

But just in case…

Archard tore open the bedroom door and ran out into the hallway. Small lights—nightlights designed to stay on in case of power failure—dotted the hall at intervals.

As he headed for the library, he savored the momentary quiet.

At least Leal wasn't blasting that infernal King Arthur series.

He rounded a corner, nearly at a skid. The door to the library was closed. He put his hand on the doorknob, and turned. It was unlocked.

Only then did he realize he might need a weapon. He scanned the hallway and saw the umbrella stand by the front door. All right. An umbrella wouldn't do much. Once he was inside the library, if he was not alone, he'd make his way to the fireplace and grab a poker.

Then he laughed nervously, telling himself he was crazy to have worked himself up into such a state.

He turned the doorknob and the heavy door to the library swung open. As far as he could tell, it was as he'd left it. The fire had nearly died out. The Cezanne still hung proudly in its place.

Archard released a sigh, then laughed, and put down the umbrella. What had he been thinking? A city-wide blackout to teach him a lesson, personally?

He had to stop fearing every shadow.

Certainly, whoever had threatened him wouldn't harm the worth of the company he was intent on acquiring?

He'd check in on the boy and the nanny on his way back to bed. If the boy was asleep, let him sleep. That was one lesson he'd learned early. If they were awake, he'd invite them into the kitchen to make hot chocolate. They'd make this into an "adventure," as his father used to suggest.

Archard went down the entry hall and turned the corner to the private quarters. He silently opened the door to the boy's room. The bed was still made.

"Leal?" he asked. No answer.

Likely the boy and nanny were still in the salon where they watched television, or perhaps out on the balcony watching the craziness below.

But that room, also, was empty.

"Leal?" he called out. "Mademoiselle Guillory?"

Nothing.

He ran through the entire apartment then, opening and slamming doors, frantically calling out names. Finally he went and sat by himself in the formal living room. And waited for his work phone to ring.

MONDAY, NOVEMBER 12, 2007, 11:25 P.M.
EIFFEL TOWER
PARIS, FRANCE

STEP, STEP, STEP, STEP. Stop on a flat landing. Turn 180 degrees. Step, step, step, step. Stop…

Mark focused on the light clang of his shoes on metal as they made their way steadily down the staircase. For what seemed like *forever* he had been following Jaime, one hand on her shoulder, as she navigated for the two of them.

But Mark couldn't see a damn thing! Instead, he was led like a blind man by Jaime, whose secret squirrel glasses must give her x-ray vision. It didn't help that there was no moon to light the way. At best, he could barely discern a slight difference in the skyline, stars, and the dark structure of the tower.

I hate this! How many more steps can there be in this place? Mark had tried to count and gave up. *I suppose it could be worse. We could be going* up *the steps!*

He laughed.

"Right about now I would love to hear something amusing," came Jaime's voice from the darkness.

"Oh, I was just thinking, 'Things could be worse. We could be going *up* the stairs.'"

"Don't say that!"

"Don't say what?" Mark was surprised at her serious response to his joke.

"I have learned *never* to say 'things could be worse.'"

"Don't tell me you, of all people, are superstitious." He smiled and squeezed her shoulder.

Jaime patted his hand. "Not superstitious, just experienced. By the way, not to change the subject, but why did you start right off in English when speaking with Daniel? You speak fluent French!"

"I appreciate the compliment to my language skills, but I am obviously not a native speaker. I have discovered it is much better to let the French show off their abilities in English than to insult them by hacking at their 'beautiful language.'" She could hear him smiling in the dark.

A last few steps and Jaime stopped.

"What's wrong?" asked Mark.

"The good news is, we're here. The entrance to the second level. There's a door. I'm looking for a panic bar of some sort. Hoping this barrier is to prevent tourists from going up, not staff from coming down." There was a slight pause, then Mark heard the sound of a click.

Jaime led them out onto a paved surface and stopped again.

"Now what?" she asked, deferring to the team member with the greatest knowledge of the tower.

"We need to find the south pillar."

"South pillar. Right. Why?"

"That's where the public stairway is."

"Great. More steps!"

"I couldn't have said it better." And the little human convoy headed out in search of their escape route.

MONDAY, NOVEMBER 12, 2007, 11:33 P.M.
UNKNOWN LOCATION
OUTSIDE PARIS, FRANCE

IT WAS SCRATCHY. So scratchy it was killing him. Killing him.

Leal pulled at the black hood, wanting to live. Wanting it to stop taking over his body. It was so scratchy, he was on overload. He banged his head. And banged his head. Scratch bugs, scratch monsters had taken over his body. He no longer had control. They were overriding his thoughts. He banged his head, trying to clear them out. Trying to take back a corner of himself. Not to be overwhelmed.

No idea of the time. Or the universe. Couldn't care. Was overtaken, his senses overwhelmed.

"Leal. Leal." It was Danièle, who was secretly Morgan le Fey. She was so far away. She was speaking, speaking to him. Words were not his friends. But she had said his name, twice. It was their code, their incantation. It meant she was saying something important. To him. He tried to grasp at the words and hide them, with the dots. The dots that floated in space, that were memories and words.

If he could live. But the scratches were winning. He banged his head again, trying to shake them loose, to kill them. But they were taking him away. Piece by piece.

MONDAY, NOVEMBER 12, 2007, 11:37 P.M.
EIFFEL TOWER
PARIS, FRANCE

ALEJANDRA CRUZ *WAS.*

She let the darkness surround her as if she were floating in her precious pod, taking in the pleasure of the chaos around her.

Sirens screamed as police tried to wend their way through stalled traffic. Hurried footsteps of frightened tourists. The muffled cries of children asking their parents why the lights were gone.

"Oh my God! Terrorists!"

She was energized. She was ready.

Alejandra leaned against the glass window of the ticket booth in the south pillar of the Eiffel Tower. To her right was the entrance to the staircase the public used to climb to the first and second levels of the tower. With nothing to power the elevators, this was the only way her targets could descend.

She had arrived about forty-five minutes earlier, just in time to see the man and woman dive out of a dark sedan and run for the closest elevator. She had watched from the shadows to see the man give something to the elevator operator, who then let the two board and ascend.

Just as well; this allowed time for the Plague of Darkness to take effect. It would make her job that much easier.

Alejandra had found a place in the shadows where she could view all pillar exits, in case her quarry came down sooner than expected. When the substations started blowing and lights went out she had an excellent vantage point to witness the ensuing panic.

The fact that her quarry had made it to the top could not be helped. There was no logical opportunity to take them out between the airport and here. But she had known what they did not, that at precisely eleven p.m., the Plague of Darkness would descend upon Paris.

Well, most of Paris. Savi had requested that one small patch of the city be left alone. That was Bradley's challenge.

Alejandra had come prepared with a small set of night vision goggles that made her look like a tourist with a pair of binoculars. She had watched the upper tower with her NVGs until she discerned two lone figures slowly but surely making their way down.

That had to be them; who else would be so foolish? No flashlight. That was brave of them, and better for her. Alejandra had moved through the darkness to her strike point by the stairway exit.

Now she was waiting. Over thirty minutes she had been waiting. Alejandra caressed the Walther P22 she held inside her coat. The Finnish SAK suppressor almost doubled the length of the weapon, but it was worth it. It would muffle the sound, creating an echo. She was not so foolish as to believe, as portrayed in the movies, that this weapon would be completely silent. But the muffled echo of the report would make it hard for others to identify where the sound came from, especially in the dark. This would make for a clean getaway.

The door to her right suddenly opened, and a woman and man emerged. It was them. Her targets.

The woman walked in front while the man followed with one hand on her shoulder. Alejandra waited, pressed against the ticket window until they cleared the doorway and the woman stopped on the landing at the top of the steps.

"Now what?" said the man, exasperated.

Alejandra took a few quiet steps to come even with the man.

Holding her goggles to her eyes with her left hand, Alejandra slowly raised her pistol and drew a bead on the woman in front.

"We should have transport pretty quickly."

Steady. Breathe. Squeeze the trigger…

MONDAY, NOVEMBER 12, 2007, 11:38 P.M.
EIFFEL TOWER
PARIS, FRANCE

MARK SHEPARD WAS SO FREAKING HAPPY to be done with stairs. He and Jaime emerged from the south pillar entrance into the cool Paris night and suddenly Jaime came to a halt.

"Now what?" he complained.

"We should have transport pretty quickly," replied Jaime.

Mark heard a faint swish of the air nearby, as if someone had passed by. Someone had.

As he squinted to try to see, dread dropped through him. The person had a gun.

A shout had nearly left his mouth when lights flashed on all around the tower. Standing immediately to Mark's left was a stunningly beautiful woman with long burgundy hair holding a pair of strange binoculars up to her eyes. And he was correct: in the woman's other hand was a long-barreled revolver, which was pointed directly at Jaime.

As the lights flashed, the woman flinched, dropping the binoculars as if she had been burned. "Shit!" she said, shaking her head. Then she took a breath and lifted the weapon to re-aim.

Mark didn't think. He didn't plan. He simply reacted. He used the only weapon he had, and took a big swing with the bottle of Champagne he had been carrying. He made contact with the woman's arm and moved the weapon off target. The extension on the front of the revolver went flying, but she did not lose her grip on the gun itself.

He dropped the bottle and launched himself in her direction. Their combined weight carried the two down a short flight of cement steps until they came to rest against a metal crowd barrier.

The woman was strong and lithe, but he had surprised her, and he was both bigger and heavier. They battled like two wrestlers, each trying to find a controlling hold. She fought like a wildcat, scratching him in the face, kneeing him in the groin. Mark didn't know how to fight dirty; he just tried to use his superior weight and strength to wrestle the weapon from her hand.

As they struggled, she got both hands on the weapon and tried to point it at his head. Mark wrapped his hands around hers and tried to force the muzzle in the opposite direction. He forced her wrists back so that the gun was now pointing toward her.

She looked at him and sneered, as if to say, "Nothing you can do will stop me."

A moment of total clarity engulfed Shepard. The sculptured features of her face, the bright emerald nose ring, the beautiful eyes filled with disdain. This was no ordinary woman. Mark knew. He *knew* that if this woman got away, Jaime was dead. He was dead. And she would be thrilled. Victorious. Fury flooded through him.

Mark squeezed his hands around hers, placing pressure on the trigger. The revolver fired, sending a bullet into the woman's brain.

No look of pain. No surprise. Suddenly the spark of awareness was simply gone.

Mark rolled off and jumped back in horror.

MONDAY, NOVEMBER 12, 2007, 11:41 P.M.
CASTEL DEL MONTE
ANDRIA, ITALY

MISSION COMPLETE? Bradley texted Alejandra. *Really sucks to be them?*

No answer.

Get out. And send photo when you can.

No answer.

Of course, it could still all be going down.

What? What's going on? Bradley texted quickly.

11:42: Still no answer.

11:45: Still no answer.

Hesitantly, he turned on the software that gave him remote access to Alejandra's phone.

Someone was scrolling through her call history.

NO NO NO NO.

He immediately wiped her phone and killed it, his heart jack-hammering.

And every point of the victory won in the last hour turned into a violent howl.

A violent howl.

MONDAY, NOVEMBER 12, 2007, 11:43 P.M.
BASE OF THE EIFFEL TOWER
PARIS, FRANCE

"JAIME. GET OUT OF THERE. *NOW.*" Her OC's voice was authoritative.

"What? How?" Jaime's first impulse had been to kneel by their assailant, who was now crumpled in a pool of her own blood.

"Get your friend into the car that is pulling up at the curb. Now. We'll take care of the shooter."

Jaime stood, looking around, and saw the black sedan pulling up. She grabbed Mark's arm and pulled. Hard. He didn't move.

She pulled again.

"Oh, my God," he said.

She took a step back and lunged at him, knocking him off balance; then, before he could plant himself again, she dragged him back toward the curb.

"Oh, my God. Oh, my God," he kept saying.

By the time Jaime jerked open the back door of the sedan, a friend of Eden was by the shooter's side, feeling for a pulse, directing shocked bystanders, giving an edited version of what had just taken place.

Jaime shoved Shepard into the car and jumped in, nearly on top of him.

The sedan pulled away.

"We're going to get you out of Paris, and into a different car," said the voice through her glasses. "Security cameras were still down, but you've both got to disappear. We'll get you a vehicle and arrange a safe house. No good can come from either you or Mark Shepard being tagged as the targets of the shooting. In fact, it could cause great harm."

Jaime wasn't arguing.

Some side streets were still dark. Apparently not all the substations were back online. Their driver seemed to know the side streets that would be neither cluttered nor cordoned off.

Jaime climbed to the other side of the back seat and turned her attention to Mark, who remained in shock. He had quit reciting, "Oh, my God," and was completely still, not saying anything. He had never been sitting up straight; now he gave in and just lay there, on the back seat, curled in a fetal position, his head in Jaime's lap.

She'd been with enough people who were in extreme shock to know there was no point in trying to jar him out of it. Instead, she ran her fingers through his hair, and continued to comb his hair gently with her fingers, solely as a point of human contact.

She exhaled and let her head drop back onto the seat. "Dear God," she said. "Dear God."

The woman they'd left was dead. She knew the woman was dead.

They'd been driving for half an hour, and had departed Paris proper when their driver turned slightly, to talk to her over his shoulder.

"Jaime, how are you? Can you drive?"

She sat up. How was she?

Her brain was turned off, for one thing. She had gone into professional mode, and was just concerned about Mark, about getting him to safety, about finding sanctuary for them both: physical, emotional, and spiritual. God willing, she wouldn't collapse until then.

"Yes. Sure."

"Okay. We're just about to reach a car. It has a SatNav programmed to get you to a safe house in Crecy la Chapelle. It's less than half an hour away. They're expecting you."

"Okay." Even as she said it, she had a memory of the muzzle of a gun pressed against the back of her head. Shit.

Get Mark to safety.

She could do it. She *would* do it.

They were on a side street. They pulled up behind a dark Volvo. Their driver clicked a key to open the doors remotely and start the engine. Then he came back to help Jaime get Mark out of the sedan. Thankfully, Mark was more pliable than he had been at the plaza beneath the tower. He walked, unseeing, to the new car and allowed himself to be deposited and buckled into the front passenger seat.

The driver also transferred the overnight bags they'd had on the plane into the back seat. When Jaime turned back around to thank him, he had already returned to the sedan and pulled away. He made a left turn two blocks ahead, and disappeared into the night.

Jaime slid into the driver's seat. The SatNav was already on.

"Everything okay to get where you're going?" Her OC spoke for the first time since the tower.

"Yes," she said, "Crecy la Chapelle."

She took off the parking brake and slid the car into gear.

"No." Mark's voice beside her gave her a start.

"What?"

"Take me home. Please."

"What?"

"To Lac-Argent. Jaime. Please. Take me home." There was pleading in his voice.

She turned to him. He was shaking. Violently.

"Did you hear that?" she asked her OC.

"Yes."

"Well?"

Jaime was torn. She knew if she got to Crecy la Chapelle, there would likely be counselors there to take over—hell, to help both Mark and her make sense of what had just happened. If they continued on to Mark's house, it would just be the two of them. And Mark's staff, of course.

Her OC came back on. "His house is less than an hour away on the A4. You'll be on it, anyway."

"And?"

"Up to you, Jaime."

"Please." It was Mark, next to her. He touched her wrist. His hands were ice.

"All right," she said. "All right."

And she drove, feeling more alone than she ever had, into the French night.

MONDAY, NOVEMBER 12, 2007, 11:55 P.M.
IN THE AIR

THE SCRATCHES DISAPPEARED.

The light. There was so much light that Leal filtered it the best he could, with his fingers.

Gravity shifted. A fantastic lifting feeling.

It felt great. The lights went down. He didn't need to filter any more.

A joy radiated from his center, with the new pull of gravity.

He gave himself over to it and floated. He was in an airplane. Did flying always feel this good?

Where was he? Where was Morgan le Fey?

The dot. The dot. The dot.

He searched infinity, testing, trying to find the right dot, the right words, from Morgan/Danièle.

"Leal. Leal."

All her words started like that.

The dot under the scratches.

"Leal. Leal. This is it. You are going on your quest. Be brave. Be bold. Save Arthur."

He'd responded: "I will. I shall. We shall return victorious."

His quest. His quest! His time had come. "When you have completed your quest, you will be a squire no longer, but a knight. A true knight of the Round Table. When you have completed your quest, you will be a squire no longer, but a knight. A true knight of the Round Table."

The words played in a circle.

He reached out. He had his bag. Morgan had made sure he had his bag. It was everything he would need.

Leal gave himself over to the feeling of flight.

MONDAY, NOVEMBER 12, 2007
UNDISCLOSED LOCATION
TERRIS

TC4 HIT THE BUTTON to open the door and admit the young agent from Monitoring.

"There's a problem with Sword 23," he said.

"Yes?" she replied.

"He appears to be in two places."

"What are you saying?"

The agent held the screen down where she could see it. And sure enough, Sword 23's locator pulsed in two locations. One in the Southern Helan Mountains, and one near the city of Yinchuan, in China.

TC4 didn't speak. *No, not this. Not now.* She considered. Then, "I'm taking that as good news."

"How so?"

"As a former Sword—and this is close hold—he has two locators. One of them, it seems, has been removed. Which means that he must be getting close to Savino. It's fairly common knowledge that Eden agents are chipped. My guess is, Wester—Savino—removed the agent chip."

"Well," said the agent, uncomfortably, "that doesn't sound like fun."

"No. But it means he's making progress. Let's watch this carefully. And let me know the moment you hear from him."

"Yes, ma'am." He turned at the door. "So, we're not thinking he's been hacked into little pieces?"

"Not yet. Because it's Sword 23. Not yet."

MONDAY, NOVEMBER 12, 2007, 11:59 P.M.
TIME ZONE 1

SIGNED, NOT BLIND, read the text.

Shanlei smiled. The Plague of Darkness had worked.

The French financier who had thought he was safe, thought he was untouchable, as was his city, had caved once the lights had gone out. Well, once the city had gone dark and he had been threatened with having his eyeballs split down the middle with an X-acto knife. Details, details.

Other item grabbed, read the next text. So Tavel, the second target, had thought their refusal would have no consequences?

The Plague of Darkness had not only gotten them their financier, it had pulled the final piece into place for the company owner and the final, most dramatic plague: Death of the Firstborn.

One young boy kidnapped.

Three hit men in place.

Ah, grand finale of plagues.

The Death of the Firstborn.

TUESDAY

TUESDAY, NOVEMBER 13, 2007, 8:06 A.M.
GOLDEN SUN VINEYARDS
NINGXIA AUTONOMOUS REGION, CHINA

YANI AWOKE AGAIN; this time because he was deposited into a chair. Dumped, more like. The chair had a soft cushion, which did nothing to stop the pain in his hip from flaring, and pulling him immediately to consciousness.

The chair also had large padded arms, to which the guards who had dragged him in cuffed both arms with nylon restraints. Twice each. They did the same with his ankles.

He was seated in a circular room. This one had a huge round table on a floor of white marble flagstones that radiated from a central circle. Lights in patterns of star constellations twinkled on the ceilings, but more notable were the three-headed torches flaming on the walls.

If you had a tasting in this room, you would be impressed.

"Good morning, Sword 23," said Creased Trouser Man. "Anyone who is following the whereabouts of your locator device thinks you're having an interesting day in the mountains even now. But let's you and I have a chat before we say good-bye."

Once again, Yani struggled to come to his senses before speaking. He hated that this man was using his Eden identity. He worked to regulate his breathing.

Physically, Yani felt ill. It was likely a combination of the drugs, jet lag, and not having eaten for many hours. Could he clear his mind to focus, even if his body was nowhere near a hundred percent?

Yani had two immediate objectives: to be thought useful enough not to be killed here and now, and to convince them he was physically weaker than he was. Creased Trouser Man must have some questions for him, or he would have simply been shot and dumped.

Yani acted as though it took effort to raise his head. He looked at the solitary man across the width of the table, and said, "Where is Mr. Latorre? I have a message for him, from Analucia."

There was a moment's hesitation. "Ah, but she is on her way to Mr. Latorre, even now. The package you received at the winery in California, even though addressed to her, was meant for you. We knew you wouldn't come alone if it was addressed to you—you would have known you were walking into a trap. But if you thought he meant for her to follow the trail, why then, you might come to us. And here you are. Far, far away from anyone you might distress by disappearing. Oh, except, of course, Mr. Shěn," He tossed a photo onto the table. It was of a man with a bullet hole through his temple.

Creased Trouser Man then put a new model Browning Buck-mark pistol on the table next to the photo.

Damn. And, Lord, have mercy.

Now? Bluff-calling time.

Yani spoke as though he was very tired. "Analucia isn't on her way to Latorre. She asked me to give him a message and arrange a meeting. And if I don't come back or contact her, she disappears again forever."

Creased Trouser Man stared at him, trying to discern the truth.

"Go ahead. Call Latorre. Ask him. If she's there, come back and shoot me. Better yet, have him come in and shoot me himself. It's been a long time. I have an apology to make."

"Nice try. But she is on the way to him."

"Ask him. If she's there, or he's heard from her…well. Nice knowing you. But if you kill me, the only one who actually knows her location, and it turns out Mr. Latorre is pissed, I won't be here to see the fireworks. Or help out."

"Then, tell me where you believe her to be."

"Can't. Can only tell Savino."

His captor considered.

"Meanwhile, might I ask where my clothes are?" Yani said. He was wearing his black boxer briefs, but nothing else.

"Simple precaution. You're dressed and you get away, we're looking for one of many tall fellows with dark hair. As it is, you get away and we're looking for the naked guy. Not that you have a chance of escape, but Mr. Latorre has pointed out that I'm 'ruthless, but not cagey.' I believe those were his words."

"You don't have to be ruthless," Yani said quietly.

"Oh, but it's such a shiny adjective," he said, standing up. He nodded to the two guards with guns. Even though his host was Chinese, Yani guessed he'd been raised with both English and Mandarin as first languages. His use of vernacular was advanced.

"If I may—while you're gone. I'm not feeling well—quite ill, actually. May I be escorted to the restroom? And when I'm returned, may I be given some water?"

Yani looked at the man in charge as if they were allies. He knew he looked pale.

The man nodded to the guards. "Have him back before I return," he said, then repeated it in Mandarin.

The men came forward with a cuff-cutter and undid his arms and feet. Yani struggled to get to his feet, and they finally came forward to help him. Once out in the corridor, one of them put an arm around his shoulder, while the other held a gun in the small of his back.

Once he reached the restroom, he signaled that he could go in by himself. The shorter guard signaled him to put his hands up, palms open, and patted him down. Which seemed unnecessary, to say the least. Then they let him go. Once inside, he splashed water on his face, and looked in the mirror, seeing a haggard version of himself looking back. Then he used the facilities, flushed, gave a loud groan, and collapsed onto the floor.

TUESDAY, NOVEMBER 13, 2007, 1:06 A.M.
CASTEL DEL MONTE
ANDRIA, ITALY

USUALLY BY NOW, Bradley would be focused on the next plague, especially as they were heading toward the finale.

But they had gotten word of Alejandra's death soon after it occurred by police scanner, corroborated by eyes on.

Alejandra's death.

Bradley could barely breathe. He hadn't realized how much of what he was doing was for her. To play with her, to interact with her, to impress her. It had been a high-stakes, complicated game. He hadn't imagined just how high-stakes it would become.

What was left, now that Alejandra was gone? The money?

The money seemed meaningless. There was no one to share it with. No one else who understood. There had been one person, only one. Many people said they'd found their soul mate, there was only one true match for them…but for Bradley, he suspected this was really true.

And she had been gorgeous.

And she had been his.

How could she be dead? His lovely, brilliant, unpredictable, chaotic Alejandra?

"Good news. No, great news!" Savino Latorre burst into the room. Bradley paused. Where had Savi been during all this?

"What?" Had the news about Alejandra somehow been mistaken? Or was he excited that they'd managed to orchestrate such a massive shutdown of the Paris power grid? That the "items" had been obtained and the financier acquired?

"Call came from China. Sword 23 knows where she is! He wants to talk with me!"

What? They'd pulled off yet another huge "plague," successfully commandeered their objective, but by doing so, lost their most valuable asset, and this is what he's on about?

Savino didn't even ask if things were in place for the next plague—the dénouement, what all the others had been leading to. All he seemed to care about was the Woman.

Well, Bradley matched him on that. All he cared about right now was a woman, also.

A woman who was lost.

TUESDAY, NOVEMBER 13, 2007, 1:07 A.M.
LAC-ARGENT, FRANCE

BEFORE GETTING ONTO THE A4, Jaime pulled over and called ahead to Mark's housekeeper, Mrs. Halpern, to let her know they were heading that way.

The night sky was clear, the moon barely edging toward a quarter's worth of light, which gave the stars the ability to blaze holes in the black tableau. That stillness, added to the lack of traffic and the quiet inside the car, gave Jaime more thinking space than she wanted.

Someone had tried to kill her. She had been moments from dead.

Instead, a woman they didn't know, had never met, whom before tonight they had had nothing against, was dead. Someone had birthed that woman, taught her to walk, perhaps dressed her in little girl dresses and little patent leather shoes. Had taken great pride in her, had great hopes for her.

And now she was dead.

Jaime had been an idiot. She had been on a mission high. Showing off for Mark.

And now, he was...well, *freaked out* wasn't a psychological term, but she didn't want to think about the reality of the situation. He had been damaged. Put it that way. Possibly scarred for life.

I'm with Minnow. So shoot me.

After hearing Mrs. Halpern's cheerful voice, Jaime had somehow convinced herself that coming to Mark's house in Lac-Argent was a good idea. He was safe here. She could stay as long as she needed to, and move on, leaving him behind.

"We found the marker, Jaime, and are working on deciphering it," said her OC as Jaime turned off the main highway onto the smaller road that led into Lac-Argent. "Thank you for your assistance. Both you and Mr. Shepard brought valuable skills to the table."

"The woman—she was dead, wasn't she?"

"Yes. I'm afraid so."

"Do we know who she was? Or why she wanted to kill me?"

A pause. "We're working on it." Then, "How are you doing? That was a terrible thing. You nearly died. We can have someone pick you up in the morning, and bring you in. We've got it from here, Jaime. You've done your part. You're off duty now."

Yeah, she'd heard that before. And…on this road, too.

"I'm okay. I'll let you know when I want to be picked up. Let me see how Shepard is doing in the morning."

"He'll need someone to talk with, also."

"I know. I'll see if he'd like us to provide someone."

" Try to get some sleep. We'll talk in the a.m."

"Thanks." Jaime signed off.

Being an Eden Operative was all about being an "agent of change," not about being a ruthless player for one side or another. You were taught to withstand torture, yes, but you were never trained to turn off your empathy or your emotions. Which made times like this a hell of a lot harder.

Jaime was now on a two-lane country road with no streetlights, passing fields, grey in the night. Maybe it was good to be coming back here, to be facing her demons. Now, nearly eleven months on, she should be ready. She had a life, a good, solid life. She had meaningful work. She had Yani, for God's sake. She had God, for Yani's sake.

She smiled.

If only Yani were here. He understood danger, scars, and roads to wholeness. He understood the enormous price that living with courage could extract. He would know what to say, to Mark, to her. He would enfold her in one of his encompassing hugs that shut out the rest of the world.

Then she reached the turn to Mark's property. The gate was open that led to his eighteenth-century chateau.

And, across the street, stood the old church tower where she had been bound and tortured.

NO NO NO NO NO.

She would take a couple of sleeping pills. She would deal with everything in the morning.

God help me, she thought.

And she knew then, with utter clarity, that coming here at this time had been a really, really bad idea.

TUESDAY, NOVEMBER 13, 2007, 8:32 A.M.
GOLDEN SUN VINEYARDS
NINGXIA AUTONOMOUS REGION, CHINA

THE FIRST GUARD OPENED THE DOOR to the marble restroom.

Not seeing his ill captive, he stepped inside, confused.

It took only moments for Yani to incapacitate him using pressure points in his arm and neck; as he crumpled to the ground, the second man came in. The room was just large enough for Yani to press himself against the wall while the man stepped inside toward his fallen compatriot.

Whom he soon ended up next to.

Yani had less than two minutes to disappear.

Once out in the hall, the most obvious place was to enter the wine cellars through an archway. Row after row of barrels ran along hallways that spanned at least a quarter of a mile in length.

This was where they would look for him first. So Yani continued down to the labyrinthine hallways that housed bottles for both the vineyard and its patrons.

He was correct; it took fewer than three minutes for the two guards to reappear, conferring with someone on walkie-talkies in Mandarin. Another guard joined them at once. After a hurried confab, they apparently decided the barrel cellar was the most likely hiding place. All three drew guns.

One of them remained in the hallway; the other two entered the cellar with the wine casks. From where he knelt behind the first row of bottle storage, Yani could hear them, likely one on each end of the walkways, going from row to row, not finding him and calling out the Chinese equivalent of "clear!"

It took a good ten minutes for them to return, empty-handed, to confer with the guard in the hallway. Apparently a very large cellar. As they spoke, other men arrived.

Now what?

The wine storage vaults, where he now waited, had to be next. He crawled to the inner end of his aisle. There was a narrow arched door between the two cellars. The problem was, the gated doorways into the main hallway were open, as were the long, arched windows looking into each area.

But he couldn't stay in the storage cellar. He crept to the doorway between, knowing that if he moved fully into either room, he would be seen from the hallway.

He didn't have long to wait.

The guards completed their plan and moved toward the storage cellar. Four of them remained behind, guarding the hallway and any doors opening onto it.

Yani pressed himself against the inner wall, ready to try to slip next door.

But he knew he was seconds from being spotted by any one of the half-dozen well-armed, angry men.

TUESDAY, NOVEMBER 13, 2007, 1:33 A.M.
LAC-ARGENT, FRANCE

THEY SAT BY THE FIREPLACE in the downstairs salon.

Mrs. Halpern brought them herbal tea and cookies that she had baked after Jaime's call.

The tea was warm and comforting. Jaime's body had no idea what time zone they were in, what meal was due, if she was wide awake or ready to pass out. She still felt an inner skeleton of adrenaline giving her body shape, holding her upright.

She had no idea when it would crumble, but she knew it would.

"She was dead?" It was Shepard, when Mrs. Halpern left them alone by the stone fireplace large enough for two men to turn a hog on a spit.

"Yes."

"God, Jaime. I'm so sorry."

"No, Mark, I'm sorry. I got you into this. I knew I was bait. I shouldn't have let you come."

"I'm a good person."

"You're a very good person."

"I mean, I'm not Bono or Bob Geldorf. I haven't cancelled third world debt or raised millions to fight AIDS in Africa, but I've done what I can. I've brought food, and water… and…"

"Mark, stop. Just stop. I mean it. You're a good person. What happened tonight does not define you. You saved my life. And your own."

"I killed a person. On purpose. I shot her. I meant to shoot her. I aimed at her and pulled the trigger. I did that. And she's dead."

The horror of it was deep behind his eyes.

"Would you rather *I* was dead? Would you rather we were both dead?"

"I didn't even know I was capable…of wanting someone dead. Let alone, of killing them. Oh, God. God, help me."

"Mark, stop. You're torturing yourself."

"I wanted her dead. I made it happen."

Dear God. See what she'd done. She should never have let a civilian accompany her into a dangerous active assignment. But she'd been showing off. She was with Mark freaking Shepard. And she'd wounded him. Again. Last time she was here, she'd brought a killer to his house. Now she'd forced him to become one.

Lord, I need your help. I can't do this by myself. Be here. Help us.

"I'm a good person."

"You're a very good person. And if someone doesn't want you to get furious enough to shoot her, she'd better not try to kill both you and a friend. Let that be a warning to anyone else. Seriously. I would have done the same. Anyone would have done the same."

"Would you have?"

Truth? She didn't know. She'd never killed someone. Gardeners—and chaplains—didn't carry weapons. But they understood those who did.

They'd been sitting on the floor. Even on the ornate carpet, though, the wood was hard. Jaime stood and went back to the wing chair that was facing the fire behind them. Mark stayed on the floor. When he spoke again, it was quietly.

"I have this temper, Jaime. I'm on my best behavior around you because I love you—or I torment myself by telling myself I do. But it's like a beast, and I can usually control it, but sometimes… sometimes, I purposely don't. Sometimes I step back into it and let it be like a circle of fire around me. And later I say it overtook me, I couldn't help myself…but there's a moment. There's always a moment when I choose to take that last backwards step. Or at least, not to fight it."

"Yeah?"

"Yeah. I hurt...Ondine...so many times. Not physically, never physically. But emotionally. But I didn't know it could make me kill. I stepped back into it tonight, Jaime. I stepped back into that rage. On purpose. In a split second."

"And you saved our lives! It was kill or be killed. You didn't let yourself shoot some person on the street! There was a woman with the muzzle of a gun pressed against my skull! That was her choice. Her decision. She put you into an impossible situation!"

"Have you ever killed anyone?" The question was quiet.

"No," she said. "But I have wished people dead."

In this very house. In the church tower across the street.

"Are you tired?" she asked. "Can you sleep? We will wade through this, Mark, we will. But I can't tell you how much it helps to be rested and fed. It's the only way we've got a fighting chance."

"So to speak."

"So to speak." Jaime smiled. At least he could see irony. A good first step.

"Did Mrs. Halpern make up a room for you?"

"She did." Jaime stood and stretched.

"Let's go on up, then." He stood. "I am tired. Will you stay with me, for a minute, while I fall asleep? I mean, in a chair. I'm just frightened. But you're tired, too. I'm sorry. What was I thinking?"

"Let's go on up."

Together they went back out into the entry hall, and climbed the wooden stairs. Jaime had earlier put her bag into her bedroom.

She'd just stay while Shepard got into bed. Then she'd repair to her own room.

At the top of the main staircase, the hall with guest bedrooms stretched off to the right. To the left was a wall with a large, carved wooden door, leading to Mark's private suite of rooms.

He opened it, and invited her inside.

Someone had laid, and lit, a fire on the hearth in the lovely large living room. Back beyond, the doors to Mark's bedroom had been opened, and a lamp by the side of the bed turned on.

He headed back. "I'll duck into the restroom, just for a moment," he was saying.

But Jaime no longer heard him. The shadows in each corner of the room were alive, and they were coalescing. Into a presence. An evil presence.

She knew it was him, coming for her. With a gun. When she was vulnerable. At her most vulnerable. Mark was gone. Help was gone.

There was nothing but snarling evil.

She screamed. And she screamed again, as it came to surround her. To overpower her.

And take her away.

TUESDAY, NOVEMBER 13, 2007, 1:43 A.M.
CASTEL DEL MONTE
ANDREA, ITALY

NO MATTER HOW HE FELT personally, it was time to start the preliminaries for the final and most dramatic plague.

Death of the Firstborn.

Bradley's most recent check-in with the hit men had been twenty-four hours earlier, though they'd each been on the job for weeks now. The kid from France had been kidnapped and was now "in house." Which meant he could be easily offed, if necessary.

Death of the Firstborn.

Death.

Bradley felt less cavalier about it now than he had when this all began.

Especially "Death of the Firstborn." That implied that the person being killed was young enough to have at least one living parent. And, also, likely, others who loved them dearly.

Chaos was fine. Intriguing. Wonderful.

Death could be so callous.

They were each expecting a penultimate check-in.

Bradley took another drink of Savino's wine, and started to dial.

TUESDAY, NOVEMBER 13, 2007, 8:45 A.M.
GOLDEN SUN VINEYARDS
NINGXIA AUTONOMOUS REGION, CHINA

A BRISK VOICE and the shuffling of a large group of people grew louder as the hostess rounded the corner leading the first of the morning's tours.

Yani could only imagine how quickly the guns disappeared.

The hostess stopped and explained in English how each of the 10,000 bottles stored in the cellar was kept at the precisely correct temperature and angle for the type of wine. She repeated the statement in Chinese. As the group moved on to the cellar of barrels where the wines aged, one woman said, "I'm sorry, but is there a restroom down here?"

"Ma'am, we're very close to finishing the tour," said the guide. "There are large restrooms upstairs near the gift shop."

"I'm afraid I can't wait," protested the woman.

"I need to stop, also," said an older man.

"But the restroom down here is a single room, made to be accessible for guests with special needs."

"If it flushes, I'll take it," said the woman.

So the entire group came to a halt in the hallway.

An unexpected, and welcome, interruption. Yani expelled the breath he didn't know he'd been holding.

The fact that civilians were now crowding the hallway gave him a moment to scope out the situation. The tour guide was chattering, trying to keep a line from forming at the single-seat restroom. She wasn't having much success.

Yani took the opportunity to slip past the open doorway into the cask room, which had already been searched. As he did, he came up short. In front of him was the back of a head of hair he recognized. It was Nancy Moore, the wine critic who had come over to write about the Zhu Winery.

What to do?

She was leaning against one of the arched windows filled with an intricate design of wrought iron.

"Nancy," he whispered. She straightened up, confused. "Behind you. Shhh."

She turned around.

"Bill?"

"Yes. Listen, I need your help. Could I talk to you for a minute? Could you slip back here without anyone noticing?"

The look on her face was a mixture of surprise, curiosity, and consternation.

He slid down below the window to the floor. She darted through the door and sat down beside him, although, given his current state, he made certain to give her enough personal space.

"Why are you still here? And—where are your clothes?"

"For reasons about which I'm not sure, I was detained here last night. Given a knockout drug on the tour. And my clothing has been appropriated. Would you be willing to help me?"

"What can I do? Get a message to Robert Zhu?"

"I'm afraid by then I may never be found. I was thinking maybe—find me some sort of clothing in the gift shop? They must have t-shirts or perhaps jackets, with the Golden Sun logo."

She looked at him with a critical eye. "What size?"

"Large anything. At this point, I'm not picky."

"Large, you sure? You're in really good shape."

"Thanks. I try. Never know when I'm going to need to impress a wine critic in my skivvies."

"Wait, so what's the plan, again? You wait here and I go buy a t-shirt and come back? Are you sure I'll be able to get past them to get back down here? Are you sure you'll still be here?"

He shook his head. "It doesn't sound likely, does it? Across the hall are a number of guards with guns, all waiting for the tour to move on, to bring me back as a prize."

"There has to be a back door here, don't you think? If we can get outside to my van driver, I'm sure I can get him to take you to the Zhu Winery. It isn't far."

"Nancy, thank you. But no. These folks are dangerous. As in, not-kidding-around dangerous. Maybe you could try getting me some clothes, and if it doesn't work, leave as you normally would and get word to Robert."

"Are you kidding? Leave you here in these circumstances? How could I live with that? I'm sure there has to be a back door. And, as I said, I have a driver just outside."

He saw the look of determination in her eyes. He knew that look on women like her. "How would you persuade him to drive me to the Zhu Winery? I'm not sure he'd want to anger one of his clients, as Golden Sun obviously is."

She opened her purse, and took out a stack of bills in Chinese currency.

"Perhaps yours is the better plan," he said. "But we're betting pretty heavily that there's a back door to this cellar."

"I'm not seeing them get all these barrels down elevators and narrow hallways, the way the tour came. My money's on a back door."

"Quite literally," Yani said. "Though I'll ask you one more time, to try the sweatshirt plan."

"In your dreams. This is the first tasting trip I've enjoyed for many a year."

"Okay. Thanks."

"Ladies and gentleman, upstairs, *please!*" The guide had clearly had enough.

Nancy and Yani needed no more nudging. They ran, ducking low, past the windows to the far side of the cellar. Then, once there were walls of casks to shield them from view, they stood and ran toward the back.

It was a cavernous room. They passed row after row of wine casks, and finally reached the back wall. Sure enough, there was a door. And sure enough, it said, in Chinese with illustrations, that the door was alarmed. Do Not Exit Except in Case of Emergency.

"This is an emergency, I'd say," said Nancy.

"I'm sure the alarm is tied in to the central system. They'll immediately know where we are." Not to mention, there was a surveillance camera pointing to the metal door.

Damn.

Nancy pointed to half a dozen barrels sitting on end, open and empty, lids beside them.

"So maybe I go for the clothing," she said. She seemed disappointed.

"And this is your idea of where I'm waiting," he said, tilting his head toward one of the barrels.

"Looks pretty big and comfortable to me," she said.

The cellar vibrated with running and shouting. Obviously, the tour had moved on, and also, enough guards had come that they were able to cover both rooms at once.

"Crap," said Nancy.

Yani held the barrel lid high. "After you," he said.

TUESDAY, NOVEMBER 13, 2007, 7:45 P.M.
BEHIND SCOTT BARRACKS
UNITED STATES MILITARY ACADEMY
WEST POINT, NEW YORK

THE RUSTLE OF LEAVES alerted Cadet Djoko Bak to the movement of something in the woods above him.

Joke stood quietly on a metal staircase behind his barracks. His eyes searched the woods that surrounded him, lamplight illuminating small patches of the woods, leaving others in deep shadow. He tried not to breathe. Was someone following him?

There, he saw it. About thirty feet away, just above him on the path, was a large white-tailed deer. It was a four-point buck, standing motionless as if waiting for the cadet to make the first move. Bak held his breath and watched. After a minute of this standoff, the buck turned and bounded up the hill, followed by the doe that had been hiding behind him.

He was obviously becoming too jumpy.

As he watched the flash of white fade into the woods, Joke wondered at the simplicity of a life focused on gathering sustenance and producing offspring. Oh how he wished for that simplicity now, for the separate lives of his homeland and West Point were about to come crashing into each other.

The cadet heard footsteps he recognized as his girlfriend Shelby coming up the staircase from below. She walked over and wrapped her arms around him from behind, with her hands across his chest.

He placed his hands on top of hers and they stood that way in the dark for a few minutes.

I wish I could just freeze this moment in time.

"Oh, I've been wanting to do this all day!" Shelby sighed and kissed him on the neck. "I'm going to be so glad when we don't have to meet in secret anymore!"

The young man didn't reply. He just stood there, feeling the warmth of her body against his back.

"And that would be your cue," she said, with a hint of laughter in her voice, "to say something like 'me too!'"

Shelby expected a saucy reply, but when he said nothing, she pulled him around so she could look him in the face.

"You're so quiet. What's wrong?"

Where do I start? My two worlds are colliding and I can do nothing to stop it.

"I received a phone call from my father."

Shelby's sharp intake of breath told him she immediately assumed some sort of family emergency such as an accident or illness. He almost wished it were that simple.

"There is great turmoil right now in my country. You remember the volcano that erupted last week, near my home city of Surabaya?"

"Yes. You said initially there was some ash, but then it died down. People were allowed to return to their homes."

"That's the problem. They were sent back home. And now it has erupted, *really* erupted, and many people have died. The government is being blamed for mishandling the situation. My father is facing disgrace. He wants me to come home."

"But, what would that achieve? How long would you be gone?"

He could tell Shelby was struggling to maintain her composure.

"I don't know, and I don't know," Bak replied. "But he needs me by his side, and I cannot deny him that."

"You could lose an entire semester's worth of credits! You wouldn't be able to graduate in May."

"That may not matter."

"What do you mean?" She stepped back from him, starting to sound hysterical.

"In my country's eyes I have learned all I need to serve in our military."

"I can't believe you're talking about throwing away everything you have here. Everything we have. After one phone call."

"Shells…" He uttered his special name for her. "I'm not saying I won't be back. I just don't know when."

He reached toward her and caressed her cheek. "I love you, but this is my home, my family. I can't abandon them."

"So you abandon me!" The young woman pulled away from him, turned, and ran down the steps.

Joke started to follow, then thought better of it. He hoped she might cool down a bit and he could make her see reason in the morning. Looking back up toward the woods with one last, wistful sigh, the dejected young man headed down the steps toward his dorm room.

TUESDAY, NOVEMBER 13, 2007, 8:45 A.M.
GOLDEN SUN VINEYARDS
NINGXIA AUTONOMOUS REGION, CHINA

THEY BOTH FIT INTO THE BARREL. But barely.

Nancy got in first and Yani handed her the lid, then climbed in across from her.

It was a tight squeeze. "Turn around," he said. "Sit against me, facing the same direction."

She turned as gracefully as she could. It was infinitely more comfortable. Except nothing was comfortable for him just now. The pain in his hip was fine until he squatted or sat on it, which had been happening on a continuous basis. Then it went from an ache to a blaze of pain. Yet the cardinal rule Yani had learned about working with civilians was that you had to act like nothing was wrong. Whatever the situation, it was something you dealt with every day.

"So what are you doing here at Golden Sun?" he whispered.

"Are you kidding? After seeing this place last night, how could I just go to Zhu's place and call it a trip? I had to check it out. So I got up early and booked one of the Breakfast Tours on my way over to Robert's place. Why are you still here? Are they really this ruthless with the competition?"

"Funny you should say that. 'Ruthless' is indeed a word they used in self-description."

The voices of the guards were growing closer, but they still hadn't reached the final vaulted room that led to outside.

"This cellar is huge," Yani whispered.

"Yeah, but, really, these oaken barrels are just for show. They likely have new, state-of-the-art stainless steel barrels at another site that can hold millions of bottles of aging wine. It's much easier to deal with in bulk, and the result is the same. Sometimes they'll add oak chips for taste, like manufacturers used to add the taste of tin to items that people were used to eating from cans but now get from plastic."

As she spoke, the footsteps and voices of the guards approached quickly, close enough that they fell completely silent.

It was clear the guards were agitated at losing a tall, undressed American.

Yani again appreciated the wisdom of sending in agents who knew the territory and were fluent in the language. Not understanding Mandarin was making him crazy.

The guards were nearly breathless with the search.

And then, an alarm went off. A loud, high-pitched alarm. It went off in bursts of three, with two-second pauses between.

Clearly, one of the guards had opened the back door.

The door-opener's boss yelled at him. As long as the door was open, some of them stepped outside to make certain there were no extraneous, running, nearly-naked Westerners.

The heavy metal door was pulled shut, and booted treads retreated toward the front of the cellar.

But just as Yani and Nancy were tempted to breathe a sigh of relief, they heard two remaining guards talking to each other.

And the men began to approach.

Apparently, they'd noticed that, of the six barrels sitting upright, only one had a lid.

For Yani, the old adage, "like shooting fish in a barrel," came to mind.

"Oh, crap," whispered Nancy.

TUESDAY, NOVEMBER 13, 2007, 2:14 A.M.
LAC-ARGENT, FRANCE

"IT'S ALL RIGHT. You're all right." The words were quiet but the voice was strong, and comforting.

Jaime opened her eyes. She was on the small divan in the sitting room of her bedroom in Mark Shepard's home. He was sitting beside her, with his arms wrapped around her.

"Can you hear me? Can you *breathe*?"

"Mark?" she asked.

"Yeah. It's okay. I'm here. You're safe."

Jaime closed her eyes again and worked on regulating her breathing. Oh, man. What had just happened?

"That was the room, wasn't it?" Shepard asked her. "We've never talked about it. But that's where you were when that monster came and kidnapped you."

"Yes," she said. "Yes."

"And, to make it worse, at the time you weren't expecting him. You didn't know he had followed you here."

"No. I thought it was you. My guard was down."

"Like tonight, when someone tried to kill you. Your guard was down."

She nodded. "Yeah, you're right. I thought we'd done it. Gotten the marker and gotten down safely."

"Just know that you're safe now. After what happened in January, I've now got two full time security guys, and the chateau is a fortress. I paid dearly to make sure the place doesn't look like a fortress—but no one is getting in here again. Ever."

"We didn't ever get to talk about it," Jaime said. "Where did he catch you? Where did you find Derrick?" His security man, who had been killed.

"Outside. By the carpark. That's a small mercy, I suppose. So inside the house still feels safe to me. But I should have thought, Jaime. Shit, I'm sorry. I should have thought."

Her heart was still pounding, but she was no longer gulping for air. "I never thought…I never knew that could happen."

More to the point, she didn't know the monster had still been there, hiding inside her head. And tonight . . . well, tonight had certainly been the perfect storm to loose him from his moorings.

"Do you want me to call someone?" he asked. "I mean, to come and get you?"

"No. No. But give me a minute."

He released her from the safety of his arms, and moved back to give her some space.

"I'm supposed to be taking care of *you*," she said.

"We're a real pair, aren't we?" he asked. "One more freaked out than the other."

Jaime turned and looked at Mark. The irony was, taking care of her, he had become cogent, coherent, and proactive.

She let herself exhale. But she was still trembling.

"Would you like some tea?" he asked.

"You've haven't got anything stronger?"

He gave a small laugh. In fact, behind the sofa on the bookshelf was a bottle of red wine, and a bottle of cognac, with glasses.

"Cognac?" he asked. "We are in the Champagne region."

"Sure," she said.

He got up, and poured the golden liquid into the bottom of two rounded glasses. He returned, and handed one to her. Then he sat against one corner of the couch. "Come here," he said.

She moved to sit back against him. He started humming. This time, to her surprise, an old hymn. *Be thou my vision, O Lord of my heart, naught be all else to me, save that Thou art. Thou my best thought, by day or by night, waking or sleeping, Thy presence, my light.*

She joined him, softly, on the second verse. Her heartbeat was nearing normal.

Afterwards, he sang another couple of songs. She closed her eyes and leaned against him. "Thanks," she said, finally, when he was done.

"Are you better?" he asked.

"Yes," she said. "For now. You?"

He nodded. "For now."

She put her glass down, stood up, and stretched. He did the same.

"Okay," he said. "Hell of a night."

"Yep."

He locked eyes with her. "Forgive me. Weird timing. But we might never be in a space that's this…emotionally intimate… again. There's something I didn't say when I had the chance. And I just want to have put it out there."

"Okay," she said.

"Back on the plane, you said I could have my choice of supermodels, so why would I choose you? And I gave you reasons. One that I didn't include was that you are gorgeous. As far as I'm concerned, you're more beautiful than any walking stick figure." He reached out and pushed at a lock of hair that had fallen forward. "Your hair. Your eyes. Your rockin' hot bod. Sorry. Sorry. But I forgot to say that. Didn't want you to think I hadn't noticed that you're beautiful. So there you have it. If nothing ever happens between us, at least I wanted you to know."

Jaime smiled. "I think it's called selective vision. But thanks. And, okay, if we're being honest, here is the part that I haven't said, but I think you know. I mean, about *us*." She closed her eyes, and tried to gather her words. "I love you so much. As a friend. And I need you to be a friend." Then, a sigh. "This is so hard. And what you just said isn't helping."

Out with it, she told herself.

She took Mark's hands. "The truth is, as you can't help but know, I find you attractive. All right, incredibly attractive. Damn it. I am married, and I meant my vows. But, more than that…even more important than that, is my relationship with my God. I have promised God that I will be a faithful follower on the journey. I will be *faithful.* So while I have promised my husband I will be faithful, I have also promised God. That is the type of person I believe I'm called to be. We're each called to be. So loving you—making love to you—would make me a different person. An unfaithful person. And as much as I want you—will likely always want you—I am not willing to become *less* to have you."

"I do understand. In fact that's probably a good part of why I love you." Mark took a step back, without releasing her hands. "It's a conundrum. So. If I promise not to continue to pursue you. If I promise not to make love to you, or write another album of songs about you, or give enough clues that journalists have figured out I've done such a thing…can I kiss you again? One final time? As a farewell to this part of our relationship, and to welcome in another?"

She reached her arms up to him, and he put his around her.

He tasted of tea and cognac, of danger and safety. In his arms, she felt longing and, then, knowledge of decisions made differently. Of other paths chosen. "Old friend," he said as they broke apart. Then, he kissed her briefly, on the cheek. "New friend."

"New old friend."

"Should I stay here in the room with you? To sleep? And I do mean *sleep*," he finally said.

"Yes," she said. "I think we both need help making it through to morning."

"And when we wake up, we wake up as friends."

"Friend of my heart," she said.

They both climbed onto the blue and white bedspread on the guest bed, leaving the light on across the room. There, together, they felt safe enough to let exhaustion overtake them.

And they slept.

TUESDAY, NOVEMBER 13, 2007, 9:07 A.M.
GOLDEN SUN VINEYARDS
NINGXIA AUTONOMOUS REGION, CHINA

YANI MOVED NANCY FORWARD as quietly as possible to give him room to maneuver. He'd have only a split second once the barrel was opened.

In the background, the alarm continued to go off at its programmed intervals.

Luckily, the first guard to reach them didn't have the courage of his convictions.

He stood before the barrel, then gingerly pried the top off. Both guards stood back. Finally, one of them stepped forward and poked at the top, slipping it forward only slightly.

Yani rolled his eyes. They hadn't moved it enough to be able to see inside. The guard stepped forward and poked at it again.

Yani took this as his opportunity to stand up and crash the barrelhead, hard, against the nearest assailant. He let the top fall, grabbed the rim of the barrel and hoisted himself out, landing on the solar plexus of the downed man. Without a pause, he grabbed, disarmed and knocked out the second guard.

"Come on," he said to Nancy, who was gamely trying to get out of the barrel. "We don't have much time."

He strode back over, and helped lift her clear.

"It seems the best route might be out the door. The alarms are already going off," he said.

"But won't they see us on camera?"

"Probably. But we'll have more of a chance outside."

As they headed for the door, Nancy slowed. "Wait—shouldn't we grab their guns?"

"Not unless you're interested in being on the losing end of a firefight."

"Oh. From the movies, it seemed like the thing to do."

The portal before them was wooden and massive, but not arched. Yani lifted the metal door-bar and pushed open the door.

As Nancy had suspected, they exited into the brisk autumn air of a loading dock. A large industrial drive came down to it, and a brick wall blocked it from view of the tourists. There were cameras everywhere.

Which meant they needed to keep moving. He took her hand and they ran to the end of the wall. No guards yet, but it would be only a matter of minutes.

"The maze," Nancy said.

Yani followed her gaze. There was indeed a tall maze made of neatly trimmed bushes that were nearly eight feet high. It was on the manicured grounds, halfway to the car park.

"Let's go."

They ran across the still-empty lawn around and into the labyrinth.

Yani leaned back against the bushes, which were hard and prickly. He straightened immediately.

"So where is this van with the driver who doesn't know he's about to get an offer he can't refuse?" he asked.

"We're fairly close to the car park. How about if I stroll out of here, and hope they don't realize you've got a friend with you. At least, not until I make it past the fountains. And, oh," she added, taking off her jacket. "For goodness sake, put this on."

He accepted gratefully. It was a London-fog style raincoat, with a warm lining. On her, it was below the knee. On him, it came mid-thigh. But he hadn't realized how cold he really was.

"You're good with trying this?" Yani asked.

"Best wine-tasting trip yet," she said. "They usually start to run into each other in my mind. Not this one."

"Thanks," he said.

But as she was about to leave their hidden vantage point, they heard two men running. They came from different parts of the chateau and met up just outside the maze.

"He's gone?" asked the first, in French. "How can he be gone?"

Yani recognized the voice immediately as Creased Trouser Man.

"We'll find him. He's here somewhere. Obviously." The response was also in French, which was one of Yani's first languages.

"Savino has a plane getting ready for takeoff. We've cleared it with local officials, which was not cheap. Savino's demanding to see this guy. And we've *lost him*?"

Yani's shoulders fell. "Damn," he said.

"What?" Nancy asked, surprised at his tone.

"It seems there's a plane I need to be on," he said.

He took off the jacket, and handed it back to her. "Thanks again," he said. "For everything."

He put his hands behind his head, fingers laced. And he strolled out of the maze, into the cold morning sun.

"That's all I ever asked," he said in French to the astonished men before him. "I'd prefer not to be killed. But I do want to talk to Savino Latorre."

TUESDAY, NOVEMBER 13, 2007, 3:07 A.M.
TAVEL APARTMENT, 7TH ARRONDISSEMENT
PARIS, FRANCE

WHEN THE PHONE CALL CAME, it was not from the "business associate."

It was from Danièle Guillory, the nanny.

"They have taken Leal," she said to Archard. She sounded distraught, but she also sounded like she was reading something. "If you don't do as they ask, you will never see him again. You will get one more phone call, today before noon. That is just before Leal will die."

She'd broken down at that point, and he'd heard a rough male voice in the background. Danièle had continued, "There is no point in involving the authorities. If you agree, your life will be happy and long. If you do not, it will be made permanently miserable, and the objective will be accomplished in other, more hostile, ways."

Then the line had gone dead.

Archard leaned back in his chair and closed his eyes. The one thing he couldn't figure out, for the life of him, was why. Why did anyone care about such a piddling company? Their revenues were in the millions, not the billions. For God's sake!

And there had been something else, something he hadn't wanted to admit, even to himself.

What if Leal didn't come back?

Anyone dying would be tragic, of course. But his own life would be so much simpler. Of course he couldn't ever say that. Couldn't admit he'd thought it, even for a second.

And then, an hour later, the phone rang again. It was Danièle. She told him breathlessly that she'd been dumped in the center of Paris. She had no money, what should she do? Should she go to the police?

He told her to take a cab back to the apartment, he would give money for the fare to the doorman downstairs. Twenty minutes later, the front door burst open, and Danièle crashed in. Into the apartment, into the library, into his life.

Oh, he knew he employed a nanny, much like he knew he paid an exorbitant amount to a special private school for his son's education. Like he knew he had in-laws, and owed taxes. Those unpleasant facts that roamed the ether of his life. The nanny came under the classification of money paid to keep things out of his hair.

"Monsieur Tavel!" she cried, and flung herself onto the ground at his feet. "Oh, monsieur, what shall we do?" The poor woman was shaking. She looked up at him, and he realized he'd never really noticed what she looked like. She was tall with thick black hair. Her eyes were also dark. He guessed her to be in her early thirties. Her face was thin, and her nose was pronounced. Otherwise, she might be pretty.

"Can you tell me where they took you? Where they took Leal?" he asked, dutifully.

"No," she shook her head. "The electricity went out, and they were in the apartment, and they found us. They knew about the back stairs. I made them let me take Leal's bag, but that was all I could grab. You know, the bag with his soldiers and his drawing tablets and his pencils."

She was talking fast, words spilling over each other. "When we reached the ground floor, they put black bags over our heads. We couldn't see anything. They stuffed us into the back of a car and made us lie down on the seats. They drove for half an hour or more. Maybe an hour. But they never took the hoods off. I don't have any idea where we were."

He should be caring about every minute detail. He didn't. It didn't matter where they'd been taken or where Leal was now. All that mattered was the call that would come before noon. But he understood that the woman must be traumatized.

"They made you read something on the phone call?"

"Yes, yes. On a landline in a dark room. Then they took Leal away. I begged them to let me stay with him. I explained to them—I tried to explain—that he's a visual thinker. They won't understand him. That he's not being difficult, but he won't necessarily hear them. He doesn't think or talk in a linear fashion, as we do. He isn't constrained by a linear version of time, or time passing. That his meltdowns aren't tantrums. But they won't understand, will they?"

Tears streaked her cheeks. "They won't understand. They'll hurt him. They'll think he's not obeying, being bad, on purpose. Oh, Leal, Leal! What do we do?"

"You did all you could," said Archard. "Leave the rest to me."

"I told them that King Arthur was his river," she said. "But they won't care, will they?"

"His river?"

"You know, the thing he cares about, that gives him focus and the kind of speech we can understand. His passion."

"What kind of speech?"

"Sometimes, he can talk in sentences, *whole* sentences, but only when he's quoting lines from King Arthur."

"Is that why he watches that damn television show time after time?"

"Yes," she said. "He lives in Camelot." Her voice got quiet, almost like she was embarrassed. "He's Merlin, you see. The outcast on the side. I'm Morgan le Fey. And you're..."

"I'm—who?"

"Ambrosius. King Ambrosius Pendragon. Merlin's secret father."

Archard stared at her.

Uncomfortable, the nanny continued, "Leal can tell you everything about Camelot. Who is related to whom. Genealogies. How big the armies are. The castles. The grail legends. It's his river."

Archard had no idea what she was talking about. Leal had a "river"?

"I gave him his bag. They'll let him keep it, don't you think? His drawing pad?"

"I have no idea."

At this, Danièle burst into tears. "What do we do? What do we do?"

That's all he needed. A hysterical woman in his house.

"Is there somewhere you can go, where you'd feel safe? Some family you could stay with?"

"I couldn't leave here!" she said, standing, suddenly completely coherent. "Leal will be back—and he needs me!"

From her tone, Archard wasn't sure exactly who needed whom.

"Yes, yes, of course."

She saw something and went over to the corner behind the door.

"One of his drawing pads," she said, like the boy was a dead saint, and this was a relic. She held it close, then she looked at Archard. "Oh, Monsieur Tavel, I am so sorry," she said. "He is your son. You should have it."

She handed over the sketchpad. It was eleven by fourteen, spiral bound. Why would he care? The boy had dozens of these, stacked all around the house.

"You will call the police?"

"I don't know," said Archard. "I will do what is best, to get the boy back."

"I will do anything to help."

"I know you will. Now please, go and get some rest."

Danièle started for the door to the hall. Archard didn't want to talk anymore, so he flipped open the sketchpad, expecting to find childish, stick-figure drawings.

Instead, he found himself staring at a page that held a professional rendering of the tower of the Chateau de Chinonceau in the Loire Valley. It was an architect's work, as it had notations of numbers and angles. He turned the page. Another turret. From the side. From above. From inside, looking up.

"Mademoiselle," he said, and the nanny turned back toward him at the hall door.

"Who has been doing these for him? Does he even know what they are?"

"The drawings?" Daniele seemed confused.

"Yes, yes. The drawings." Was he paying some damn architect to entertain his "special" son?

"Why…those are his, sir. I thought you knew."

"Leal drew these? My eleven-year-old son?"

"Yes. He loves castles. Especially turrets, because he loves circles. And spinning."

"How did he learn?"

"How to do architectural renderings? Remember when he took that art class two years ago? We never made it into the children's room at the college. He sat in the cloakroom of the hall where the architectural class met, until the professor found him. Well, found *us*." She looked uncomfortable. "He was going to kick us out. But when he saw Leal's notebook, he found him a little desk and some instruments. He let Leal sit in the back of the class. His name was Professor Paquet." She flushed. "He was wonderful. Is wonderful. It turns out that drawing turrets is what they call a splinter skill. Something Leal does really well because his brain just…thinks that way."

She hesitated a moment, and then said, "The electricity is back? The alarms…?"

"Yes," said Archard. "We are now perfectly safe."

After she left, he sat in the firelight and flipped page after page of drawings of the turrets at chateaux they'd visited, and some they hadn't. In fine detail.

Leal? Really? What surprised him most wasn't the expertise of thc drawings. It was thc thought that there might be a boy in there.

TUESDAY, NOVEMBER 13, 2007, 12:37 P.M.
IN THE AIR, FLYING WEST OVER THE NINGXIA AUTONOMOUS REGION, CHINA

THEY'D RETURNED HIS CLOTHES.

Yani had also asked for more bandages because the wounds on his hip from removal of the chip were still bleeding if he moved around a lot.

Of course, he hadn't mentioned he had a second chip.

At the airport, they'd all walked together onto the private plane. He still had his travelling papers from Robert Zhu, and Savino—or someone—had clearly greased the wheels.

There was a small bedroom at the back of the plane, where he was taken, instructed to lie down on the bed, and handcuffed with another nylon restraint to a handle on the bedside table. The table was bolted to the floor.

They left the door to the cabin open, so he was in sight at all times, but they could confer and go about their own business privately and he couldn't hear.

They hadn't needed to cuff him. He wasn't going to escape until they reached Savino Latorre. Of course, he couldn't tell them that. The angle of his cuffed arm, and the pressure from lying on his hip let him know it was going to be a very uncomfortable journey—and, likely a long one, depending on where in the world Savino was.

He tried to think of the man he'd known Savino to be. Back when he was Wester, was there any indication that he was capable of something as large and atrocious as the Wheel of Plagues? What had happened to him in the intervening decades to send him in this direction? Or was he acting at the behest of someone else?

He held a grudge against Yani; that was now certain. And, as rude as Yani might have been to him, it certainly was not of the level of slight that would cause you to murder someone.

Normally.

After his conversation in the Paris park with Savino, Yani was sent on one more mission as a European agent, which he'd completed as asked. To the letter, of course. And much more quickly than expected. As usual. Terris dwellers were so easily manipulated, it was astounding.

As an agent, Yani was good. He was the best. And he'd known it.

He'd found it to be an odd thing, transitioning from the Steppe to the Terris world, especially after his immersive training as an agent. In the Steppe, he was young, thought of as naïve, someone who was just beginning to earn respect. In the Steppe, the women all knew their worth and their abilities and were not interested in a young man who was both still mourning his mother and full of himself.

In the Terris world, however, he easily knew more than most people. The women were very easily impressed, and readily available.

He hadn't been back to that time, in his mind, for so long. He had been angry then—purposefully careless, too easily good at the job. But he pushed the bounds. Much was forgiven because he was Mara's son, Simeon's son. Adara's brother. But his mother was gone, and he hated Eden. Hated God. Hated them all.

Yani had been clever and callous. He drove them crazy by performing whatever duty they asked of him as an Operative. But he acted shallowly. He was vain; proud of himself and offhand about responsibility.

And then finally, after a successful mission, he was called in by his Operative Coordinator. They met in a safe house in Gstaad. She had been stationed there, but was packing up, which caught him off guard. She had thick brown hair, with golden highlights. Her eyes were blue gray and perfectly set. She wore a straight skirt and silk blouse.

Yani expected yet another "congratulations, but" talking-to. He knew he could talk his way out of any situation. He was not worried.

"What's all this?" he nodded to her packed bags and boxes.

"This is it," she said. "My last day as Operative Coordinator, mid-European command. Which leads me to ask, do you have anything to say for yourself?"

"About what?" he said. "Another successful mission."

She stopped what she was doing and looked at him. Really looked at him. For the first time, he was slightly nervous.

"So you're moving on? You'll no longer be my supervisor?"

She nodded curtly. He moved to stand near her. He softly touched the hair by her face. It was silk. "Then, may I say how extraordinarily beautiful you are?"

He could tell by her expression that he'd crossed the line. So, if he was already in trouble… he put his whole hand on the back of her neck and gently ran his fingers through her hair.

He said, "Can this be off the record?"

"Yes," she said. "I think it would be best, as on top of everything else, you've made a pass at an Operative Coordinator."

"I thought you said you weren't, any more."

"That's correct. I'm about to become your TC."

"Oh."

"Yes. Oh. Not that I have any interest in becoming the next in your long line of sexual partners in any case. Here is the problem, the one many of us have been dealing with for the length of your training and career. You are extraordinarily blessed. Under normal circumstances, you would have become a top-notch Operative. You could have made a lot of difference in the world. We could have counted on you for many things.

"It's true you've been through hard times. Here's what you might not know. It's difficult times that make a leader a leader.

But you refused help. Acted out. Threw away all the opportunities presented to you."

"But—I brought every mission to completion."

"Every mission, except the most crucial. Which was to become the man we needed you to be."

For the first time, Yani had no answer.

His superior sat, looking up at him with an expression of disappointment that burned through his skin, down inside of him. "We are now going on the record."

"Yes, ma'am."

"Operative Sword 23, I'm very sorry to inform you that, by unanimous decision, you are being released from the responsibilities and privileges of your Operative status."

Her words spun around him. He grasped at them. "Ma'am, I—No! I mean—please reconsider."

"How many times we have reconsidered. I'm sorry. Perhaps you will come to think of this as good news. You are now free, in the Terris world, as you have so long wished. You may bed whomever you please. You may spend as much money as you'd like. You may have whatever kind of life you choose to fashion for yourself."

"Please. No. I beg you."

"No one is ever dismissed for one or two bad decisions. No—you've worked hard to get here. I wouldn't wish you on my successor. It ends here."

"Have I no second chance? Am I never to work again? Am I… cast out? Forever? With no warning?"

"You have had years of warnings," she said sadly. "If you wish, you may make a life for yourself here in the Terris world, and be free of your promises. If you'd like, you may return to this address sixty days from today, and tell us whether you would rather be assigned somewhere inside Eden."

She grabbed a suitcase and walked past him. As she opened the door, he said, "Ma'am?" His voice was filled with anguish. She turned back to look at him. Broad, silent tears were coursing down his face.

His broken voice conveyed only three words. "Pray for me."

And she was gone.

Perhaps it was the fact that Yani remembered that day so clearly that made him feel that surely Wester could be brought back, also. Yani knew that not only did he feel he had to stop any more destruction, he wanted a chance to talk to the man he'd once known.

TUESDAY, NOVEMBER 13, 2007, 7:00 A.M.
AIRPORT, ITALY

THE SUN WAS BRIGHT, but the angle was not intrusive. Leal smiled as he spun and spun. They were on their way. It didn't even bother him much to be back in the grip of gravity.

"You are going on your quest. Be brave. Be bold. Save Arthur." The words Morgan spoke.

"I will. I shall. We will return victorious."

His quest. His quest! The day had come. "When you have completed your quest, you will be a squire no longer, but a knight. A true knight of the Round Table." That was what Ambrosius said. Yes. Yes! "Be brave. Be bold. Save Arthur."

He didn't hear what the two men said. They opened the door to his conveyance, and he climbed in with a smile.

"Be brave, be bold," he said cheerfully to the man sitting next to him. "Be brave, be bold."

These were good dots. Very very good.

TUESDAY, NOVEMBER 13, 2007, 10:00 A.M.
AEROPORTO DEL SALENTO
BRINDISI, ITALY

BY THE TIME THEY LANDED, Yani had no idea where in the world they were.

They'd made three stops to refuel, but since the window covers were down in his compartment, he wasn't able to read signs on the ground to see what language they were in. By the light from outside in the rest of the plane, he'd known they were travelling west. His best guess was that Savi was bringing him to somewhere in Western Europe.

He'd explained to Creased Trouser Man that he wasn't going to try to escape. He just wanted to talk to Mr. Latorre. He'd only escaped when he thought it likely they might want to kill him. He'd given himself up to be taken to the boss. He wanted to be on the plane.

They'd kept one hand cuffed, but had allowed him enough movement to stay off of his hip, and also to be able to eat some bread and drink some tea. That, with some sleep, was starting to restore him.

They wouldn't tell him when or where he was meeting Latorre—Wester.

After he'd last spoken to Wester in that Paris park, and after the meeting in which his OC had let him go, Yani had found his Operative apartment locked, his possessions in a locker at the train station, with two thousand cash. He travelled to Paris and rented a small flat. He went out and drank himself into a stupor. When he awoke, he had no purpose. He didn't leave the house. He didn't eat. He didn't do anything, except despair.

It was there that his older sister Adara found him. She also lived and worked in the Terris world, as a Messenger. She brought soup, and forced him to eat. She sang to him, songs their mother used to sing. Slowly, he started talking about his mother. His anger and frustration all seeped out, not as a roar, but as an oozing of toxic emotion.

After this, after crying in front of Adara—which he had never done—and after the walls surrounding his bluster and bravado fell, he realized he'd blown the one thing he was good at, the one purpose he had found for his life. He was despondent.

Adara took him out into the countryside, to a retreat run by a former Gardener. Yani stayed there for the remainder of the sixty days. As time went by, he spoke often with the Gardener, and spent a lot of time in the chapel.

When the days were up, Yani returned to the safe house in Gstaad. He told the four on the assembled Operative council that he was no longer interested in his old amusements. He also admitted he would be very sad to leave the Terris world, but couldn't consider living forever outside Eden. If he had to choose one, he would choose Eden. But mostly he had discovered, through his great mistakes, that he couldn't live without purpose. He hoped that they would somehow find somewhere he could work and be useful. Other than that, he knew he'd lost his right to ask anything.

He was taken back to Eden. After deliberations, he was allowed back to Mountaintop. He was told that if he were to regain Operative status, it would be after retraining to work in a new part of the Terris world, the Middle East. He spent a year at Mountaintop retraining. While there, it was as if he were a different person. He was quiet, introspective, studious. The irony was that things seemed harder for him than they once had: mostly because he now had something to lose.

After two years back at work in the Terris world, he came back to Eden for his first sabbatical. While he was there, the woman who had been his Operative Coordinator, who was finishing a vacation herself, asked to meet with him over tea. With trembling and hesitation, he agreed.

She said she had been deeply moved by his request for prayer, and that she had prayed for him, daily, since that time. Even though she didn't oversee the Middle East, she'd kept track of him. She'd been gratified by his progress, by the glowing reports she now got back from his colleagues.

He thanked her for taking the very difficult step that had led him to confront his demons, and had made possible a new life.

Back in the Terris world, they continued to meet every few months for tea. As she was preparing to leave after one particularly deep conversation, she stopped him.

"I do have one question about our first meeting," she said. "Did you actually find me attractive? Or was that just one of your pick-up lines?"

Surprised, and somewhat chagrined, he said, "I called you 'extraordinarily beautiful.' It wasn't one of my pick-up lines. Despite the inappropriateness of the situation, I was glad I had the chance to be truthful."

"You were sincere?"

"How can you doubt it? When you remain…so extraordinarily beautiful."

"I'm no longer your supervisor," she said.

Yani was quiet. "And yet…I've heard nothing from you to lead me to believe—"

He was silenced by her kiss. Nothing was ever the same, for either of them. They married within the year.

Maybe that was why, slim as it might be, Yani held out hope for Wester. Sometimes, miracles did happen.

This time, when they landed, everyone got up. The jet had parked by a general aviation hangar. Someone came and cut the zip cuff. There were three guns trained on him when he stood up. So maybe their trust wasn't complete.

They forced him to put his hands behind his back and cuffed his wrists together. Which was fine. He wasn't going to escape until they'd reached their destination. Meanwhile, he was very curious about where they were, and where they were going to end up.

The air outside the airplane door was chill but not cold. The signs were in Italian. They thanked him for using the Aeroporto del Salento, in Brindisi, Italy.

Ah, okay.

Three men walked behind him, close enough that the casual observer wouldn't see Yani's handcuffs. They were headed for a much smaller plane. A shorter flight. To a nearby location, likely somewhere inside Italy.

Yani's Italian was passable. Back on home turf. He breathed out, and relaxed a bit.

Which caused him to inhale enough chloroform from the cloth placed over his nose and mouth to lose consciousness quickly. The men behind him grabbed his arms as he collapsed and hoisted him onto a seat inside the Cessna Skyhawk.

The package will be delivered within the hour, texted Creased Trouser Man as he climbed into the co-pilot's seat for takeoff.

TUESDAY, NOVEMBER 13, 2007, 10:45 A.M.
TIME ZONE 1
TERRIS

THIS TIME, IT WASN'T A FLOOR AGENT from monitoring. It was Sword 23's Operative Coordinator who came into the command center.

"What is it?" asked TC4.

"Sword 23. The chip that was still moving, that we presumed to be him."

"Yes?"

"It's disappeared."

"You mean, stopped moving?"

"No. Landed at the Aeroporto del Salento in Brindisi, Italy. Got on another plane, flew into the southern interior. Got close to the coast, and vanished."

"Chips don't just vanish."

"We've looked at the monitors, at the history. You can do the same."

"No one simply disappears. Meeting in five. Let's decide who we'll send in."

TUESDAY, NOVEMBER 13, 2007, 11:06 A.M.
TAVEL APARTMENT, 7TH ARRONDISSEMENT
PARIS, FRANCE

ARCHARD STUMBLED BLINDLY down the hallway of his apartment. It was full daylight, but he felt like he was walking in utter darkness. He was not a man used to being out of control.

As he approached the den, he heard the DVD of that annoying King Arthur series playing. Damn kid…wait. What?

He went over to the doorway.

The nanny was sitting there, staring at the television, which was blaring Leal's favorite show.

She looked up. "They said they would call before noon," she said. She was shaking.

"Yes."

"What will happen?"

"I'll give them what they want."

"Do you think we can trust them? They were cruel," she said.

"They said if I gave them what they wanted, they'd give Leal back. They'd tell us where to find him." Archard trusted them as much as he'd trust a fox with a chicken, but he needed to calm her.

Archard realized he was holding Leal's drawing pad.

He said, "This is the show? The one he watches?"

"Yes."

"Is this the first episode?"

"No, it's the third."

"Could we start at the beginning?" Archard asked.

Nodding, Morgan le Fey picked up the remote. And Archard sat down, as well.

TUESDAY, NOVEMBER 13, 2007, 11:08 A.M.
TIME ZONE 1
TERRIS

WHEN THE SMALL GREEN LIGHT FLASHED, TC4 knew it was the call she'd been expecting.

"Jaime," she said. "Are you all right?"

"Well, we made it through the night. Both Shepard and I finally got some sleep. In fact, he's still asleep."

"Thanks to your work, we were able to follow the path to the next marker. We hope this one will get us to Wester's location, or at least pretty close. It's more challenging, though. We're still working on it. But thank you. We've got it from here. You're officially done with this mission. Please let me know when you'd like to get to the safe house, with the masseuses and counselors. And when you're ready to go home."

"Yeah, thanks. I'll figure that out shortly. Meanwhile, are you getting closer? The deadline on the website counting down to the Death of the Firstborn, that's still going. Less than six hours remaining."

"We're on it."

"Okay. And, out of curiosity, where did you find the marker? What was that building that was lit up?"

"You'll appreciate this. It was the Museum of Wine."

"Ah. That is what they meant by 'the ancient brotherhood.' So wait—what is more difficult about this one?"

"The wording. It might be some sort of inner knowledge that would be shared only by that group in the Vintner's Cup."

"Oh—wasn't Yani—Sword 23—in the group, also? Can't he help you with it?"

Here it came. The difficult part.

"He is currently unavailable for questions."

"What does that mean?"

Silence.

"Okay. Wrong way to ask, I realize. It's an active mission."

Terris Coordinator 4 was still looking for an opening, a question she *could* answer.

"Sword 23 is still on the mission?"

"Still assigned, yes."

"What are you not telling me?"

She heard the sudden fear in Jaime's voice. This is why it was a bad idea to have loved ones on the same mission.

"Is he all right?"

"We don't know. We have no evidence that he's not."

"Where is he?"

"His last known location was in southern Italy."

"So where is he now?"

"You know I can't tell you that. We have no reason to believe any harm has befallen him."

"May not tell me that, or *can't* tell me that? Do you know where he is?"

"We're on it, Jaime. We've got it covered."

"Tell me. Just say, 'yes' if you know where he is. That's all I'm asking."

"Jaime, don't worry. It's Sword 23. And we've got it handled."

"Please, no," she said, and she hung up.

TUESDAY, NOVEMBER 13, 2007, 11:22 A.M.
LAC-ARGENT, FRANCE

JAIME WAS SITTING on the window seat in her suite's dressing room when she heard Shepard get up.

"Morning," he said, as he padded past her into the bathroom.

"Morning," she answered, seemingly enthralled by the back garden. She didn't turn to look at him.

The toilet flushed, the bathroom door opened, and Mark came out, stretching, to stand behind her.

"How are you?" he asked.

Jaime wasn't one who cried easily. In fact, she could control herself, nearly always. She saved the tears for private times, behind closed doors.

"What? What's wrong?"

"It's Yani. He's missing."

"Missing? What do you mean? How do you know?"

"I don't know much. They can't tell me anything, really. He's still on assignment. They don't know that he's dead. But he's missing."

"Jaime, are you sure? What did they say, exactly?"

"It's hard to explain. But they couldn't tell me they know where he is."

"That can't be unusual, can it? To go off the grid?"

"They always know where we are."

With that one statement, she'd said too much and too little. She saw a million questions dart behind his eyes.

"Oh, my God, Mark, I'm afraid—" Emotion choked her words. "I'm with…men…who do important, brave things. And then, they marry me—and they die."

She couldn't help it. She began to sob. He grabbed her, and held her close, as she cried for another man.

"Marrying you doesn't kill people," he said. "We don't know that Yani is dead!"

"He can't be. I just…couldn't stand it."

Mark sat down beside her. "What do you know? Did they tell you anything about where he is?"

"He's also following Wester, the fellow who's been leaving the markers. They said the last place he was is in Italy. Southern Italy. They also said they'd found the next marker. The building the lights were leading to was the Museum of Wine. But there's something in it they can't decipher, some insider reference."

"So, what do you think?" Mark asked.

"About what?"

"I guess we can't really just go to Southern Italy. That's a rather large area. So, I guess we go back and try to decipher the marker at the Museum of Wine?"

"Mark, we can't. I'm off the mission. We've done our part. No one will take us to Paris. Or take us to Italy."

"We don't need anyone to take us. I've got a car. And a plane."

"No. I can't ask you to do that. Look at the trouble I've caused in your life, already."

"You've caused? I'm sorry. At which point did I tell you I wanted to leave, and you forced me to come along? I believe I've been making my own choices here. And…it would help me to go and try to do something more to help, rather than to sit around here dwelling on the recent past."

"But—"

"My guess is Free Winds—or whomever you've been talking to—already has people headed for Southern Italy. We can certainly head that way. But first, we're only a little more than an hour from Paris. Let's go see what this last marker says while it's still there.

I'll have the plane waiting to take us wherever we want to go." He looked at her. "That's if you want to. If they've told you to sit tight and that's what you want to do, that's okay." He was quiet. "But neither of us is really a sitting around sort of person."

"You've got that right," Jaime responded. They could visit the Museum of Wine. What could it hurt?

"We could each use a shower and a change of clothes. I'll have Mrs. Halpern lay a breakfast, then we're on our way." Mark stood, and helped her to her feet. He turned to head back to his own suite of rooms.

Jaime kept one of his hands in hers.

"Thanks," she said. "Thanks."

TUESDAY, NOVEMBER 13, 2007, 11:38 A.M.
CASTEL DEL MONTE
ANDRIA, ITALY

YANI FELT LIKE "DEATH WARMED OVER" would be a kind description.

Between jet lag, the infernal sedatives they kept giving him, and the bizarre positions in which he'd been zip-tied, he was not crazy about the idea of waking up. He was nauseous. His head throbbed. He was dehydrated. Every muscle group screamed for prominence in the fiery pain department.

At least the room where he was currently held was not brightly lit. Thank God for small blessings.

He opened his eyes to yet another surprise: he was not bound. He was in an ornately carved chair with deep, firm cushions the color of Merlot. There was a medieval hearth, with a lit wood fire. The walls were crafted of large grey stones. At first, they seemed curved and circular. Then, in the dim firelight, he realized they were flat and octagonal. There was a thick woven rug on the floor and tapestries on the walls.

It was as if he'd awakened eight hundred years in the past. All that was missing was the wolfhound sleeping at his feet.

It took a few moments in the flickering firelight for him to see that there was a low wooden table next to him, and a chair matching his on the other side of it. There was a decanter of wine on the table, and two silver chalices.

Seriously.

There was a man sitting in the other chair. He was facing away from the fire, so his features were in shadow.

"Where is she?" he said.

"Wester?" Yani asked. "Yacov?"

"Yes. I'm sure I'm the man you've least wanted to meet again in this lifetime."

Not even close, thought Yani. But not wanting to insult him, he said, "In fact, I've been trying to find you. I even went to China, looking. Then gave myself up to your lieutenants so they'd bring me to you. And here we are."

"Where is she? You're alive because you said you knew where she was. That she had a message for me."

"Analucia," Yani said. "Ah, Yacov, weren't those the days? The three of us were so young and high-spirited."

"And you've stolen her from me?"

"No. Not at all. She and I were never more than friends. Neither of us ever wanted it to be otherwise. We spoke of you often, with kindness."

"I'm told you've married."

For the first time, a cold drop of fear slipped inside Yani's thoughts. How did he know this? Or did he? Was this old information? Or was Wester more current, and more dangerous, than Yani had supposed?

Wester held up a five by seven photo. It was black and white. It was Jaime and himself. From three days earlier. Their wedding at Cadet Chapel. Even Yani hadn't seen this photo.

Damn.

"You're going to tell me where she is," Yacov stated simply. "And then I'm going to kill you."

"I have to say, that isn't a very persuasive argument for me being forthcoming," said Yani, surprised. He'd expected promises in exchange for revealed information, rather than threats. Was there a trick there, somewhere? Or was Wester not making complete sense?

"I'm going to kill you anyway," shrugged Wester conversationally. "And you owe me."

"I do owe you an apology," said the former friend with darker hair. Yani's hair had gotten curlier the longer it had gone without being washed. "I'm afraid last time we met, I wasn't as kind as I might have been. For that, I'm sorry. However, that being said, Analucia—as you well know—has a mind of her own. I'm afraid there's nothing either of us can do to persuade her to do something against her will."

"So you've got her hidden."

"What? Why would you say that?"

"She isn't here with you, that I can see. Yet you've said you have a message from her. Let's have it."

"She is very fond of you. You know that. She chooses to live where she will."

"She is being held *against her will*! Why are you lying to me like this? You have her imprisoned in the Steppe!"

Wester had gone from having a reasonable tone to a fury within one sentence. Yani sat, contemplating, assessing.

"Yacov, she is not imprisoned. She is free to move about as she pleases. She is waiting to hear from me, that you are well, where you are." If nothing else, Yani had to buy time.

Unexpectedly, this had a calming effect.

"You can get a message to her?"

The truth was, he could get a message to those who could get a message to her. Same thing. "Yes."

"Then—" Wester reached over and took the crystal stopper from the wine decanter on the table between them. "Do you remember the wines she loved? The smoothness? Yani, this is for her!" And now, Wester was young, guileless and enthusiastic. As if his rage from only moments before had never happened.

He poured two glasses. He lifted one and gestured that Yani should take the other.

Yani hesitated only a moment. Surely, if they were poured from the same decanter, it should be all right, not drugged or poisoned? Or did Wester plan for them to die side by side?

Wester swirled the wine and smelled it.

Yani bought time by doing the same. The bouquet was earthy and mysterious. Undertones of vanilla and violet, perhaps pears… but there were hidden complexities.

Yacov took a long draught. Yani gambled and did the same.

The character was sonorous, velvety and elegant. Very robust, very smooth. Dark berry side notes, and more…

"It is a grape I made for her," Wester said. "A special blend with the Negroamaro variety.

The wine had reminded Yani of Analucia. And Wester. And their group in the Steppe. And then he knew how, and why. And he was furious.

"Yacov, you tricked me," Yani said. "When we left our home together, you brought out cuttings of the Amal grapevines. You must have! Why? We can't bring unknown species out. The risk isn't worth it! That would be a foolish way to reveal things best kept hidden! Why would you do this? How selfish can you be? This wine is good—too good!"

Wester looked at him with a hard, calculating stare. "No one will find out about the precious grapes that don't grow here in the Terris world. Even if they did, who's going to jump to the conclusion that they must come from a hidden society? No one," he said. He stood. "I almost forgot myself. It is a gift for *her*. You are the only other one who knows the secret. And you will be dead."

Wester stalked to the door. "Guards!" he called out. "Chain him!"

Two guards—dressed in modern garb and carrying assault rifles—came into the room. As they did, Yani looked out into the hall and saw at least three more heavily armed men. This would not be the time to run.

The two strong men grabbed Yani and dragged him back to where metal chains were set deeply into the wall. They shoved him to the ground onto his stomach, pulling his hands behind him, roughly. Then they brought out the heavy plastic zip ties and bound his hands together before slipping the twenty-first century cuffs through the ancient metal chains.

And then they left, pulling the door closed behind them, and locking it from outside.

Yani sat, deeply thirsty, yet with the taste of forbidden wine still on his tongue.

TUESDAY, NOVEMBER 13, 2007, 1:06 P.M.
LE MUSÉE DU VIN
PARIS, FRANCE

THE MUSEUM OF WINE was located on Charles Dickens Square across the Seine and slightly south of the Eiffel Tower.

Mark was out of rock star mode. It amazed Jaime how slight changes served as a competent disguise. He still wore jeans, but had exchanged his pressed white shirt for a dark green t-shirt and his fedora for a grey knit cap that hid most of his hair. He'd also added sunglasses and a slight slouch. No one gave them a second look. Or, if they did, it was of the "did anyone ever say you look like that singer?" variety.

They arrived at the museum, bought tickets for a self guided tour, and went in. It was much like walking back three or four centuries in time, into arched stone walkways and earth-cooled air.

Jaime tried to remain calm. Mark was correct that doing something beat fretting, but what if they couldn't find the marker? Or they found it and couldn't make any more sense of it than the other agents? Or they made sense of it and it led somewhere that had nothing to do with Yani, or stopping whatever international horror was behind the plagues?

The last one had said, *Where the monks find solace.* What did that mean? Didn't monks find solace everywhere here? According to the brochure, a group of monks known as the Tiny Brothers of the Abbey of Passy were granted land on a wooded hill by the Seine in the late 1400s. They soon discovered the remains of Roman quarries and used the excavations as the beginnings of their own wine cellars. They'd cultivated a small vineyard, making wines that were popular with Louis XIII. However, they were closed and their lands confiscated after the unpleasantness at the end of the 1700s. The arched rooms and walkways had been used for a while as wine cellars for the restaurants in the Eiffel Tower, then had been purchased by the *Conseil des Échansons de France* and turned into a museum dedicated to the history of wine making.

Although Wester's marker had alluded to the "ancient brotherhood," the *Conseil* had only been started in the 1950s. "I think he meant the winemaking brotherhood in a much broader sense," said Mark.

"Okay, so which monks? Where are the monks?" asked Jaime.

They moved together through rooms with displays of mannequins enacting highlights of the history of wine. Napoleon was there, as were Louis Pasteur and Balzac, along with unknown vintners and coopers of various eras.

"This is getting frustrating," whispered Jaime.

"What's left to see?" asked Mark.

"Just the restaurant. And the gift shop which will offer a complementary glass of wine."

It wasn't hard to imagine the arched walkways alive with monks in brown homespun. But none were present today, finding solace or otherwise. Jaime was stalking past the vault that served as a restaurant when Mark caught her arm.

"Look," he said, furtively pointing.

The restaurant itself was in a long corridor under rounded stone ceilings. Undoubtedly there were fancier settings at night, but now the flagstones were dotted with square or rectangular brown tables, at which sat folding chairs with bright orange cushions. It looked considerably more casual than Jaime expected.

"At the far end," Mark added.

Jaime's eyes swept the cavern to where he pointed. The room ended in a tableau of a vineyard, in which three Tiny Brothers of the Abbey were trying out the vino.

Three monks.

"Okay," said Jaime.

"Let's sit for a minute and catch our breath," suggested her companion. He walked casually through the eatery. There was one table at the end. They stood beside it, studying the tableau with intention.

The painting in the background was the abbey itself, up on a hill overlooking the river. In the foreground were large casks of wine. One brother was holding a glass up to examine it; the center monk was sitting at a cask which was upended to serve as a table, and the third—the only monk who was hooded—was pouring wine from a large wooden cask.

"It has to be here," whispered Mark. "But where?"

Jaime took out her regular glasses—not being on assignment, she'd turned off her Eden glasses and left them in the car—and squinted. "There," she said, surreptitiously pointing toward the barrel where the hooded monk stood.

"Oh. I see."

Jaime turned on the camera on her phone. "Cover me," she said, and almost smiled. "I'm going in."

And she stepped over the roping and into the exhibit. She looked around quickly to make sure no one was watching them, and then she focused the shot. Someone had carved three lines of symbols into the wood of the barrel. It wasn't deep; in fact, it likely had been done with a pen or other everyday writing instrument. And they were small enough to be unnoticeable. She snapped a photo of it. Three times.

Then she and Mark wandered back toward a table in the middle of the restaurant, where they would hopefully look like a couple of tourists planning their next excursion online.

For years, Jaime had carried a small notebook and pencil with her, and now she transcribed the symbols, leaving room underneath for translation. She took a first quick pass through, writing out the words she knew. Then she pulled up a cheat sheet on her phone, and studiously added other symbols as she went.

"So," said Mark, "just where have you been that you've learned modern-day Sumerian?"

"Would you believe me if I said modern day Sumeria?" She didn't even look up.

"No," he said, and she shook her head, concurrently.

"I see now—it's this one line they couldn't translate. I don't know these symbols, and they aren't in my dictionary."

"What *can* you translate?"

"It's something about a marriage and a grape..." She was stumped. "I don't know. How did I think I could know? If the experts couldn't decipher it... I'm a neophyte at this. What was I thinking? Where is he, Mark? What do we do?"

She sat, deflated. "Let me look one more time."

Jaime glanced about and then walked back up to the display. She stepped over the ropes. As she did, she saw a man in chef's whites emerge from the side door to the kitchen.

She didn't care. She walked straight to the carved barrelhead.

"What am I not seeing?" she said to herself, teeth gritted.

"The caret."

It was a soft female voice behind her.

"What?" Jaime asked, startled.

"Right here," the woman with thick black hair and a camel-colored faux leather jacket said quietly.

"That means it's the beginning of another dialect."

Jaime looked at her, completely confused. Mark was starting to lose his argument with the chef, who was gesticulating now toward the two women inside of the wine display.

"When you change to the Renault dialect, it becomes phonetic. I believe it says that the long-awaited grape hybrid has come to fruition. Then it spells out, 'Vigneti Paradiso Ritrovato. Puglia.'"

The chef started heading their way. The unidentified woman strolled back to the edge of the display, Jaime not far behind.

"*Je suis désolée*," said the woman to the kitchen worker. "We were arguing over whether he was pouring a certain kind of wine."

"You're not allowed in the display!" he said.

"Yes, yes, I'm sorry. We didn't hurt anything," she said with an easy smile. "Come, friends," she said to Mark and Jaime. "Our reservation is later."

The three of them exited the vaulted room, the kitchen worker standing protectively, arms crossed, in front of the display as they left.

"What did it say?" Jaime asked, breathlessly, as they reached the gift shop.

"Vigneti Paradiso Ritrovato, which is apparently a vineyard in Puglia," said the woman. "I believe Puglia is in Italy. Any ideas about the fastest way to get there?"

"Who are you?" Jaime asked, flummoxed.

"I'm a Gardener," she said. "I came to see if I could help."

TUESDAY, NOVEMBER 13, 2007, 2:10 P.M.
CASTEL DEL MONTE
ANDRIA, ITALY

LEAL WAS TERRIFIED.

Men, very large, angry men, were carrying him. Controlling him. Not letting go.

He struggled to catch their words, but the words flew too fast.

"Damn kid runs," he had heard.

"Something wrong. Some kind of idiot," he had heard.

He panicked.

He didn't have control of his body. Or the dots.

Leal had been so thrilled. Castle. They'd come to a castle!

"You are going on your quest. Be brave. Be bold. Save Arthur. I will. I shall. We shall return victorious." He'd said it. They had stared. He'd said it again. Used their words. In order!

Run. Castles. Draw. Draw. Draw.

Why were they so very angry? Why were they hurting him so much?

Where was Morgan? Had she lied? Where was he? Why was there no one who could understand?

Screaming. Screaming.

Thrown. Hurt.

Screaming. Screaming.

Rolling. Rolling.

Dots. Quiet. Dots.

Exhausted, finally, Leal raised his head.
And everything was all right. Everything was worth it.
He had found King Arthur.

TUESDAY, NOVEMBER 13, 2007, 2:32 P.M. FRENCH TIME
UNDISCLOSED LOCATION
TERRIS

"HOW CLOSE ARE YOU?" TC4 asked the special team they'd sent into Italy.

"Landing now."

"It's confirmed. Our last ping from his locator came from Castel del Monte in Andria."

"Okay. We're heading that way."

"Waiting to hear."

"Roger that."

And the Eden Operative ended the call as the airplane rolled to a halt.

TUESDAY, NOVEMBER 13, 2007, 2:40 P.M.
CASTEL DEL MONTE
ANDRIA, ITALY

YANI HAD THOUGHT that—between his extreme thirst, his headache and daunting pain—short of his being shot, his situation couldn't get much worse.

He had been wrong. The little boy who was thrown into the locked room with him had screamed. And screamed. For nearly half an hour.

Yani had used techniques he had been taught at Mountaintop, in Eden, for withstanding torture. He released himself from his physical situation, and went into his secret cave, hidden deep inside the mountain. He heard the stream; he even tasted it. He relaxed.

He didn't know how long after the screaming had stopped that he returned to the locked room with the fireplace.

The young boy was quiet, looking in his direction, expression filled with wonder. The boy wouldn't meet his eyes, but said, "Be brave. Be bold. Save Arthur. I will. I shall. We shall return victorious."

Hmm.

The boy repeated, "Be brave. Be bold. Save Arthur. I will. I shall. We shall return victorious. Arthur. Arthur."

Then, more urgently, "Be brave. Be bold. Save Arthur. I will. I shall. We shall return victorious. Arthur. Arthur."

He was getting agitated. The same words, over and over. He'd added, "Arthur. Arthur."

It reminded Yani of another young boy he'd known, many years ago. He thought perhaps "Arthur" was the name of the person to whom the boy spoke. The boy was waiting for an appropriate response. Now he was panicking. "Be brave. Be bold. Save Arthur. I will. I shall. We shall return victorious. Arthur. Arthur."

This time, Yani spoke quietly. "What does Arthur say?"

The boy didn't hesitate.

"When you have completed your quest, you will be a squire no longer, but a true knight of the Round Table. When you have completed your quest, you will be a squire no longer, but a true knight of the Round Table."

Ah, *King* Arthur. Yani spoke with certainty. "When you have completed your quest, you will be a squire no more, but a true knight of the Round Table."

The boy lit up. "Be brave. Be bold. Save Arthur. I will. I shall. We shall return victorious."

Yani said again, "When you have completed your quest, you will be a squire no longer, but a true knight of the Round Table." Then he added, "What is your name, boy?" in his best Arthurian voice.

"Why, I am Merlin, young Merlin, at your service."

"Young Merlin, you will become a great wizard, and I a great king. But now, we must escape."

"How can I help you?"

"Is there any water?" Yani asked. It probably didn't go with the narrative, but it would certainly help.

The boy ran his hands over his face. Then he walked the perimeter of the room, touching things. Across the room, hidden from Yani's view by the chairs, was something that had an electrical hum.

"Open?" asked the boy.

"Yes. Please open it," said Yani.

"Wine for your chalice," said the boy. "Water for your bag."

"Bring me water, Merlin," said Yani. "For my bag."

There was an opening sound and a thud. The boy scuttled

sideways, with a large bottle of spring water. Yani nearly swooned with relief.

"Merlin, I am held prisoner. My hands are bound. Can you open the bottle for me, and help me to drink?"

"I must free you, my lord," said the boy. And he dropped the bottle. "I must free you, my lord."

"Can you bring me the water, first?"

"Be brave. Be bold. Save Arthur. I will. I shall. We shall return victorious."

"When you have completed your quest, you will be a squire no longer, but a true knight of the Round Table," repeated Yani. "But Merlin, why does Arthur say this? You shall never be a knight. You are more important than that."

"You know and I know," the boy said. "But it must remain secret still." Then, "Save Arthur," said the boy. He was carrying a bag. He reached inside, and took out a pair of scissors. He offered them to Yani. "I cannot cut," the boy said.

Yani tried to move his hands behind him. "I cannot cut, either, Merlin," he said. "We must be clever. Can you walk behind me? Can you cut off the cuffs?"

"Is this our quest?" asked the boy.

"Yes," said Yani. "You can cut the ropes off."

The boy didn't have very advanced motor skills. Every third or fourth try, he could open the scissors correctly over the strong plastic bands, but he couldn't close them together more than once.

"Be brave," said Yani. "Be bold. Cut hard."

"Be brave. Be bold. Cut hard." He noticed the boy was speaking in an English accent. The boy snapped at the cord, and then snapped again.

"Yes, Merlin, you're getting it!"

He tried a final time, pushing the scissors hard under the taut plastic. They scraped Yani's wrist, but he made no noise. "Cut hard, young wizard," said Yani.

The boy chomped down on the scissors with all his might, and then did it again. And the plastic broke!

"Arthur, you are saved," said the boy.

Not quite. But Yani with his one hand free could reach around with the scissors and cut the other one off. That freed him from the metal cuff on the wall as well. He sighed deeply and scooted across the floor to the water bottle Merlin had brought him.

"Thank you, powerful wizard," he said. He took the cap off and drank deeply. He closed his eyes and felt his strength eking back.

Then he opened his eyes. He remembered the vocal marker the boy had given him to repeat a name as a way to command attention. "Merlin. Merlin," he said. The boy looked his way. "Do you know where we are?"

"We are in the castle of the evil sorcerer!" he said.

"The castle of the evil sorcerer," replied Yani. He sighed, remembering the well-armed guards in the hallway. He'd gotten a drink of water, and that was good. Wonderful, in fact. But he was no less stuck, and now, he had a boy to look after. "You don't happen to know how to get out of this place, do you?" he asked. "Is there a secret door?"

"Shall I show you?" the boy said. "Shall I show you the castle?"

"Yes, O Merlin," said Yani. "Do you have a crystal ball?"

"Yes," he said. "Yes, I do."

And he walked across the room to pick up his bag.

TUESDAY, NOVEMBER 13, 2007, 2:40 P.M.
AIRBORNE BETWEEN FRANCE AND ITALY

MARK SHEPARD LOOKED AT HIS PHONE and sighed.

How many texts could he get in one day from outraged bandmates, publicists, and label execs? The album dropped in five days now. He'd done the interviews for the majors, *Rolling Stone* and *People* and *Spin*, months ago. He could catch up on the dailies and radio/television tomorrow or the next day. Chill, folks.

When they produced an album, there was satisfaction and creativity in the composing, the putting the pieces together, the producing of the tracks. But the best part—for Mark, anyway—was knowing that the new music was about to be unleashed on a waiting world. That people would be singing, and playing, and even studying lyrics, for years to come.

This was the time he would usually be involved in all of this. Talking to reporters who had already heard the tunes. Pressing flesh, doing television, meeting fans.

Instead, he was on his jet with the woman he loved, going to save her husband, after having killed an assassin.

There had to be a song in there, somewhere.

He sat by himself, as Jaime sat across from him, chatting with this mystery woman they'd picked up at the Museum of Wine. It was clear the two of them were talking, but not really talking. That this woman was part of whatever organization Jaime worked for. Part of him wanted to say, "Look, just go in the back of the plane and have your secret conversation." But he didn't.

Why was he here?
He could have just put the plane and the pilot at their disposal.
But he needed closure. Somehow. Closure.
He turned off his cellphone and closed his eyes.

TUESDAY, NOVEMBER 13, 2007, 2:58 P.M.
CASTEL DEL MONTE
ANDRIA, ITALY

YOUNG MERLIN RUMMAGED in his bag. He didn't pull out a crystal ball, but a drawing pad.

"What is it?" Yani asked. Did he have a picture of a wizard and a crystal ball? Or a magic wand?

Merlin opened the pad and shuffled through the papers. He then handed Yani the drawing pad, open at the page with this drawing:

Yani looked at it, confused. Then it occurred to him that the room he was in was the same shape as the octagons on the floorplan.

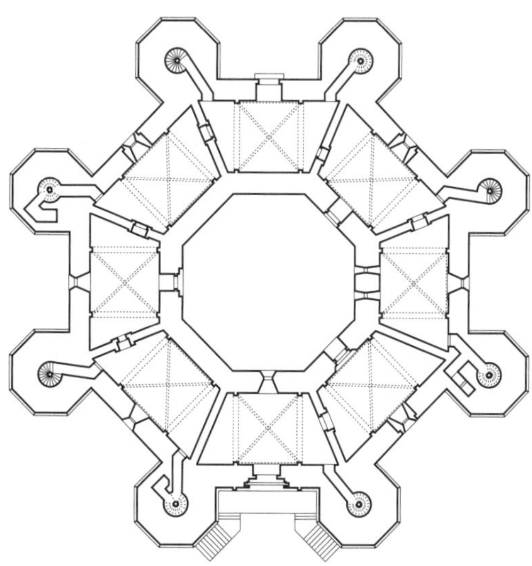

"Where did you get this, Merlin?"

No answer.

"Merlin? Merlin, did you draw this? Is this where we are?"

The boy was looking at the ground. He nodded.

"You have magical powers indeed."

That was all it took. He pointed at the drawing, and spoke, this time in French: "Main floor. Main floor. One above. Didn't go there. Three underneath. Big room. *Big* room. People, lots and lots. People." He indicated himself and Yani. "Underneath. All the way down. Under the ground."

Merlin was trying so very hard, and he was succeeding—speaking in words in what now sounded like his native language. Words that didn't seem Arthurian.

"Then, what are these? Here in the towers?" Yani asked, also in French.

"Right there, a staircase. Up and down. Up and down."

"It looks like this is only one turret over," Yani said.

"Yes, yes. Yes. One over. Another secret. A panel. Fireplace. I saw it when I saw you. Upstairs, also."

A panel? Yani leapt to his feet and went over. He felt around the panels. He knocked on each—until one sounded hollow.

"Push the panel. Mordred, where have you been hiding?" The boy had returned to quoted dialogue in English.

"Should we go through here, Merlin? To escape?"

"Yes, save Arthur. Save Arthur. Be bold. Be brave."

Yani continued pushing on the panel, until he found the spring lock. When it opened, he found that it led a step down to a tunnel that was four feet tall.

He looked inside the dark tunnel. He looked at the boy beside him.

"Be bold. Be brave," he said. And he stepped through the door.

TUESDAY, NOVEMBER 13, 2007, 3:10 P.M.
CASTEL DEL MONTE
ANDRIA, ITALY

SAVINO LATORRE WALKED into the underground command station he and Bradley had spent ten years designing. It seemed to Bradley that Savi was looking at things and people without actually seeing them.

"Change of plans," Savi said. "Our plagues have done their job. You can cancel some of the Deaths of the Firstborn, already. They're caving left and right. Shanlei is very impressed."

"Whom do I cancel?"

"Well, Prince William. He was mostly for show, anyway. And maybe that little French kid who's running around here. But he's not for certain. Shanlei needs all the papers, signed, before the hit men are cancelled for good. Also with the politicians. They've said yes, but nothing signed yet, nothing signed."

Bradley breathed a sigh of relief. When it came right down to it, he simply didn't want any more death on his hands.

And yet, the orders he was giving were temporary stays of execution. Not final cancels.

Not to mention, something was wrong with Savino Latorre.

All the way around, Bradley had a bad feeling. Who was this Shanlei, anyway? And what in the world was he going to all this trouble to set up?

Did Shanlei care that sometimes it seemed like Savino was losing it? Did he even know? Or was that, also, part of the plan? Was Savino going to survive this?

Was Bradley going to survive this?

Yes, Bradley had a bad feeling indeed. Something was very, very wrong.

TUESDAY, NOVEMBER 13, 2007, 3:14 P.M.
CASTEL DEL MONTE
ANDRIA, ITALY

YANI CRAWLED THROUGH the darkened tunnel, Merlin behind him. He was relieved to reach the next octagonal tower, and to find that the matching panel in that room had swung open easily.

"Up and up," said Merlin. And sure enough, there was no fireplace in this tower. Instead, there was a rounded wall in the middle of it. Merlin led him around to the other side, where there was an entrance to a circular staircase.

The staircase was of brown-rose colored stone, and it ascended quickly. Yani was dizzy before they reached the floor just above. He would have liked to have stopped to see what was on this floor—if it was indeed the "big room" Merlin had described, but he knew if he got separated from Merlin and the boy was found, they'd both be in trouble.

Instead, they wound their way up, to the next floor. "Out this way," said Merlin. "Be brave. Be brave."

"We will be victorious," agreed Yani.

They came out of the stairwell into an empty octagonal tower. Merlin was not stopping. He darted, quickly, into the hall. The hallway ran along the interiors of the rooms inside the eight towers. Each one formed a trapezoid: smaller toward the inside, and longer toward the outside.

"Fly, fly! Castle!" said Merlin.

Yani looked through a window into the central courtyard of the castle where they were being held. The courtyard was open at the top, nothing but Italian sky. At least, Yani assumed it was Italian, from the last place they'd landed.

Young Merlin stood then, as if he didn't know where to go.

The hallway wasn't the best stopping place, so Yani guided them both through a door way topped by a pointed Gothic arch.

Merlin, who hadn't been thrilled about being guided, even by Arthur, wrenched his shoulder free. But then he stopped, stood stock still and squealed with delight. "The Grail! The Grail!" he clapped. And he began to spin.

The room they were in was gorgeous. Marble covered the walls halfway up. There was a marble desk with an old globe and an opened ancient manuscript. Four marble steps led up to a Gothic church window.

"The quest! The quest! The quest! The quest!" the boy was chanting while he spun.

"Merlin!" said Yani. "You must be quiet!"

But the boy didn't hear him.

It seemed that someone nearby had heard Merlin, however. Heavy footfalls sounded in the hallway outside.

Now what? Yani shut and barred the door. It didn't buy them much time, but it would buy some.

Had the guards discovered they were missing? Or were they just making rounds?

Yani turned and surveyed the room. His gaze landed on the altar cloth. It was perhaps two feet wide and eight feet long, stretching from the floor, over the altar and back to the floor.

"Merlin. Merlin!" he said. "The scissors!"

The boy thrust the bag toward him. Yani fished out the scissors and quickly made a six-inch incision in the center of one end of the cloth. Then he grabbed both sides and pulled. It tore open like the Red Sea. He soon had two lengths, totaling sixteen feet. He grabbed two ends and did two powerful knots. Then he ran up the four steps and tied one end to the center marble column of the window. A glance outside told him they were too far up to jump. But they could possibly rappel.

He ran and grabbed Merlin, who, shocked, began to kick and scream.

Whether the guards had been searching for them or not, the ruckus inside the room was enough to capture their attention. Purposeful shouts rang through the corridor, then banging on the door. Someone called for a key.

Yani paused. How could he possibly get safely out the window and to the ground with the boy fighting him, tooth and nail? "Merlin!" he said. "Merlin! We have to fly! But you have to hold on!"

Yani climbed out through the window, balancing on the small ledge, the rope in both hands. Dear God. Merlin looked up at him then.

"You must hold on. Hold on to my neck. And put your legs around my waist. We have to escape. Be brave. Be bold. Hang on!"

And to his amazement, the boy jumped from the window onto him, his arms around Yani's neck, his feet around his waist.

And down they went.

There was a smaller window just below them, but they rappelled past. Yani heard a commotion above, and dropped the last ten feet to the ground. Merlin landed with him.

As it turned out, the castle was set in a bare circle on a hilltop. There were trees and some scraggly bushes among tall dried grasses about twenty feet out from the castle. They wouldn't provide much cover, but it was their only option.

Yani grabbed Merlin and said, "Be bold, be brave."

He ran.

They reached the nearest tree, which was too thin to hide behind. Instead, Yani grabbed Merlin, dragged him behind a large bush, and pulled him down.

As he did, he heard the guards, having breached the room, gathering at the open window. They were shouting.

"Quiet!" he said to Merlin.

But the boy wrestled to be free. What should Yani do? He understood that Merlin didn't seem to like being touched. If he let him go, would he settle down? If he didn't let him go, certainly the motion would catch the attention of the guards.

Yani let go of the boy, who got to his knees and started to make a break for it.

No! Yani had to catch him before he broke free of the tall grasses.

As he thought this, he heard gunfire. The men were heavily armed, of course. And they'd seen movement.

Shit.

Merlin used his new freedom to stand and begin running through the tall grass.

Yani made one calculated leap, and landed on top of the boy.

Merlin fell to the earth beneath him.

And a bullet tore into Yani.

TUESDAY, NOVEMBER 13, 2007, 3:30 P.M.
TIME ZONE 1

SHANLEI WAS VERY PLEASED with the way things had gone.

Very, very pleased.

Now, it was time to add the final piece in the quilt, giving the framework needed to amass the resources that would bring ultimate power. The last square, the press conference during which the governor of Colorado in the United States would announce the change in policy which would clear the way for Shanlei's holding company to successfully acquire rights to natural resources, was about to begin.

The governor came out to face the cameras, smiling. She made a few comments and answered some puff questions from the reporters. She looked at her teleprompters. Everyone was ready to take notes.

Then, she looked away. Her eyes focused in the distance. She stood up straighter. She smiled, and looked directly at the reporters.

"Ladies and gentlemen of the press," she said. "I stand here today to assert my previous stand about keeping control of our great natural resources in our own country, our own state."

What? Shanlei jumped up, enraged. *What? Who did she think she was?*

Livid, Shanlei reached for the phone and dialed, hands shaking with anger. "The hit is on! The governor doesn't know with whom she is dealing! The hit is *on*!"

TUESDAY, NOVEMBER 13, 2007, 3:40 P.M.
CASTEL DEL MONTE
ANDRIA, ITALY

THE FORCE OF THE BULLET flung Yani aside. He tried to hold onto Merlin, but the boy gave an anguished cry, twisted to break free, leapt up, and started to run.

Yani raised his head to watch. The boy didn't run past the trees and away, nor did he head back for the castle. He ran in the direction of the castle, but his trajectory would take him past it. Yani guessed he didn't have a plan. Merlin was just running.

Don't shoot, don't shoot, don't shoot, Yani incanted as both a prayer and a silent directive.

The guards on the second floor of the castle saw the boy immediately. The captain yelled, "Hold your fire!" in Italian. Then the men in the window shouted to point out the boy to the group of guards who were pulling around the side of the building in a small truck.

The truck stopped only a few yards from Yani, the corrugated metal back was opened from within and a dozen armed men hit the ground. They headed after Merlin on foot.

A second vehicle, this one a sedan, screeched around in the opposite direction.

They had the boy hemmed in.

It took five guards to block his way, before one of them was finally able to capture the boy and pinion his arms behind him.

As this happened, Yani took a moment of self-assessment. The bullet had torn into his left shoulder. He raised himself on his opposite arm, and felt the front of his shirt. It was blood-soaked and torn. The bullet had passed through. Thank God for small blessings.

Now what? The boy was screaming like a banshee.

A man who'd gotten out of the sedan was obviously in charge. He indicated that they should bind the boy and throw him into the back of the truck, which was more easily said than done.

Yani had to make a decision, and he had to make it quickly.

It was clear they had not yet discovered that he was missing, also. There really was no point in staying here. The grounds were so bare past the trees that he could easily be spotted heading away. And where would he head to? Nothing else was in sight. He couldn't travel far in this condition.

His only real option was to go with the boy.

He looked at the tree that was five feet beyond him. The small delivery truck had come to a stop underneath it. He could have easily climbed the tree and found a perch on top of the truck, if he had been unharmed. But could he do it now?

There was no choice. He'd have to climb with one arm.

He'd have to ignore the pain.

The armed men were all still struggling with the screaming boy and shouting frantic instructions to each other. It wasn't hard to reach the tree unobserved and make the hop to the lowest branch. There were three more he had to maneuver, his left arm useless at his side. He decided to climb one branch farther and drop down. It was a calculated risk.

If anyone remained inside the truck, they'd hear him and the game would be up.

He took a deep breath and dropped as lightly as he could. The landing jarred him enough that the pain in his shoulder exploded. He gritted his teeth and sank to his knees, took a breath, and made himself lie prone.

He slithered to the square front of the cargo hold. He reached out his right arm and took a good grasp of the front lip. Then, knowing the position in which he'd ride, he pulled his arm back to his side.

They were coming back now, carrying the boy, who was crying, and still struggling to break free.

One of the guards, tired of the situation, hit him, hard, with the back of his hand.

It didn't stop him. It made him struggle more.

Another guard hit him.

As they threw Merlin into the back of the truck, Yani heard a cry. Two men climbed in the back with him; two more got into the truck's cab in front.

The roof vibrated as the motor was started. As they started to move forward, Yani stretched his good arm forward and dug his fingers into the front lip of the hold. He moaned as he moved his left arm sideways, trying to move it forward. He was able to move his elbow. He pulled himself slightly sideways so that both hands could hold on. He could feel something tear as he did it. Damn. But he grabbed the lip.

He said a fervent prayer that they wouldn't go speeding down a highway. There was no way he could hold on.

TUESDAY, NOVEMBER 13, 2007, 4:11 P.M.
AVIOSUPERFICIE CERASO
BARI, ITALY

THEY LANDED at a small private airport, as close as possible to the address they'd gotten at the Museum of Wine.

Jaime was feeling uneasy about coming to Italy without alerting her Operative Coordinator. When they'd touched down and were walking to the car their pilot had ordered to meet them, Jaime pulled the other Gardener to the side.

"Does your OC know you're following this trail?" she asked.

The woman shook her head. "I'm not an active agent," she said. "I don't have an OC."

"I've got to call in," said Jaime. "Should I mention you?"

"I'd prefer you didn't, at least for the time being."

Jaime's OC picked up on the second ring. "You're in Italy," the OC said.

"Yeah," Jaime admitted. "I seem to have this problem with sitting still. What's going on? Have you heard from him? Do we have people here?"

"Give me a minute," the OC said, and Jaime was put on hold.

She'd never done anything like this: taken off on her own. Would her TC kill her? Would Yani kill her? Would she get demoted? Or de-agented?

Shoot.

Really, she didn't care. She just wanted to help save her fellow agent.

Her freaking husband.

"You still there?" It was her OC.

"Yes."

"Okay. There's bad news and good news. The bad news is that we sent a team to Sword 23's last known location, a place called Castel del Monte, in Andria. The roads were closed, and local police were stopping all vehicles heading that way. Our people were intercepted and detained. They were able to call out. They feel like the local authorities were just under orders to keep outsiders from the Castel; they aren't detaining them for any specific reason. They feel that if they co-operate, they'll be let go very soon. Still, they haven't been able to make it to their location."

"And the good news?"

"Sword 23 is moving again. We can follow him."

Relief flooded her. "Where? Where is he?"

"At a location in Minervino Merge."

"Minervino Merge? That's where we're headed. To a vineyard there."

"The one referenced in the final marker?"

"Yes."

"There's a good chance that's where he is. Is anyone with you?"

Jaime wasn't sure if her OC was referencing Mark or the Gardener, but in any case, she said, "Yes."

"What we want you to do is get there, lay low, avoid detection, and get the lay of the land. Our team should be able to free themselves from the locals in Andria pretty quickly. Your entire mission is to be able to point them toward Sword 23. You hear that? You find, you point. *They* go in."

"It sounds like a plan."

"Okay. Be careful. These people aren't kidding around. They're dangerous. Keep in contact and stay out of sight. Let us know what you find. Don't take on impossible odds. Wait for the cavalry to get there."

"Yes, ma'am."

Mark and the Gardener were looking at her expectantly.
"Okay," she said, somewhat relieved. "We're official. Let's visit the Vigneti Paradiso Ritrovato."

TUESDAY, NOVEMBER 13, 2007, 4:14 P.M.
VIGNETI PARADISO RITROVATO
MINERVINO MERGE, ITALY

THE TRIP TOOK about fifteen minutes along back roads.

Yani couldn't see much from his position. Finally they turned up a flat road that wound through a magnificent vineyard. Vines planted in graceful half-circles were curtsied down toward a river. It was a beautiful property.

All the vineyards in the Steppe had vines in curved waves, as well. Oh, Yacov, what were you doing?

When the truck finally came to a stop, it was in front of wide steps leading down to a building front built into the rise of a hill. Signs in Italian welcomed guests to the wine cellar.

A portly man came around the corner from a wide drive. He stood expectantly as the truck rolled to a stop and the engine was killed.

The driver and guard disembarked from the front. The door to the back of the truck rolled up.

"Get up, kid, move," said one of them.

"What's wrong with him?" asked the driver.

"Nothing! He was fine a moment ago. He was rolling all over the place."

The boy apparently was lying inert, as the men from the back joined those from the cab to check-in with the newcomer. The moment Yani heard the voice, he knew the new arrival was Wester, himself.

So this was the man's grand estate.

There was clanking from the truck, as something clashed against metal. The boy had apparently waited until their attention was diverted. Then he scrambled to his feet, jumped, and made a run for it.

Shouts from the men.

"Oh, for God's sake," said Savino. "Just shoot him. We're getting what we need from his father. Once papers are signed, it doesn't matter whether the boy makes it home or not."

Two of the guards went into firing stance.

"Wait!" roared Yani. He struggled to his feet. It was not graceful. But then he stood on the top of the truck, staring at the open-mouthed guards.

"Yacov," he said, in Italian. "Let the boy go. You know he can't hurt you, can't tell anyone anything. It's me you want. Let's talk now."

"Get down right now!" roared Wester.

"The boy?" asked the guard, as Merlin ran down the path, as fast as his legs could take him.

"Forget about the boy. Get Sword 23 down. *Right now.*"

Yani considered his best option. He walked to the front of the truck, sat down, and jumped down onto the cab. Crap, that hurt.

From there, two of the guards grabbed him and pulled him roughly to the ground, shoving him to his knees. He screamed through gritted teeth.

The larger of the two guards put the muzzle of his gun to Yani's head, at which point Wester said, "Don't kill him. Yet."

Instead, they grabbed Yani and pulled him to his feet. The pain nearly made him weep. He glanced down and saw the front of his shirt was soaked with blood; more all the time. One guard held Yani on each side. His left shoulder burned as if seared with a branding iron. It made the pain in his hip seem inconsequential.

"What do we do with this one?" the leader, who'd been driving, asked Wester, concerning Yani. "He's like a greased pig. He always gets away." He was more formally dressed than the others, in a dark suit and white shirt. "If it was my job to keep him from running . . ."

"Yes, yes, what?" replied Wester.

"I'd break his legs."

Yani couldn't help but notice the man had picked up a shiny black tire iron. Oh, hell.

"You do realize I've been shot," he said. "And I'm losing blood?"

The man in the dark suit sliced the air with the iron.

"I'm tired of you running," said Wester. "In fact, I'm just tired of you." He turned back to the well-dressed guard. "Fine. Break one leg. Then bring him down into the conference room."

Yani tried to catch the eye of the man with the tire iron, just in case he still had a shred of humanity. What he saw, instead, was an intense pleasure and a relishing of what he was about to do.

Yani looked away.

There was one loud crash, and he felt his tibia snap.

He moaned and sagged from the pain. The men dragged him over to the stairs.

"Welcome to Vigneti Paradiso Ritrovato," said Yacov Wester. "I've waited a long time for this."

TUESDAY, NOVEMBER 13, 2007, 4:52 P.M.
VIGNETI PARADISO RITROVATO
MINERVINO MERGE, ITALY

THEY ARRIVED at the Vigneti Paradiso Ritrovato to find large notices up about the forthcoming Grand Opening, but today the signs said "closed."

Jaime, Mark, and the Gardener had the car drive them up to the parking lot, and then they asked the driver to leave. They would call for pick-up.

From there, they took off on foot, following a sign with an arrow pointing to the estate.

The vineyards through which the path ran were mature and graceful. The surprising thing was that these rows of vines weren't in straight lines, but curved, making long graceful half circles.

Jaime expected to be turned back by guards, or at least estate workers, but so far they hadn't run into anyone.

All that changed when they came to the edge of the vineyards, and stood overlooking a palatial home and arrows pointing toward the cellars.

Here there was a long driveway, bordered by trees, that ended in a circle around a large fountain in front of the dozen marble steps up to the entrance to the estate.

"What do you think?" Jaime asked. "The house or the cellars?"

"I have a feeling 'business' of this type isn't done at home," said the Gardener. "Let's head for the cellars."

There were half a dozen luxury cars in front of the house. Men were coming and going, calling out to each other in Italian.

They stayed low and amongst the vines, duckwalking to stay out of sight, until they reached the back of the house. Then they headed back toward the entry to the cellars.

Wide stone steps led down to a main entrance, designed for large groups of wine enthusiasts. On one side, farther along, was a metal door that rolled up and down for deliveries. On the side closer to them down the berm, was a single wooden door. They conferred without speaking, and decided to head for the single door.

It opened into a short hallway, which then split into three directions. They could hear men arguing in Italian down the hallway to the left, but they were out of sight.

That left two choices.

Just then, a boy, probably ten or eleven, came hurtling down the central hallway. He collapsed against a wall. He looked up quickly at Jaime, and then away again.

"Morgan?" he asked, staring at the floor.

"I'm Jaime," she said.

He slumped, defeated. "Be bold. Save Arthur. I will. I shall. We shall return victorious," he said, but he was slurring his words. "Save Arthur. Save Arthur."

"Does someone need help?" asked Jaime.

"Save Arthur," said the boy.

"So I guess we go this way," said Mark. And they pressed forward, down the corridor from which the boy had come.

TUESDAY, NOVEMBER 13, 2007, 4:52 P.M.
VIGNETI PARADISO RITROVATO
MINERVINO MERGE, ITALY

"I CAN HELP YOU; you know I can. Let me have a phone, and I will get Analucia here today."

"A phone? How stupid do you think I am?" Yacov had asked. "Oh, for God's sake. He doesn't get it!"

"There must be some way I can help," Yani said again. He was playing for time. Even if he was killed now, his chip would bring Eden Operatives to this place. It would be helpful if Yacov was here when they arrived. So, he'd try to buy time.

Wester nodded to the tire-iron man. This was not good news for Yani.

"The other one?" asked the man, in Italian.

Wester gave a dismissive, "whatever" sign with his hands.

"Yacov, it's me. What are you doing? Why are you doing this? I've said I'll help you. You don't need to use force. Simply tell me what you want."

Even though the bullet hadn't severed any major arteries, Yani would indeed bleed out, eventually, if the flow wasn't staunched. The man with the tire iron was heading his way, again with the gleam in his eye.

"Dear God," Yani muttered under his breath as the second of nausea engulfed him..

He heard the sharp crack of his bone. Crap. Crap. He gave a low scream and then gasped for breath. He would pass out from blood loss long before he died, but being trussed up in this upright position meant any chance of checking out would be a while in coming.

If only he could get word to his OC about Wester, that there was some sort of serious mental condition at play.

Wester seemed to be enjoying the fact that Yani was being killed by inches—well, okay, by yards, now. “Good, good,” he said to tire-iron man. “I’ve got it from here. Go find the kid.”

The man gave Yani a parting glance of disappointment. Apparently, he had more ideas for tire iron use that weren’t approved by AAA.

Once they were alone, Wester started talking, nonstop. “Yes, the curves, and the circles, as we discussed. Perfect. The perfect idea. The perfect layout. You should be proud. So proud. And look at the grapes. Perfect. The perfect grape. The color of the sky before a storm, the color of your eyes, my love.”

Waves of pain from the breaking of his second leg continued to course through Yani. It brought bile to his mouth. Although he was currently being killed slowly, there was a gun on the table, which meant by inches could turn to immediately, on Wester’s whim.

“I can bring her,” said Yani.

“Yes, I know. The years we wasted. The time you were kept from me,” Wester was saying now, to—whom? No one was there.

And then—then Wester approached the long wooden table. The one that held the gun. He picked it up, pointed it at Yani’s heart, and smiled.

TUESDAY, NOVEMBER 13, 2007, 4:58 P.M.
VIGNETI PARADISO RITROVATO
MINERVINO MERGE, ITALY

JAIME, MARK, AND THE GARDENER headed down their hall, which ended in another hall, and a black door with a rounded top.

They heard talking coming from inside.

Should they go in? Jaime's Operative Coordinator had told her to stay out of sight and simply locate Sword 23. Was he here? Were they close?

They had no idea how many people were inside the room, and how heavily armed. The three of them, on the other hand, had nothing. It did seem stupid to burst in.

Then she heard a commanding voice from within say, "I've got it from here. Go find the kid."

Someone was coming toward the door. There was no time for the three of them to disperse or hide.

Jaime kicked into Operative mode. All they had was the element of surprise, and that would last approximately two seconds. "Try to trip him from behind," she hissed to Mark, pulling her two companions to the other side of the door.

The man stomped out. Jaime was surprised to find that, if he had a gun, it was still holstered. Instead, he was swinging a tire iron. He closed the door behind him turned the other direction to head down the hall. They took advantage of that instant of surprise to go for it. Both Mark and the other Gardener went for his legs, and Jaime pushed him, hard, from behind.

He went down, the tire iron flying down the hall.

It was only a momentary victory, however. The guy was huge, and he was strong. It was all Mark could do to keep hold of one of his arms, as Jaime pulled out her Eden "drop cloth" and fought into position to place it over his nose and mouth.

The effect was immediate. His muscles went slack and he collapsed onto the floor.

"Whoa," said Mark.

"He'll be okay," Jaime whispered. "For better or worse. But not for a while!"

And then she heard another voice say, "I can bring her."

It was Yani.

Jaime threw open the door.

There was a portly man holding a Beretta. He was talking, in English.

Jaime didn't hear what he was saying.

The man at whom he was pointing the gun was Yani. And he was not in good shape.

There was a hook on the wall. Yani's hands were cuffed, and the center of the cuffs was strung over the hook.

The front of Yani's shirt was covered with blood. And he was sagging from handcuffs on the wall, unable to stand, and little wonder. The lower bones in both legs were askew. Broken.

Oh, God!

She launched herself forward, toward the man with the gun. He heard her and spun around, now aiming the barrel toward her. He pulled the trigger. It missed her by inches.

"How annoying. Who is this? Who is this?" asked Wester. "You need to leave. Leave, my dear, I must kill this one, and then we will get on with the grand opening. The time has finally come! The wine! The grapes! The Analucia! How happy are you? Are we? What joy!"

"Yacov." The Gardener who'd come in with them stepped forward and put her hand on Wester's shoulder.

"It is everything I hoped. Everything I planned. Stunning. He will be dead, and we will go on."

"Yacov, it's me."

Yacov Wester looked at the woman standing beside him. "What? You need to stand to the side. Everyone will get a taste, very shortly. Very shortly. Once this one is dead, we will all drink. We will all raise a glass."

Then Yani looked at her. A look of surprise crossed his face. "You're here?" he asked. "Analucia?"

The Gardener smiled at him, then turned back to Wester. "Yacov, it's me. Analucia. I've come. What is it you have to show me?" she asked.

"Analucia? Yes. She's here. Isn't she lovely? Everything I said she would be. And I'm so sorry, my love, so sorry. The lost years. But now we're together."

"You don't need to be sorry," said Analucia. "I've had other work, important work. I couldn't come to see you. But now I'm here. Put the gun away, please."

But Wester didn't look at her, didn't even seem to hear her.

"Sorry, let me get on with this, then we'll see you all, talk to you all. Even give you a taste, if the lady says we may."

It dawned on Jaime that the Analucia he was talking to was not the real Analucia, who was standing right next to him. The person he was talking to was not, in fact, there at all. He was clearly delusional. Now what?

Wester raised the gun, aiming straight at Yani's head.

"Good-bye," he said. "Good-bye to my former friend, now my enemy."

And he squeezed the trigger.

TUESDAY, NOVEMBER 13, 2007, 5:04 P.M.
VIGNETI PARADISO RITROVATO
MINERVINO MERGE, ITALY

"WHY DON'T YOU ANSWER your fucking phone?" Bradley yelled as he stormed toward the room to which the guards had pointed him. "Shanlei wants me to—"

There was a guard lying crumpled outside the door. What the—?

The sound of the gunshot reverberated off the walls, ceiling, and floors. It was loud and shattering and stopped him in his tracks.

Bradley took a risk and threw open the door. It had been Savino who'd fired the gun, just as he was tackled from behind by a tall, faintly familiar, male stranger who forced his arm to go high, the bullet shattering the stucco on the ceiling.

What was going on?

Bradley recognized the man hung up on the wall—it was the fellow who had escaped from the castle earlier. But now there was this other man and two women, one with black hair, who had been talking to Savino, practically hanging off of him, until the shot.

Well, the dark-haired woman had knocked Savino to the floor, and she had the gun now. What was going on?

Bradley didn't wait to see if Savino would emerge with the upper hand. He turned and ran from the room.

As he did, it clicked into place: where he'd seen the other woman and the tall man before. They'd been Alejandra's targets. One of them, instead, had killed Alejandra.

"Guards!" he yelled, running from the room. "Guards!"

TUESDAY, NOVEMBER 13, 2007, 5:08 P.M.
VIGNETI PARADISO RITROVATO
MINERVINO MERGE, ITALY

BRADLEY CAME TO A SQUARE CORNER and made a hard right turn, running fully into the person who had been heading in his direction. Momentarily shaken, he stepped back.

It was Xiaofan, the woman who cared for Savino. Maybe she could get through to him.

"Thank God you're here!" Bradley said. "Savino needs you—he's talking crazy. But there are three outsiders in the room with him. We need guards!"

"What?" she said. "Something's wrong with Savino?"

"I don't know…he was shooting someone, but they got the gun away from him, and there's been more gunfire. Did you pass any guards?"

"Yes," she said. "But what are you doing here? What's going on?"

"The authorities have Castel del Monte closed, but that's okay. They don't know to look for the hidden basement. The control room has better locks than they could figure out, in any case! But things are crazy. Do you talk to Shanlei? Have you talked to him lately? First, I was told to cancel all the hits on the Firstborn. Fine with me. I'm tired of this. Tired of death! But now this Shanlei wants me to re-engage hit man three. But we'd pulled the plug. Is that what Savino wants? I take my orders from Savino Latorre."

As if to make his point, he turned his phone around. On it, a contact reading H3 was displayed.

"Shanlei told you to call this person?"

"Yes."

Bradley stopped. Everything had gone crazy. The mysterious Shanlei was giving orders, Savino was in a shoot-out, the Castel was closed, Alejandra was dead. It was…chaos.

"I think…I think you do what Shanlei says," said the woman.

"Ah, but of course. You work for Shanlei, Xiaofan," said Bradley, realizing his error.

"No, I don't," she said simply.

"What?" He was shocked to see that she'd pulled out a handgun—a Kahr PM9. She took aim and pumped two rounds into the center of his chest.

As he collapsed onto the ground, she picked up his phone, with H3 still displayed.

She hit "dial."

"Yeah," was all the voice said.

"You're live."

Shanlei tucked the phone into the wide scarf at her waist, and headed out for the waiting car. Her work here was done.

Finally. Her work here was done.

TUESDAY, NOVEMBER 13, 2007, 5:36 P.M.
VIGNETI PARADISO RITROVATO
MINERVINO MERGE, ITALY

"ARE YOU ALL RIGHT?" Jaime ran over to Yani, where he hung from the hook on the wall.

They locked eyes, and the absurdity of the question hit them both. Jaime laughed. Yani managed a smile.

"Analucia, can you keep Savino here in the room?" Jaime asked. The woman had already noticed a pair of zip-tie cuffs on the table and had managed to get Savino's hands behind his back. He lay on the floor, seemingly, now, completely out of it.

"Mark, help over here?"

But Mark was already at Yani's side. "We're going to need to lift him up just enough to get the cuffs off the hook," Jaime said. Then she looked at Yani, really looked at his condition, not knowing how to go about it.

"There's no good way," Yani breathed. "Just lift me up and let me lie down on the floor."

Jaime and Mark counted to three, lifted him, and did their best to lower him gently to the ground.

Then Mark picked up the gun in case someone else unwelcome came through the door.

Jaime grabbed her phone and dialed in.

"You're there, we see that. Have you been able to scope out the situation? Should our ground team come there, or go to Castel del Monte?" asked TC4, who was on the line as well.

"Here," Jaime said. "Come to the vineyard first. We've got Wester and we've got Sword 23, but he's badly injured, and Savino is having some sort of delusions. We need medical help right away."

"Hang tight. The team's heading your way right now. Are there guards? Are there guns?"

"We've seen both. Don't know how many."

"Where are you?"

"In the wine cellar, down a main hall. Sword 23 has been shot, and both legs broken. We can't move him. I'll do my best to staunch the blood flow. But please hurry!"

"We've been standing by. The ground team and a medical helicopter have been standing by. Will there be a place to land?"

"Easily."

"Can you sit tight?"

"Yes."

"I don't hear anything in the hall," said Mark, and he opened the door. He stepped over the unconscious man and sneaked gingerly to where the hall turned a corner.

"What do you see?"

"Another body," he said. "But no more guards."

"*Stay put,*" said TC4. "The ground team will be there in ten."

Jaime turned her attention back to Sword 23. "Are you in a lot of pain?" she asked, then grimaced. "Sorry, I keep asking stupid questions. But you're probably not in the mood to discuss your favorite color."

"God, what would I do without you?" Yani asked. "Vermillion."

TUESDAY, NOVEMBER 13, 2007, 6:06 P.M.
VIGNETI PARADISO RITROVATO
MINERVINO MERGE, ITALY

IT WASN'T LONG before they heard shouting and footfalls in the hall as the Operative team arrived. An airlift helicopter with a medical team landed at the vineyards as soon as the ground team gave the all clear.

Yani watched from his stretcher as his wife filled in the ground team with what she knew. The team would come to debrief him next, after his bleeding was stabilized. He knew they'd want to get himself, Savino, Analucia, Jaime, and Mark out of there before the local authorities arrived. The best way to answer unwelcome questions was to have them not come up in the first place.

"There," said the physician, who was done with a preliminary bandage for his gunshot wound, and had started a transfusion. "That should hold you to the plane. Is the pain being managed?"

"Much better," said Yani.

"Okay, you can talk to these guys, but quickly."

"Good to see you, Sword 23," said the first one.

"Glad to see you, too," Yani responded. "Here's what I know. Not much."

He described Castel del Monte—the underground rooms, and the existence of a control room. Yani also informed them about Wester's state of mind, and that there had to be someone else, someone with more reach and power—and coherence—running the operation.

Yani also described the link with the Golden Sun Vineyard in China.

"Thanks.," said the team leader. "Now let's get you and Wester out of here while we can. With all these questions outstanding, it seems our best move will be to stabilize him and see what he will—and can—tell us."

They had Yani on a gurney, and as they rolled him to the helicopter, Analucia came over to the stretcher. "Hey, old friend," she said.

"Nice of you to come," Yani said. "You didn't have to."

"How could I not? Although, wow, what a situation."

"You're living in his mind now, not so much walking the earth," Yani said.

"It's bizarre."

"So, do you have any theories, any ideas about what was going on with Yacov?" Yani asked.

"No. You'd seen him more recently than I had, by a decade at least. I really know nothing except about what's happened in the last hour. Except—" she lowered her voice. "I tasted the wine. Drop dead marvelous, Yani. Apparently, he hasn't always been crazy!"

"Oh, man. The story of this vineyard is going to end tragically, no matter what happens."

"Here, take a bottle with you." She smiled and slipped one beneath the sheet on his gurney. "Until we meet again."

The helipad was to the front of the estate. As Yani neared the 'copter, he held up his hand, and yelled to be heard.

"Wait!" he said to Jaime. "Where's the boy? Merlin? Where is he?"

"The little boy who told us where you were?" she asked.

"He's all right," one of the team spoke loudly. "We found him floating in the front fountain. He seems fine. He seems calm."

"Jaime," Yani said. "I can't get over to him. But could you, please? Say his name, twice. Say 'Merlin, Merlin,' and then tell him that he has completed his quest. He may go home."

“Then hurry back,” said the team member. “We’re lifting you outta here.”

“That reminds me,” Yani said. “The boy has a bag, with colors and a drawing pad and a pair of scissors. Inside the drawing pad is a sticker with his name and address. I have a feeling that whoever else lives at that address will have some more insight as to what is happening here.”

“Got it,” said the man, and Yani’s gurney was put aboard.

Jaime came running back. “Not sure he heard me,” she yelled.

“He did,” Yani said. “Or he might hear you later. Great kid. I’ll check in on him when we’ve both gotten our sea legs back.”

“Yeah, let’s work on that part for a while,” his wife smiled.

TUESDAY, NOVEMBER 13, 2007, 6:04 P.M.
IN THE AIR

FROM HER AIRPLANE, Shanlei could see the emergency vehicles surrounding Castel del Monte.

Too bad that Savino's damn personal vendetta had brought the authorities so close to the hub. That hidden control room represented a sizeable investment.

Ah, well. This phase was over. And anyone with critical information had been dispatched. Bradley was dead. Alejandra was dead. That code writer was dead. And Savino Latorre was so far gone, he would certainly never come back.

And, even if he did, he had never met Shanlei, and could give them little information.

All he would know was that Xiaofan had disappeared.

Shanlei knew there was not much time to revel in these successes. The final phase of acquiring a majority of the world's most valuable resources was about to begin.

It could happen with or without that final "square." But it would be so much easier with it.

So, there would be only one Death of the Firstborn.

But hopefully it would bring the final piece to the quilt.

TUESDAY, NOVEMBER 13, 2007, 6:04 P.M.
IN THE AIR

ALL HE KNEW WAS THAT, ONCE AGAIN, it wasn't his plane.

Instead, he was on an airplane that was heading somewhere, over water. South? Southeast? Southwest?

Mark Shepard sat with his head in his hands, completely exhausted.

This was an unusual type of plane, he knew that. There were rooms in the rear that seemed to be a hospital suite. Which was good, because Jaime's husband had been through some hard times.

Not long after they'd managed to secure the room where they'd found Jaime's husband, the men and women that Jaime had referred to as "her SWAT team" had arrived and had immediately evacuated Yani, Jaime, Mark, and Savino Latorre. Yes, they'd brought Latorre along. Not left him to rot in the local jail, as Mark would have been tempted to do, or forced him to explain what was going on, or be shot "by accident." Instead, now, he was in the medical suite next to Yani's.

A couple members of the SWAT team had stayed behind to debrief the local authorities.

Now, they were all here, on someone else's plane. Including Mark.

He was feeling better. Energized. Jazzed, even. The fact he'd been able to help take down that guard, been able to disarm Savino and help with Yani, gave him back some of the feeling of control he felt he'd lost at the Eiffel Tower.

Granted, he was tired, hungry, and overwhelmed by the events of the past seventy-two hours. Was it really only three days ago he'd been at Jaime's wedding?

And only days from now, he had a new album coming out. An album of damn good songs. Excessively good songs. About lusting after another man's wife. When he'd written them, it had felt hopeless and romantic.

Now it felt stupid.

And he was going to have to talk about it. Ad nauseam.

The joke was, that was the safest thing for him to be thinking about.

As if on cue, Jaime plunked down next to him, where he sat in a comfortable, private room on the aft side of the airplane.

She seemed happy.

"How is he?" Mark asked.

"He'll survive," Jaime said, smiling. "Thank you so much, Mark. Not exactly the honeymoon of my dreams, but I'll take it."

"So, what's the deal here? Where are we going? I do have an album coming out, and a bunch of really angry band mates. Am I being whisked away to be debriefed? Will I ever be seen again?"

She laughed. "Not becoming a drama king, surely?"

"I believe a drama queen—or king—drama ruler—is someone who treats situations as more fraught than they actually are. I don't know that anyone would be able to do that, given the last few days."

"I'm sorry, Mark, it's been…really something. Strenuous. Stressful. But no one is taking you anywhere against your will. Wait—wait—I know you weren't exactly asked, before you boarded the plane. From the moment we land, you will be free to ask to be taken anywhere you'd like to go.

"But hear me out. Here's the default plan. We will land at a safe house/clinic on a very pleasant island. Yani and Savino will be seen to. You and I will each be given a very nice meal, massages, offered a hot tub and a good night's sleep. We will each be offered a counselor to talk to. And believe me, I'm going to talk with mine.

I'd advise you to do the same. These are good people, wise people, Mark. They understand what you've just gone through, which would take a lot of explaining back home. And they won't tell a soul. Privacy isn't an issue. They want to serve no other purpose than to help you talk through all this and deal with whatever issues it's brought up. Then, you'll be offered a good breakfast and a plane trip to wherever is best for you to meet up with your band."

She smiled. "So, you can decide to leave the minute we touch down. But you'll be so far ahead if you decide to spend the night."

As if to prove her point, a young man arrived pushing a trolley with heaped bowls of strawberries, blueberries and pears. There was also a teapot and, from the aroma, some savory scones.

"May I serve you some tea?" he asked. Mark realized he was starving.

"I'm heading back to Yani, just to see how he's doing. We should be landing soon. I'll see you then," Jaime said, and she hopped up. It was clear she was smitten. With her damn husband. Mark smiled wryly.

As he sat back to sip his tea, another man came to stand at the door to the cabin. "Hello," he said. "I'm Evan Moser, from Free Winds. Thank you so much for all you did to bring this situation to resolution. Your tenacity and courage have been very much appreciated."

"Oh. Yes. You're welcome."

"May I?" he gestured to the chair recently vacated by Jaime.

"Sure. Fine." Mark took a healthy bite of the cheese and herb scone. "Oh. Wait. Are you one of the counselors Jaime was just talking about?"

"Guilty as charged. You certainly don't need to talk about everything that's gone down over the last few days, but I'd love to hear your take on it, if you're up for it."

Oh, hell.

"It must have been a surprise, as you were leaving to find out what had happened to your satellite, to have your old friend Jaime boarding your plane."

Mark looked at Evan. Was he irked that Evan knew this much, or was he slightly relieved? Jaime was right. Mark explaining to a normal therapist why he had a satellite, a plane, and an old friend who was an hour's bride boarding another plane with him would take a hell of a lot of explaining.

"You want to shut the door?" Mark asked.

"Good idea," said Evan.

TUESDAY, NOVEMBER 13, 2007, 7:14 P.M.
ON THE ISLAND

YANI SMILED AT THE WOMAN before him. "You've given me a lot to think about," he said. "Ah, and here's just the person with whom I need to consult."

Jaime walked into his room from the hallway. Her hair was wet; his guess was that she'd had a massage and a shower. It was good to see her, here and safe. He gave a contented sigh and sat back against the pillows.

The side door of his room was open to a terrace; birdsong punctuated the breeze as the birds prepared for nightfall. The pace of the waves soothed the rough edges of the past few days.

"How are you feeling?" Jaime asked.

"Right now, pretty fine," he said. The Steppe was very advanced medically, which was why it had been worth it to fly him and Wester more than two hours away to one of their venues. Pain medication and anesthesia were without side effects, for all practical purposes. Except, well, he felt pretty fine.

"Jaime, come in," said Jocasta, the woman who was the head of his medical team. She wore white linen pants, a blue shirt, and a white blazer. There was another woman there as well, whom Yani knew well, but he was fairly certain Jaime had not yet met. They closed the hallway door as Jaime came in.

"Repair went well," said his doctor. "We were able to do a lot on the plane ride here. The bullet hole is mending, and his legs will take a while to set, but they were both clean breaks."

As happy as Yani was, he did realize he wouldn't be running races any time soon.

"Which brings us to our first big question. As you're both aware, he would heal much more quickly and more completely in the Steppe. Pure and simple. He would be ready to travel by the next door opening, and he'd likely be back, in good shape, by spring."

"I'd be stuck there for at least six months," Yani said quietly. "Possibly longer. Not that we don't both love the Steppe…but there are certain times in a husband's life when his wife needs tending to. The six months after his wedding seem to be such a time."

Jaime smiled. "Thanks for thinking of me. But if you would heal so much more quickly and thoroughly in Eden, it would certainly be selfish of me to keep you here."

He could tell she meant every word. He could also tell it was killing her. He looked her squarely in the eye. "I'm not going anywhere for six months or longer," he said. "End of discussion. I'll heal just fine Terris-side."

"Which brings us to our next discussion topic," said the second woman. She had chestnut skin, deep black hair, and wore a red sari.

"In that case, I'll excuse myself and check back later," said the physician.

"Have you had time to tell Jaime what I asked you about?" the remaining woman asked.

"No. I've just awakened, and she's just back. Jaime, this is Isla, by the way. Isla, Jaime."

"Very nice to meet you." The women smiled at each other.

The woman exuded energy and vigor. She also looked to be about sixty, which was older than most Steppe dwellers who lived topside usually appeared. Yani could tell Jaime was curious.

"Would *you* mind telling her?" Yani said to Isla. He was alert, but he wanted Jaime to hear it correctly the first time.

"I was sent here to offer Sword 23 a new course of action. One of the four Terris Coordinators will be retiring in three years. It's time her successor was chosen. I was dispatched to see if Sword 23 would be interested in retraining."

"What would that mean?" Jaime asked.

"It's not often that we have someone like your husband, who has been both an active Operative and a Sword. He knows the key players and the operations in a way very few people do. But being a Terris Coordinator is a very specific and highly skilled position."

"I would continue as an active agent while I retrained," Yani said. He hoped his eagerness was not too easily read. "And once I was in the position, I would be able to stay in one place."

"Wouldn't you get bored staying in one place?" Jaime asked.

"Being a TC is not exactly a paper-pushing desk job," Yani replied. He wasn't sure why he was hesitant to mention it would make it easier to raise a family.

"I will leave you two to talk a bit. There is much to discuss," said Isla. "So glad to see you on the mend."

And then they were alone.

"It sounds like what they're offering you is a great honor," said Jaime.

"It's true."

"I'm very proud of you."

"Thanks. I'm proud of you, also."

"So, do you have any idea what was going on with Wester and the plagues?"

"They hope to know more once they have him stabilized, of course. But they did find the large control room under Castel del Monte that was apparently the hub of the operation."

"So you're here, and you're safe, and on the mend," said Jaime. "Are you sure you don't want to go to Eden?"

"No. I want to stay here with you. And begin to retrain," he said with a smile. "And help them figure out exactly what was going on, and why. My guess is, we're nowhere near getting to the bottom of this thing."

"So how do we play this? If I tell my superiors you've been injured and hospitalized, I can likely get my leave extended. Then what do we do? Do I stay here with you for the last four days of my leave? That doesn't make sense."

"We need to move our stuff out of Quarters 60," said Yani. "We were going to be back on Saturday to do that before Chaplain Thomsen and Carol got back."

"I'm thinking, if I go back and work for a couple of days while you're doing your initial therapies, do some paperwork and move the part of our stuff that isn't in storage, I can come back and be with you for a week or so while you heal."

Yani added, "I was also hoping we could reschedule our honeymoon for as soon as I'm more than a bit better."

"The cadets are off over Christmas. I bet you'll be better by then. Let me see about getting another leave late next month."

"Sounds good," he said. "I would be mightily disappointed to have missed our whole honeymoon if I wasn't so darn glad that we're both still alive."

"With you, I'm guessing that will always be blessing number one." Jaime shook her head and smiled.

"And, dear God, wife, I certainly need a good amount of time alone with you."

"You'd need to be careful. I might take advantage of such a situation."

"Full advantage."

There was another knock on the door. In walked a strapping, tall man. A grin overspread his face when he saw Yani.

He was a current Sword. The Swords were the twelve men who knew how to get in and out of Eden at any given time. It was a rare honor, and the reason Jaime had first met Yani. The newcomer was Sword 31. Yani had played a large part in his training. He'd been the Sword to take Jaime and Yani back to the Steppe together for their Eden wedding.

"You do know how to show off," said Sword 31.

"Yeah, well, I do my best," replied Yani.

Jaime smiled at him. "Good to see you," she said. "Did you come in case Yani chose to go back?"

"Eh. Nobody expected him to."

Jaime's eyes clearly asked, "Then, why?"

Yani responded, “I think I know.”

“I’m actually here to see if I can borrow your wife for half an hour or so.”

“Yes. You certainly can.”

“What?” Jaime asked, intrigued.

“I’ll stop back in a few, when we’re ready.”

And he left the room.

“What’s going on?” she asked Yani.

“Trust me. Something you’ll want to be a part of. But meanwhile, we do seem to have a few minutes to ourselves.”

“Yeah?” said Jaime, moving to lock the door. “So, let’s see. Two broken legs, wounds in hip, and a gunshot wound through the shoulder. Any parts of you that are still up for grabs?”

TUESDAY, NOVEMBER 13, 2007, 8:02 P.M.
ON THE ISLAND

MARK SHEPARD KNOCKED on the door of the room to which he'd been directed.

Jaime had been correct. Talking with Evan, having a massage and a hot tub, along with a great dinner with Jaime and Yani, Isla and some of the locals, along with a truly fabulous bottle of wine had made things seem much more handle-able. He'd been able to reach the band and his publicist to let them know he'd be back, ready to rock and roll, the next morning.

He'd gone out to his terrace, under a black velvet sky, strumming on a guitar he'd borrowed and making notes on the beginning of some lyrics, when he'd been told someone wanted to talk to him.

Shepard decided nothing could surprise him anymore.

The woman who'd invited him led him down the colorful corridor to a closed door. She nodded at it, and at him, and left.

He knocked.

The door was opened by Jaime.

"Hi," she said. "Come in."

Mark walked into the room. There was a fireplace, with lit logs, and a wooden table near it. A tall, brown-haired man whom Mark didn't recognize was seated at the table and got up as he entered. They were the only three people in the room. Jaime closed the door behind him.

"Mark, this is Sword 31," said Jaime. "Sword 31, Mark Shepard."

The three of them sat.

Shepard was inexplicably nervous, even with Jaime smiling at him. There was something in the air that hinted at "momentous occasion."

"I'm very pleased to meet you," said Sword 31. He had a commanding presence. Mark tried to guess his age, but gave it up almost immediately. "Mark, you've been working with Free Winds for several years now," he said. "And the truth is, we know you to be a man of character. A man of his word, who is what he says he is, who lives out his commitments."

"Okay," said Mark.

"The truth is, we were interested in you even before Free Winds started financing some of BeCause's projects. You're uniquely creative and talented. Someone whose input we'd value. Someone who we believe could grow and profit from what we have, as well."

Mark looked at Jaime. "You suspected Free Winds was more than a funding source," she said.

"Is this gonna be good?" he asked her.

"Yes. It's gonna be good," Jaime answered.

"Here's the thing," said Sword 31, in an echo of what Sword 23 had once said to Jaime. "Free Winds is the offshoot of an altruistic society. The one place on earth that exists for the good of its neighbors. There's not much coming and going, but agents of this society are quietly at work bringing peace and healing throughout the world. It's also very technologically advanced, because many of the world's great teachers, thinkers, and scientists have come to lend support. One must be invited to join this society, and must be willing to leave everything behind."

"What are you talking about?" asked Mark. "Where is this alleged society?"

"That's the interesting part. You can't know. Only the twelve know. Once you're invited, you may have time to think about it. You can talk to Jaime, who has been there. If you decide you want to go, you won't be able to tell anyone. You'll simply disappear, for a minimum of three years. Some choose never to return. It won't become clear until you're there, how you feel you're called."

Mark looked at Jaime. "He's kidding."

Jaime said, "Mark, do you remember those three years that I was missing, presumed dead?"

"You're telling me…wait, no…"

"You don't need to make up your mind now," said Sword 31. "All we need now is your promise that you won't talk to anyone other than Jaime or other Gardeners about this."

"Gardeners?" asked Mark.

Sword 31 looked at Jaime, and gave a small nod. She said, "It's Eden, Mark. The Garden of Eden still exists."

Mark stared at her.

"Believe me, I know exactly what you're thinking right now," Jaime said. "I wasn't even given time to think about it and put things in order."

"The Garden of Eden."

"You said you thought there was more to Free Winds," Jaime said. "And, by the way, if you're looking for a whole bunch of women who won't give a fig that you're a rock star, do I have the travel opportunity for you."

Sword 31 looked a bit taken aback. Perhaps that wasn't a part of the usual spiel.

"You're not…joking?" was all Mark could say.

"Go ahead and ask questions. We can't answer everything, but we'll answer what we can," said Sword 31. He looked completely serious.

"The Garden…" Mark stuttered.

"Of Eden," Jaime finished.

"Holy crap."

"Well said."

TUESDAY, NOVEMBER 13, 2007, 1:30 P.M.
CADET CENTRAL AREA
UNITED STATES MILITARY ACADEMY
WEST POINT, NEW YORK

"HEY, SHELBY, YOU COMING TO LUNCH?" one of Cadet Fairfield's friends yelled from the dorm hallway.

"Nah, you go on without me," she replied, attempting to affect as much nonchalance as she could muster. But the truth was, Shelby chose to hide in her room right now, rather than face the prying eyes of friends who might wonder why her face was so puffy.

She had tried, for an hour, to do her physics homework but couldn't concentrate. All she could do was sit and stare out the window. And cry. And then stare some more.

Her cell phone pinged. Text message. It was the fifth in a string of messages from her boyfriend.

Shells, we have to talk.

I must see you.

I may be leaving tomorrow.

Don't leave it like this.

Please respond.

Each time a new text message arrived she picked up her phone, glanced at the content, then set it back down again.

Her eyes fell upon the class ring she wore so proudly. All of the Firsties (Seniors) had received their West Point rings in a grand ceremony at the beginning of this semester. Her personal design included her birthstone, an emerald, in the center, surrounded by diamonds.

Shelby had been stirred by it, so excited about the tradition it represented, especially for her. It was the practice to melt rings from previous classes into the gold that would be cast into the new rings. This way each graduate carried a piece of the past on his or her finger. Shelby's father, West Point Class of '80, had died of cancer during her first year at West Point. At his request, his ring was included in the melt for his daughter's class.

Now, she looked at her ring and felt nothing. What did it all mean? What was the purpose?

Oh, Dad, I feel so lost. What would you tell me to do now?

Maybe it would help to call her mother and talk. Where was she this week? At the governors' conference or back home in Denver?

Just as she was reaching for the phone a tentative knock fell on her doorframe. Shelby looked up to see the one who had caused her all this misery. And, *damn it*, she had to admit he looked as miserable as she felt.

"Shelby, please, talk to me."

Cadet Bak stood in the doorway, arms out pleadingly, but made no attempt to enter the room.

"Are you leaving?"

"Yes, tomorrow. The paperwork is all approved."

"Then what's left to say?"

"A lot!" At this point he stepped in and sat on the edge of the bed, ignoring the fact that she had not invited him into the room. "I have to go home for awhile. I'm not sure how soon I'll be able to come back, but that is not the end of our relationship. We knew this was not going to be easy, there would be some separations."

"Yes, but not so soon! I just have this feeling that if we head off in different directions, our lives will diverge, and we won't need each other anymore."

"Oh, Shells, I need you in my life. But right now what I really need is your support as I try to help my family. This trip home could mess up all my plans for graduation, but I have every intention of coming back here."

It wasn't until that moment that Shelby realized how all of this had overturned Joke's plans, his future. All she had been thinking about was her problem, and now she felt very selfish.

With all the courage she could muster, Shelby tried to push past her own sorrow and reach out to him. "What can I do to help?"

His eyes lit up, as he saw the ice beginning to melt.

"Pray for me. Pray for my family." He paused, and then looked sheepish. "And it wouldn't hurt to have a good set of notes from Middle Eastern culture when I return!"

"Count on it!"

He stood up and grabbed her into a big hug. At that moment, she didn't care if someone walked in and caught them in an illegal PDA. It was worth it, and might have to last for a very long time.

CODA

WEDNESDAY, NOVEMBER 14, 2007, 6:55 P.M.
CADET CHAPEL
UNITED STATES MILITARY ACADEMY
WEST POINT, NEW YORK

IT WAS GOOD TO BE BACK. Back on solid ground. In the house of God, where the chaplain felt most at home.

Jaime had come through the secret study entrance from the chaplain residence of Cadet Chapel into the vestry. The lights above the altar were still glowing, which told her the choir director was probably still down in the basement and had not left for the evening.

As she walked down the side aisle toward the basement steps she noticed, barely visible in the dim light, someone sitting at the far back of the sanctuary.

Who could be there at this time of night?

Curious, the chaplain cut through one of the pews to the center aisle, and walked toward the back. It did not escape her that just a few days before she had walked this same path, sun streaming through the stained glass windows, cameras flashing, escorted by her husband.

Now it was dark, so dark that she was right on top of the lone figure before she could identify her. She recognized one of the cadets from the Chapel choir, Shelby Fairfield, sitting quietly in the last pew.

"Good evening, ma'am," said the young woman. There was a listless quality to her voice that concerned Jaime.

"Shelby? Why are you sitting here in the dark?"

"We just finished handbell practice. And I didn't feel like going back down to my room."

Suddenly, she started crying. Jaime sat down next to her.

"I take it this has nothing to do with bell rehearsal. What's wrong?"

"The *future*, that's what's wrong!" Her words were tinged with anger. "I thought I had my life all figured out, now everything is messed up."

Welcome to the real world, Jaime thought.

"So, your best laid plans have come crashing down around you?"

"I don't know. My fiancé—well, boyfriend—I'm not sure what to call him now..."

She paused, trying to find her words. Jaime just sat still and waited.

"He left today to return to his home country for an emergency. Problem is, we don't know how long he will be away. I'm afraid his father will try to convince him not to come back. We haven't even figured out how we want to handle our relationship yet, and now he's gone. I need more time. But we may never have this chance again."

"You may be right." Jaime was very matter of fact. Shelby looked at her, surprised. "What? You want me to say 'everything is going to be fine?' That you and this mystery cadet will live happily ever after? I don't know that, anymore than I know that it won't work out." Jaime tried to keep her tone gentle, if her words were not.

"I just want some clarity."

"I understand. Here is the only clarity I've got. Each day is a new challenge, Shelby, and we don't know what life is going to throw at us. But there is one thing that is absolutely clear for me: God gives you and me the resources to handle those challenges, and stands by us to face them."

"Each day...one day at a time, huh?"

"Wasn't that how you got through Beast Barracks three years ago?"

She laughed. "Yeah, couldn't see past the end of the day, let alone the week!"

"But you made it through. Didn't you?"

"Yes, ma'am, but this is so much more difficult than our Basic Training ever was."

Jaime knew that a few platitudes were not going to make the young woman's pain go away. So they both sat, quietly contemplating the challenges that were before them.

As they sat, Jaime heard the heavy side door of the chapel swing open. It was the door kiddingly known as the "Bride's Escape," because it was near the altar and offered an escape route for a last minute change of mind.

Stepping out of the doorway into the dimly lit corridor was a tall man wearing a long overcoat. He turned away from them, stepped over the velvet rope by the organ console and moved up toward the altar. He was obviously looking for someone.

Jaime almost called out to him, until she noticed what he was carrying. Jaime's blood froze. In his silhouette she could clearly see the man held a pistol in his right hand.

She placed one hand on the cadet's knee. Gaining her attention, Jaime motioned very quickly for her to remain quiet. The young woman looked at her with confusion, but immediately obeyed.

This was not good. Was it someone sent by Savi? A friend of the woman in Paris?

Jaime hoped with all her heart the man had not seen them in the dark. Her mind quickly ran through escape routes, and she realized that the intruder was between them and their only way to leave the building. The massive entry doors behind them could only be opened with a sizeable skeleton key, which she did not happen to be carrying. The doors had no "panic bars."

Concluding that anywhere was better than sitting in the open, she motioned for Shelby to follow her, then dropped down to the floor and crawled to the side aisle. The cadet followed in kind. Using a large pillar for cover, they both stood, then silently moved further back into the darkness.

Jaime kicked herself for not carrying her cell phone with her, or better yet, her Eden glasses. But who would have thought she needed them in the chapel?

Still, their best bet was to find a good hiding place and call for help. She prayed that Cadet Fairfield, like every other young red-blooded American kid, would be carrying her phone.

Jaime pulled Shelby through the doorway into the chapel foyer, where the stairway up to the roof was located.

The stone circular staircase was guarded by a four-foot high metal accordion gate which was padlocked to keep visitors from wandering that way. Most of the cadet chimers who came to ring the tower bells didn't bother with the padlock and simply vaulted the gate. Jaime knew where the key was, but couldn't afford the time to unlock the gate. She motioned for Shelby to go first, and the young woman scrambled over it with ease. For Jaime it was not quite as easy. The cadet—still obviously confused—gave her a hand. She got one leg over, and the gate rattled. She stopped, holding her breath. Hearing nothing, she brought the other leg over and they began to work their way up the circular staircase.

"Have you got your cell phone with you?" Jaime whispered as they moved up the steps.

"Yes, of course. What's going on?"

"As soon as we reach the top of this tower, you're going to call the police."

Shelby stopped and stared at the chaplain, fear in her eyes. "But who is that man? Why are we running from him?"

Jaime shook her head and gave the young woman a little push to keep her going up the stairs.

The two reached the top of the steps, where a plywood door was being held in place by a large cinder block. They slid the block out just enough to squeeze past the door, then ascended a short set of wooden steps to the passageway that ran above the high, arched ceiling of the sanctuary.

Jaime stopped and motioned for Shelby to pull out her cell phone.

"Do you have the number for the MPs?" she whispered.

"No, but I have CGR, and they can call the police." CGR was slang for the Cadet Guard Room, a twenty-four seven duty station in the Cadet Central Area.

"Do it."

"What do I tell them?"

"There's an intruder in the chapel. I believe he's armed and dangerous."

Now Shelby looked very frightened, but dialed the number. While she quietly spoke on the phone, Jaime cracked the door they had just passed through and listened for sounds of someone following. She thought she heard the rattle of the gate below. It was the same rattle it made when she so clumsily climbed over.

She closed the door and pushed the young woman in the opposite direction.

The two were now traversing a wooden catwalk that enabled bell chimers to reach the bell tower without actually stepping on the curved ceiling of the sanctuary. Just in time, Jaime remembered that there were metal crossbars at intervals across the walkway. They were at eye level, and would clothesline you if you didn't duck. The two women tiptoed down the catwalk, crouching just enough to miss the crossbars.

They ducked through a short brick passage into the bell chimers' lair, and Jaime looked around for a good hiding place. In the center was a large square platform where a set of long wooden levers with heavy cables were linked to the bells in the chamber above. There was also a couch and some tables, but nothing that would have provided sufficient hiding space. In one corner was a small, metal, circular staircase that went up three stories past the tower bells and to the roof.

Jaime heard the creak of the plywood doorway at the other end of the catwalk they had just traversed. Crap.

There was a small clang and a muffled expletive. Jaime almost giggled. Whoever was following them had walked into one of the metal crossbars in the dark.

She and Shelby looked at each other, and both came to the same conclusion. They had to keep moving. The metal staircase was their only escape. But they both knew it only went up. It was also a dead end.

Shelby took the lead, using only the light from her cellphone. Jaime followed, understanding how Mark had felt on the Eiffel Tower. As they moved up past the giant bells she could feel a cool breeze coming through the screened windows. Could they hide on this level? No, better keep moving up. She motioned for the cadet to continue.

Two more stories up, into total darkness, and they reached the doorway to the roof. It was supposed to be locked, but the chimers had learned how to jimmy it open. Jaime quietly turned the knob, and it opened. Grateful that she didn't need to add excess noise by messing with the latch, she pushed the door open and the two stepped out into the night.

It was a small, square roof, designed like a castle turret, with high walls and two shoulder-width view ports cut into each side of the square. You could step up and actually stand in one of the view ports for a better view, but this was discouraged as there was no fence or railing. The view was spectacular. A few weeks before, when the Cadet Chapel Choir had a lock-in, she had stood up here late at night with thirty cadets as they marveled at the beauty of the lights on the Hudson River.

Now, Jaime didn't particularly care about the view. She wanted to know that help was on the way.

"Shelby. Contact the police again. See where they are."

The cadet moved away from the door and began speaking into her phone in a muffled tone. Then she put her phone away and whispered, "All they can tell me is the MPs are on their way."

Jaime stood in the corner behind the door, so that if it opened she would be hidden from view. She motioned for Shelby to come stand behind her.

They waited, listening for sirens, and watching for any sign that the intruder was coming through the door. Jaime prayed the sirens came first.

Then the doorknob rattled very slightly.

If Jaime had not been staring at it she might not have noticed. It turned, very slowly and quietly.

The door pushed open, noiselessly, about six inches. Jaime's eyes were now accustomed to the starlight, and she observed the muzzle of a revolver peek through. A few moments later, and the muzzle was followed by the full weapon and the hand which held it.

As soon as the man's elbow had cleared the doorway, Jaime kicked with all her might, slamming the door on the man, catching his arm in the door. He yelled with pain, and dropped the revolver, which went scooting across the metal tower roofing.

Jaime dove across the roof, grabbing the weapon as it slid. She rolled onto her back and immediately brought the gun to bear on the intruder, clicking the safety off with her thumb. The man was on one knee, breathing heavily, holding his arm as if it might be broken.

"Don't move," she said, trying to sound much more in charge than she felt at the moment. Keeping the weapon pointed at him she slowly stood up.

Multiple emergency vehicles could be heard screeching into the parking lot below. "They're here!" blurted the cadet, who had been holding back a scream. She pulled her phone back out to see if she could guide the officers up to the tower.

The chaplain and the hit man stared at each other, a frozen tableau, each waiting for the other to make the next move.

Jaime decided to break the ice.

"Why were you trying to kill me? Who sent you?"

"Lady," the man almost laughed. "I have no interest in you. I don't even know who you are." His eyes darted to the girl, where she'd been looking over the edge of the tower, waving at the police while she spoke directions into her phone.

"What? You're chasing *me*?" Shelby whirled back toward the man. "What did I ever do to you?"

"Not you, kid. Someone else. Somebody didn't do what my employer wanted her to do. You were payback."

Shelby stepped out to Jaime's side, confused for a moment, then said, "My mother?"

"Whoever it was really ticked off the wrong people." As he said this he straightened himself up into a full stand. "And my employer can be *very* nasty when unhappy."

The man started to edge toward the closest view port.

"Just hold it right there," said Jaime, with as much authority as she could muster. "The police will be up here any minute."

"I know," he said with finality. "They really do 'have this place surrounded,' that's not just some movie quote." He looked over the edge at the flashing lights below. "And as I said, my employer gets very nasty when unhappy. No point in living if I'm looking over my shoulder. Not to mention, I have a hundred percent success rate. And if I'm going down, I'm going down with one hundred percent."

With that, he hurtled himself forward.

Too late, Jaime saw that he'd positioned himself so that Shelby was between him and the nearest view portal. She had a split second to respond. She dropped the gun and grabbed the girl with both hands, flinging her forward onto the roof as the hit man hurtled toward her. He grabbed her shoulder, but Jaime's weight was on top of her, and Shelby smacked the roof, hard, as she fell.

The man couldn't have stopped himself if he'd tried. As Jaime left the girl on the metal floor and rolled back for the gun, he went flying forward, flying off the bell tower, and disappeared into the night.

Shelby screamed as the man disappeared over the ledge. Then there was quiet. Jaime stepped to the opening and looked down to see the broken body of their assailant sprawled on the walkway below.

The young woman started to move as if to look for herself, and Jaime threw her arms around the girl. She didn't need to see this. Didn't need the memories that would haunt her in the night.

The girl sobbed hysterically against her shoulder, and they remained there, unmoving, until the police finally found them.

WEDNESDAY, NOVEMBER 14, 2007, 10:55 P.M.
CADET CHAPEL RESIDENCE
UNITED STATES MILITARY ACADEMY
WEST POINT, NEW YORK

JAIME SAT ALONE in the dark wood-paneled dining room that seemed like a college hall at Oxford or Cambridge. The MPs and police, and even the CIA, had come and gone.

Shelby was back with her friends. Her family was on their way.

Family and friends. Loved ones.

And all the messiness they brought about. Oddly, that seemed to be what life was about.

Jaime stood, exhausted. She went out into the hallway and grabbed her carry-on. Instead of unpacking tonight, she'd just brush her teeth, pull on a t-shirt, and fall into bed.

There was still a lot to figure out. And, most likely, another madman to take on.

As she unzipped the outer compartment and grabbed her toiletry kit, she felt something else.

She pulled out a CD. The new one, by Borderland. Signed simply, "Love, Mark."

Family and friends, and all their messiness.

She shook her head, and put the CD into the player down in the living room. She brushed her teeth in the downstairs bathroom, and collapsed onto the sofa, letting Mark's inimitable voice surround her as she drifted off to sleep.

CÔTE DE BEAUNE
BURGUNDY, FRANCE

DOTS AND DOTS. Stars and stars.

Nighttime. Quiet. Dark. Floating in stars. Flying.

Happy.

Be bold. Be brave. Save Arthur.

Quest. Victorious. Quest.

Surrounded by happiness. Surrounded by stars.

"Be bold. Be brave. Save Arthur," said his father, Ambrosius, who floated beside him.

And Merlin smiled.

ACKNOWLEGEMENTS

The authors would like to thank the following people for sharing their expertise: Samuel Amber for advice about satellites and low earth orbits; Maria Laurendau for her understanding of the workings of portable ultrasound machines; Andrew Lastowecky for the introduction to his lovely Teodozia; and the members of the autism community who so openly shared with us. On that topic, we would like to add that Leal is one specific boy, and any way in which he is not the person the reader would find most helpful is attributable to the authors alone.

Many thanks to our early readers, Robert Owens Scott, Mary Ann O'Roark, Marilynn Fryer, Kirk Vandezande, Lisa Pennington, Cherei McCarter, Laura Kendall, Karen Diefendorf, Bradley Diefendorf, Susan Hirsh Prager Kriegel, Karen Johnson Sorge, Lynda Sherer, Kris Gerling, Mary Gaskill for their wisdom and insight that truly paved the way.

To those who made the book a book: Editors Margaret Diehl and Sharon Honeycutt whose expert work made things fall into place; Ailsa Campbell, our fantastic copy editor who knows just how long to let each wine breathe, and the gang at Arundel, especially Karen Lee who put all the pieces together in production and Brie Eltz who made marketing fun as it possibly can be. To Christian Fuenfhausen for expert cover design and Mie Kurahara for interiors; and Steven Saus, for unusually fine e-book conversion.

To all of our friends who happily visited the Eiffel Tower while we were locked in dark rooms writing about it, we forgive you.

And, as always, to the readers of Eden, who continue to be our reason to write.

Many, many thanks.

Visit us at EdenThrillers.com

SharonsSuperSecretEdenBlog.com

A portion of the proceeds of this book will be given to autism research.

SHARON LINNÉA is the author of the new mystery *These Violent Delights* as well as the three Eden Thrillers. She has also written award-winning biographies of Raoul Wallenberg and Hawaii's Princess Kaiulani. She lives outside New York City with her family. Visit her at SharonLinnea.com

B.K. SHERER holds a Master of Divinity degree from Princeton Theological Seminary and a Doctorate of Education from Oklahoma State University. A Presbyterian minister, she currently serves on active duty as a chaplain in the US Army. The authors first collaborated on a play about the French Underground for their sixth grade talent show in Springfield, Missouri, and have been friends ever since.

EDENTHRILLERS.COM

A portion of the proceeds of this book will go to the Wounded Warrior Project, (WoundedWarriorProject.org) which supports soldiers and the families of soldiers who have been severely wounded in the service of their country.